MARKED AS QUEEN OF HEARTS

A Rolling Brook Novel

Blye Donovan

Marked as Queen of Hearts Copyright © 2023 Blye Donovan

This is a work of fiction. The names, characters, places, and events portrayed in this book are products of the author's imagination or are used fictitiously. Any similarity to real persons, living or dead, or real events is purely coincidental.

No part of this book may be reproduced, or stored in a retrieval system, or transmitted in any form or by any means—electronic, mechanical, photocopying, recording, or otherwise—without express written permission of the author.

Warning: the unauthorized reproduction or distribution of this copyrighted work is illegal. Criminal copyright infringement, including infringement without monetary gain, is investigated by the FBI and is punishable by up to five years in prison and a fine of $250,000.

All rights reserved.

ISBN: 9798986768342
Imprint: Independently published
Cover Design by Central Covers.
Series Logo Design by K.B. Barrett Designs.

DEDICATION

To all the survivors who know emotional wounds can be the toughest to heal.

"...the most painful goodbyes are the ones that are left unsaid and never explained."
\- Jonathan Harnisch

"Death must be so beautiful. To lie in the soft brown earth, with the grasses waving above one's head, and listen to silence. To have no yesterday, and no tomorrow. To forget time, to forgive life, to be at peace."
\- Oscar Wilde

"What is stronger than the human heart which shatters over and over and still lives."
\- Rupi Kaur

"...nothing of jealousy, no risk of bliss, the wide, white eye; the perfect parting kiss."
\- David Harsent

INTRODUCTION

Okay, readers. Think of this as a **Stop Sign**. Please take a quick pause with me here while I run through some important information regarding this book.

This story has some dark themes commonly included in **content warnings**. Because the *last* thing I want to do is hurt anyone in the process of healing, I'm going to tell you what that content is. However, they will include **spoilers**. So, if you don't have any triggers you need a warning about and don't want to read a spoiler, please turn the page.

Some of the triggers I'm about to mention have personally touched my life, and in a way, imbuing this story with them was cathartic for me. If you have similarly struggled, my heart goes out to you.

This book contains content involving: thinking and talking about miscarriage and sexual assault, as well as mentioning attempted suicide and attempting suicide. Additionally, it has profanity, gore, violence, and talking about necrophilia.

Now, if that hasn't scared you away, please dive into

Rafe and Tori's love story. Because that's what this book is, *really*. It's about two characters who have been through a lot but manage to overcome it for their second chance at love.

Note:

"Necrophilia, a sexual attraction to corpses, is a rare disorder that has been known since ancient times. According to Herodotus, the ancient Egyptians took precautions against necrophilia by prohibiting the corpses of the wives of men of rank from being delivered immediately to the embalmers, for fear that the embalmers would violate them."

(Rosman, J. P., & Resnick, P. J. (1989). Sexual Attraction to Corpses: A Psychiatric Review of Necrophilia. *Bull Am Acad Psychiatry Law*, *17*(2). https://doi.org/10 February 2023)

CHAPTER 1

Rafe

The overhead light flickered in Captain Rafe Alonso's office, mirroring his mood, which was equally unsteady. He glanced at it with a scowl, and the thing buzzed at him in response.

Dammit! The fluorescent bulb looked ready to die, and he'd have to put in an order to replace it.

Just what he needed . . . *more* paperwork.

Shuffling witness statements into a folder, Rafe swiveled in his desk chair to place it in the filing cabinet. As he turned around, a flying object nearly hit him.

A box of playing cards landed on his desk. He automatically recoiled, his back snapping straight, his muscles tensing, before he looked up to see Lieutenant Jameson leaning against the doorframe of his office with arms crossed over his chest.

The massive redhead had been his friend since they'd gone to the police academy together nearly two decades ago, but Jameson didn't know Rafe hadn't been able to look at a deck of cards, much less touch them, since . . .

He swallowed against the memories churning his stomach, his olive skin blanching.

"You up for a game tonight, Alonso? The Redlands are hosting." Jameson's grin was a taunt. He'd been trying to get Rafe to join their weekly poker game since he'd moved to town.

He forced himself to relax as he reached for the deck to toss it back at his friend. He was glad he'd tucked away the file he had spread across his desk, or there'd have been a mass of papers to reorganize. "Can't. Unlike my slacker Lieutenant, I've got work to do."

He raised an eyebrow to mask his unease at seeing those cards, and Jameson laughed, unoffended. "You work too hard, *Captain*."

The title still sounded foreign to his ears. He'd taken the job as a small-town police captain a little over a month ago. Technically, it was a promotion, but it didn't feel that way to Rafe. Moving to Rolling Brook from Chicago was supposed to be a chance to slow down—have *less* work on his plate—but he was still getting his feet under him in the new position. The amount of extra paperwork at the top meant a lot of late nights and weekends.

Or maybe he just liked taking work home. It gave him something to do instead of staring at the boxes he'd yet to unpack.

He blinked to find Jameson had moved and now stood in front of his desk.

"Hey, you okay?" His friend's light blue eyes searched

Rafe's face before he reached up and rubbed at his muscled neck. His voice lowered as he dropped his hand. "I know it's the anniversary, man. Join us. It'll take your mind off it."

Rafe's shoulders wanted to slump as the familiar weight pulled on his chest, but he kept them straight, shaking his head. "Thanks, but I really do have shit to do tonight."

Jameson sighed but gave him his space. "All right, well, if you change your mind . . . you know where to find us."

He forced a smile, though it didn't quite reach his dark brown eyes. "I do."

The redhead nodded, his brow furrowing. He opened his mouth as if he planned to say something else before he changed his mind and left.

When his friend was out of sight, Rafe's posture fell. With a heavy sigh, he dropped his head into his hands, his fingers gripping the dark waves on top, and squeezed his eyes shut.

He'd been doing his best *not* to think about the fact that a year ago today, the hardest case he'd ever been on had ended. A case that still haunted his dreams and made him give up being a detective. The cards had brought it to the forefront of his mind.

The Suit of Hearts Slasher.

Or so the media had dubbed the man responsible for the serial murders committed across Chicago—the man Rafe had finally apprehended. At each crime scene, the killer had left behind a playing card from the suit of hearts.

Rafe pulled in a shaky breath when his stomach roiled and lifted his head. Jameson had meant well, but asking him to play poker—seeing the box of cards—had images flashing through his mind. Images he wished he could forget.

The victims started to scroll through his memory in a vivid horror show. He scrubbed a hand across the five o'clock shadow he could never get rid of and stood, ignoring the pain in his gut as it knotted into a bundle of tight snarls. A scowl twisted his expression, turning down the corners of his full lips, and he made a decision. He wasn't going to let the anniversary affect him.

If he did, that sick bastard won, even if he *was* serving life in prison.

Determined to think about anything else, Rafe shrugged into his suit jacket. He hadn't lied to his lieutenant. A pile of paperwork waited for him on his desk at home. The work would keep his thoughts busy, and to combat the loss of appetite thinking about *that* case inevitably caused, he'd stop at the grocer's to get what he needed to make his favorite dinner—spaghetti carbonara.

Squaring broad shoulders, he ignored the heaviness in his chest and locked up his office for the night.

* * * *

Rafe

Pipkin's buzzed with activity when Rafe walked in. The tiny grocery was busier than he'd expected it to be. Apparently, Friday after work was the store's rush hour. As the only place to buy provisions inside the town, he'd come here often since he moved. Most people shopped at the big chain store on the outskirts, but he had no desire to drive all the way out there.

Pipkin's was conveniently located in the town's historical area. The location meant it had limited space, even though it sat on a bigger corner lot. Because it was compact, no spot within remained unused. A glance around revealed all four walls crowded top to toe with items. But by now, Rafe had become familiar with where things were stored.

Growing up with an Italian mother meant food was everything to him, and he enjoyed cooking. His mom had moved to the U.S. for his dad, bringing her favorite dishes and her language. Rafe not only made a mean *risotto alla Milanese*, but he also spoke Italian.

He picked up a wire basket from the stand near the door, then gave the woman with two very upset toddlers a wide berth. One of the little ones screamed, their face crumpling as he walked by, and Rafe flinched. The sound existed on a decibel level of its own.

He liked little kids, but he didn't have a lot of experience with them. As far as he knew, he didn't have any siblings, and the one chance he'd had . . . well, *that* hadn't turned out as planned.

Probably for the best.

He knew jack shit about being a father. His own had left before he could walk, and his mother had never remarried. Thinking about the man used to make him angry, but these days, his absent parent barely registered. He didn't remember his dad and had no contact with the man—ever.

Rafe ducked down an aisle of dry goods when the

screaming suddenly stopped. In its place, the sound of the local radio station played out on low from tiny speakers in the ceiling.

He grabbed the box of pasta he needed, then headed for the meat section, where he became absorbed in an internal debate over whether to use pancetta or regular bacon for the carbonara since Pipkin's stock didn't run to guanciale.

"Captain . . . Captain . . . Captain Alonso!"

At hearing his name attached to the title, Rafe spun around. His head was still getting used to hearing it, and sometimes, it didn't register that people were talking to *him*.

An older woman with gray curls and exasperated blue eyes stared up at him. "Where were you, Captain? I must've said your name five times."

He forced a smile and managed not to point out that 'Captain' wasn't his name. "I'm sorry. Can I help you with something?"

She blinked, her eyes going wide at his smile before her features settled into a neutral expression. "Well, yes, but I wanted to introduce myself. I'm Sissy Rowlins. I run the local chapter of Children's Relief, and we've been trying to get in touch with you all week about the Christmas toy drive."

His eyebrows shot up.

Christmas?

September had barely begun, and the air hadn't turned. "Forgive me, Ms. Rowlins, but I don't understand what that has to do with me."

She huffed out a breath as her right hand went to her

hip. The other gripped a bottle of white wine the size of which made Rafe's lips twitch. Maybe it was book club night, or Sissy liked to party. The mental image of the older woman slamming back the wine nearly made him laugh aloud before she drew his attention to her toy problem.

"We need your permission to put a dropoff box at the station. We've done it every year for the past five but with the turnover . . ." She cleared her throat. "Well, we didn't want to assume."

Ah, now her accosting him made sense. The turnover of police captains hadn't been a smooth transition for Rolling Brook. He didn't have all the details but knew the previous captain had been charged after an Internal Affairs investigation.

"Of course. The Rolling Brook Police Department is happy to support the . . ." Rafe tried to remember what charity she'd said she was a part of. When the name didn't come to him, he settled for "Children." He smiled again and hoped he could end this conversation soon.

Sissy nodded her head. "Good."

"When do you need to set up the dropoff?"

"We put up the boxes on the first of December. You can expect to hear from us then."

"Great. Have a good evening, Ms. Rowlins."

After she bustled off, he shook his head. He hadn't gotten used to everyone knowing who he was. Rolling Brook was a far cry from the anonymity of the city. He'd grown up in Chicago and had spent most of his life there. Living in this small town was proving to be an adjustment.

Turning, he reached for the pancetta. It would be better

for the dish—hands down—and he wasn't sure why he'd debated it for so long. He'd dropped the meat into the wire basket he carried when a flash of red caught his eye. As he glanced up, a surge of shock bowled through him, and he felt like the linoleum dropped away, leaving him suspended in midair.

While he struggled to steady himself, the beeping of the cash register behind him and the murmured voices within the shop faded into nothing.

Victoria Graham.

The woman he hadn't seen in over a decade—hadn't known if he'd ever see again—was right there. Perusing the row of apple varieties not ten feet from him.

Right. Fucking. There.

His grip tensed on the shopping basket, and he stiffened, afraid to blink or breathe lest she disappear.

Tori fucking Graham.

He couldn't believe it.

Why is she in my grocery store? And why does she have to be so damn impossible to miss?

His chest tightened at the sight of her bright red hair waving around her shoulders. She wore a simple T-shirt and jeans, but the outfit couldn't disguise those curves. His eyes lingered on her perfectly round ass before traveling back to her flaming red hair. He was both desperate and apprehensive for her to turn her deep, emerald-green eyes on him—eyes which had been able to see straight into his soul.

But what scared Rafe the most was her smile. Tori had a smile that could stop a man's heart from a mile away.

When her gaze slid in his direction, he sucked in a much-needed breath.

Those big green eyes went wide, and she froze. She recognized him.

He could hardly breathe as he waited to see if she would run or approach. But then she smiled the smile that still made his stomach jump.

And took a step. Toward him.

Holy fuck.

He tried not to have a meltdown when she stopped two feet away. Her scent reached his nose and flooded him with memories. It was the same—warm like the first rays of sunshine after a rain and as sultry as the smell of narcissus blooms.

Sun and sex.

It suited her perfectly.

"Hi, Rafe." Her voice came out even—no sign of the nerves plaguing *him*. And her smile looked genuine. Because of that, something in his chest loosened a fraction.

"Tori"—his greeting sounded strangled in comparison, and he swallowed to wet his dry throat—"what are you doing here?"

She laughed. The sound was like music, washing over him in a familiar caress. "Nice to see you too," she teased with her damn smile.

"I, uh, yeah . . ." He scratched at the back of his neck as his tongue tied itself in knots. "Good to see you."

Her emerald eyes gleamed with laughter at his fumbling, and Rafe wondered why she didn't seem as shocked to see him as he was to see her.

"I'm writing a book."

He'd known she'd become a writer. He'd kept up with her career, reading every book she'd ever published, but he wasn't sure why she mentioned it now. "What?"

"You asked why I'm here." Her smile blasted him again. "I'm working on a book."

Why Rolling Brook when she's a crime fiction author? A city seemed more appropriate.

He blinked and attempted to pull his thoughts together. "Oh, that's . . . uh, great."

So, she'd be staying here. As the possibility of seeing more of her sank in, his pulse drummed in excited panic.

But for how long?

"It is. I want—" Her cell rang, and she stopped midsentence as she searched for it in her giant purse. The thing looked like a beach bag and was half as big as she was. When she finally found the phone, her eyes shot to his. "I'm sorry. I have to take this."

"No problem." He nodded, at a loss of what more he wanted to say.

She gave him another of those kilowatt smiles. "I'll see you around . . . Raffaello."

He didn't like being called Raffaello any more than she liked being called Victoria. Or at least she hadn't . . . *before.* It was something they'd bonded over. When they were young and green. So damn green.

She laughed at the scowl on his face over her use of his full name, but then she left with a wave before he could respond.

He sighed and scrubbed at his chest as the weight he'd

been battling all day pulled against it. Over the years, he'd imagined what he'd say to Tori if he ever saw her again, but all of the practiced lines had abandoned him. The apology he desperately wanted to give had sat on the tip of his tongue, halted at the sight of her.

He stared after her until she disappeared through the front door of the grocery store. She was just as bright and beautiful as he remembered, and he felt grimy in comparison—especially today. The years hadn't dulled her shine, but they'd darkened his.

The memory of the last time he'd let her walk away flashed before his eyes, and regret punched him in the stomach, stealing all the air from his lungs.

He should've at least gotten her number.

Fuck!

Adrenaline kickstarted Rafe's feet as he flew out the door, sending the bell overhead jangling to scan the parking lot for a shock of red hair, but it was nowhere in sight. Only a handful of cars and a street empty of her unmistakable color.

"You didn't pay for those."

He spun around to find a young woman pointing at the basket of groceries he'd walked out with.

"Dammit," he grumbled under his breath. He'd been so distracted by Tori he'd forgotten where he was and what he was doing. "Sorry," he told the clerk. "Let's fix that."

When she gave him a skeptical look, he handed her the basket and motioned for her to lead the way inside.

He glanced over his shoulder one last time.

Gone.

Tori was gone.

But if she were staying in town, he'd find her.

CHAPTER 2

Tori

Tori had been staring at a blank screen for the last hour. The bright white of the empty document felt jarring now that the light had dimmed in the room she'd turned into her workspace. It had everything she needed to put words on the page: a desk for writing, a reading chair for research, and a bookshelf filled with ways to procrastinate.

But the words hadn't come.

The tiny bungalow she'd rented came fully furnished, and she had it on a month-to-month basis. She planned to leave before Christmas, though the owner had informed her she could stay until the end of the year. With her lack of progress on the book, Tori wondered if she'd need to stay until the spring.

With a frustrated sigh, she gave up and closed the lid of her laptop. The sun had set while she'd been working, but she'd been oblivious to its descent, focusing solely on the story she was supposed to be writing.

Her literary agent wanted the first three chapters of the book she'd pitched, but she hadn't written a single word.

Well, that's not true.

She *had*, but she'd deleted them.

Across the small white writing desk, she stared through the window, looking out onto the town's park. The oak and pine trees still had their greenery, though she looked forward to when the air would cool and the leaves would turn colors. Los Angeles had been her home for the last few years, and the climate in Southern California had made her miss the change in seasons. While she'd enjoy experiencing fall, her deadline loomed in the distance, not nearly far away enough.

But at this rate, she'd likely still be in Rolling Brook for that.

Tori groaned and slouched in the desk chair, her head falling back as she shut her eyes. With her lids lowered, the man she'd been trying *not* to think about for the last hour invaded her thoughts.

Rafe Alonso.

She'd mentally prepared herself to see him again, but running into him at the grocery store was still a shock. When she'd glanced over, it had felt like being in a car crash, where time would slow down right before the moment of impact.

And what an impact.

The sight of Rafe had slammed into her, along with all the memories—good and bad. Her stomach burned as the bad ones intruded. With a deep breath, she pushed those back into the box she kept them in. Dwelling on past hurts would get her nowhere she wanted to go. Hadn't she learned that the hard way?

Besides, she couldn't crumble; she had a book to write.

Her original plan had been to call him, then set up a meeting. She'd wanted to lead with the reason she'd moved here—to interview him for her book. That way, they could keep things on a professional level, leaving those memories in the past where they belonged.

But her body's response to seeing him had been anything but professional. She hadn't believed it was possible, but the man had gotten more handsome. His face had been sharper, more . . . chiseled, as though the years had worn away any softness from his youth. But the same scruff had covered it. She'd always loved its scratchiness under her palms.

Her belly tightened as she remembered the feel of it on *other* parts of her body.

Rafe's nose had always been strong under those brows as dark as his wavy hair. He'd worn it longer than when she'd last seen him, at least on top. The sides had been buzzed, and the look had made her ovaries sing. Plus, those eyes. They were sinful. Like melted dark chocolate, she wanted it to be poured all over her.

She shook the thought out of her head.

That's not why you're here.

She was here to talk to Rafe about the serial killer case he'd worked on. *Not* to get caught up in the past. But if she wanted his help, they would have to acknowledge their history. You couldn't spend nearly three years with someone, think they were *the* someone . . .

Tori sighed as the memories threatened to drag her under. She'd been so young and so wrong, and when it had ended . . . the *way* it did . . .

The burning in her gut reignited at the thought. After that, she expected things would be awkward between them—at first.

She took a deep breath and washed away the memories on the exhale. She'd made her peace with their fallout and hoped Rafe had, too, because she needed his insight for the book she wanted to write. Despite what it had cost her, she'd let him go, had moved on, and truthfully, hadn't expected to ever see him again.

Until the Suit of Hearts Slasher had made headlines.

Suddenly, his name was everywhere as the lead detective tracking down the killer. She'd followed every article, devoured every detail for news of the case.

The idea for a book had already sparked by the time Rafe caught the slasher. After close to a year of planning and researching, she'd realized she needed the help of someone with firsthand experience.

She needed Rafe.

Her heart squeezed like she'd dropped it in a vise, and she rubbed a hand over it.

No, what she *needed* was a new plan.

Should she call his office on Monday and try to set up a meeting? Or would it be better to ask for his help in person?

She debated but decided to use the weekend to work out her next move now that he knew she was in Rolling Brook.

At least he hadn't seemed angry at seeing her, just surprised—well, stunned. Tori frowned as her thoughts reverted to his appearance.

Apart from shocked, he'd seemed . . . troubled. The color of his eyes had been the same, but they hadn't sparkled as they'd used to. He'd appeared weighed down. Those broad shoulders she'd always loved had been tired, as though each year had added a load when it passed.

I wonder how he's be—

Something cold and wet touched her hand, and she jumped. Opening her eyes, she chuckled at the nose pushed into her palm. It was attached to the shaggy face of her silver labradoodle.

"Yes, Toby. I know it's dinner time." He'd been resting peacefully on the floor at her feet, but he never failed to remind her of his strict feeding schedule.

After a quick pat on Toby's head, she stood and headed for the kitchen. He trailed after her, his nails clicking on the hardwood floors.

She paused at the kitchen entrance to flip on the switch. The room had been updated with overhead can-light fixtures; they gleamed off quartz countertops. Stainless steel appliances and new cabinets in a dark blue shade completed the HGTV look.

Despite the updates, it still had its traditional layout, with a cute picture window above the sink looking out over the fenced backyard. It was big enough to allow Toby room to run in, even if he rarely wanted to. At the mere age of five, he'd become a lazy old man. He spent most of the day snoozing at her feet or begging for treats.

And she loved him for it. For the companionship only a dog could give.

Tori moved to the pantry beside the refrigerator and retrieved the bag of freeze-dried food she'd brought for Toby. Her attempt at getting groceries for herself had been cut short by seeing Rafe and then receiving the call from her agent.

She'd been putting the woman off for days and knew she'd had to answer . . . or she'd just used the call as a stalling technique.

She frowned, holding the bowl of dog food suspended in her hand.

Is that what she'd done? Run from Rafe at the first opportunity?

Toby barked and broke her from her reverie. Shaking off those thoughts, she set his bowl by the back door. She smiled as he sat and waited until she gave him the signal to dig in. He kept her from being lonely and provided someone to talk to and cuddle with.

She stroked the dog's spine. He'd been black as night as a puppy, but as he'd aged, his color had leached away into the dapper gray gentleman she viewed him as now. His hair was caught somewhere between a poodle's curl and a lab's smoothness. He'd shed too much for the family who had initially bought him, needing a hypoallergenic dog for their little boy. But she'd been happy to take him off their hands. That had been over four years ago, and she had no regrets.

She chuckled as Toby scarfed down his dinner. He'd yet to live up to his namesake when it came to hunting anything but food. Sherlock Holmes would be less than impressed with this Toby. His primal instincts were only good for sniffing out treats she'd forgotten she'd left in a pocket or a purse. Those he could find without fail. But anything else? He was uninterested.

She loved him regardless. Toby was the sole man in her life—the only one she'd wanted in her life for quite some time.

Her stomach ached at the thought, and she wasn't sure if it complained out of hunger or something else— something she didn't want to acknowledge.

Giving Toby one more pat, she went in search of her own dinner, even though the thought of a pair of dark eyes had her craving something other than food.

* * * *

Tori

Tori smiled as she stopped in front of the window of a hardware store with a whimsical display of tools. Wrenches, screwdrivers, and more trappings she didn't know the name of were artfully arranged into a humanistic scene.

A workshop?

She stared at the flashlight with jigsaw blades for arms. It sawed into a tiny block of wood held up by Allen wrenches like an offering to a god. She shook her head with a chuckle.

Someone has a twisted sense of humor.

The honk of a car horn had her turning, but it wasn't

the angry blast of a driver with road rage she expected from living in the city. Only a neighborly wave as the driver passed a friend on the street.

As she took in the small town, the afternoon sun warmed her face. The main street of mom-and-pop stores stood awash in various bright colors, the shop windows baring hand-painted signs. It was almost as if she'd stepped back in time.

Or into a Hallmark movie.

Rolling Brook's serenity contrasted with the bustle of L.A. she'd grown accustomed to. She'd always loved the grit and grime of the city, though. Growing up in suburbia, Tori had craved the noise and the crowds. She hadn't looked back when she left home for college in Chicago.

But standing on the corner of the picturesque street with the breeze ruffling her hair, her chest ached with a longing that slowly widened into a pit of loneliness. About a year ago, she'd begun feeling dissatisfied—with her work, her life, all of it. Being in this small town gave her hope of filling in the pit. She'd needed a change in scenery—in more ways than one.

She ambled on her way to the library with that aim in mind. She'd been trying and failing to write at home. When she'd still been experiencing writer's block this morning, she'd taken Toby on a walk through the park and returned to the grocery store, but as soon as she'd sat down to write—nothing. Nothing had helped break through the wall she was up against, so she'd thought trying to write somewhere new might help her scale it.

She continued along the brick pedestrian walkway,

passing and noting what Rolling Brook had to offer. When the bright red awning of a coffee shop caught her eye, she vowed to visit it soon. As she passed by the door, a young couple exited, and the scent of freshly ground beans hit her nostrils. She breathed in deeply, savoring the appetizing aroma. Too bad she'd already had four cups today. If she went for another, she might be up all night.

Peeking through the entryway, she saw black chairs, warm wooden tables, and a stained concrete floor in a deep cherry. The colors made her think of the different stages of the coffee-making process, and she wondered if that had been the designer's intention. After one last pining glance, she turned the corner and saw the town library up ahead.

The cinder-block building dated to the 1950s, and with its mint green paint, it was impossible to miss. It looked to be all on one level, and she wondered how extensive their collection might be. The longest face of the building, covered in steel, international-style windows, spread the length of the block.

Tori passed through an opening in the low breeze-block wall surrounding the property. The library set back from the sidewalk and had a small lawn with freshly mowed grass, tables with umbrellas, and a couple of benches. If her computer battery weren't forever dying on her, she wouldn't have minded sitting outside to write. But since it did, she needed an outlet and preferably a quiet corner to hole herself up in.

She walked up the wide-set stairs and pulled the glass front doors open. When she entered, the cooler air sent a cold chill racing over her and raised goosebumps on her arms. The open floorplan of the library's single level made it appear spacious. In the center, row after row of racked books stood waiting.

Unable to help herself, she wandered to the fiction section, bypassing the circulation desk—which was currently unmonitored—and a children's area partitioned off with stacking cubes in primary colors. The sound of a child's giggle, followed by the unmistakable hushing noise of their mother, sent a pang of sorrow to her heart.

She hadn't experienced that in years.

Seeing Rafe brought too many things she'd hoped never to deal with again to the surface. She absently rubbed the spot as she wound her way through the stacks of books.

Her fingers traced the spines as her eyes scanned the filing codes.

G-a, G-e, G-o . . . there! She found the author she was looking for and pulled the book from the shelf.

"Oh, that's a good one."

She jumped at the wispy voice and spun around to find an older woman with short dark hair streaked in gray.

The woman smiled as she addressed Tori, her light green eyes crinkling as she tapped a long, wrinkled finger on the book she held. "Kept me riveted."

Tori returned the smile as her chest ballooned with pride. "Really?"

The woman pushed her cat-eye glasses further up her nose. "Yes. It's brilliant. Have you read T. E. Graham before?"

Her face split into a grin. "Actually, I *am* T. E. Graham."

The woman blinked, her expression turning quizzical.

"*You're* T. E. Graham?"

"Yes." Tori wasn't taken aback by the woman's surprise.

She'd intentionally kept her full name and her photo off her books. Not that she felt ashamed, but it never hurt to add to the air of mystery when you wrote books meant to keep people on the edge of their seats.

And when she'd first been published, she hadn't wanted anyone to know who she was. She'd been trying so hard to start over. Be someone new.

You are someone new.

Tori blinked away the memories to find the woman shaking her head.

"I always thought you were a man." She chuckled, and Tori joined in. "Well, I'm very pleased to meet you. I'm Meg."

"Tori Elizabeth Graham"—she smiled and clasped Meg's outstretched hand—"nice to meet you."

"What brings you to Rolling Brook?"

"I'm working on a book. I hope—"

"Really! That's fascinating. You know what? You should do a signing while you're here." Meg's hand landed on Tori's arm as the older woman became excited. "How long are you staying for?"

Her glee faded at the reminder of her deadline. A line marred her brow as she responded, "I'm not sure. I'm sorry, but that's not why I'm here. I've got a deadline to meet and need to get some serious word count in." She swallowed against the anxiety rising up her throat. She'd fallen so far behind already.

Thankfully, Meg didn't seem put off by her response. "Well, I'm the extent of the library staff, dear." She patted

Tori's hand. "You let me know if you change your mind."

She nodded, grateful to drop the subject. "Is there a quiet desk by an outlet I can use?"

Meg nodded. "There is. I try to keep the whole place quiet for people reading or working, but I think I have just the spot for you."

When she beckoned, Tori placed her latest release on the shelf and followed Meg to a table in the back corner of the library. It hid, wedged behind a tall stack of non-fiction books so that you couldn't see into the rest of the building. A window graced the wall behind the table, adding a lovely glow from the natural light.

When Meg stopped, Tori set her bag on the small wooden desk. "This is perfect. Thank you."

"You're welcome. If you need anything, you can find me at Circulation." She smiled before leaving Tori to it.

Two hours later, when her phone buzzed and broke her concentration, there were at least words on the page.

That was progress, right?

She cracked her neck and stretched her arms over her head. She had a bad habit of hunching forward over her laptop when she fell deep into what she was writing.

Now, she felt a pop and winced. Thirty-four wasn't that old, but already, she thought she could use regular chiropractic care.

I guess it's a hazard of the job.

She reached for her tote bag and pulled out her phone. The buzzing had been a text message from a number she didn't recognize.

When she selected the message, she found a notice from

the local county's automated information system. She'd signed up for alerts as soon as she'd decided to stay in town, partially out of habit but also her limitless curiosity. Living in the city, she'd learned to use the system for traffic delays, changes to bus routes, or natural disaster notices like wildfire evacuations.

Curious about what Dale County needed to warn her of, she opened the text message.

DCSO: Human remains discovered in wooded area off Lesco Drive. Identity, cause of death, not yet known.

The Dale County Sheriff's Office had found a body. Tori didn't know if that was a regular occurrence for the area, but the part of her that loved a juicy story wanted to know every sordid detail. Her brain sped ahead with ideas of how she could use this in her book.

Was the body male or female? Was there evidence of foul play? Or was this a tragic accident?

Her writer's brain weaved a story with the answers it supplied. She could use some of this when she wrote the first victim of her fictional serial killer.

Pulse racing with excitement, she closed her laptop and shoved it in her bag. She needed more information.

Making quick strides through the library, she waved at Meg as she breezed past.

Where the heck is Lesco Drive?

Tori didn't know, but she determined to find out.

CHAPTER 3

Rafe

Rafe stared down at the face of the murdered young woman. Tendrils of red hair spread across the dark soil she'd been deposited upon. Her light blue eyes were vacant, staring at nothing. His gaze took in every feature: the short button nose, the high, rounded cheeks, the cupid's bow mouth. It hung open slightly, the lips bluish-purple in color, which wasn't the result of lipstick.

Not Tori.

He worked to steady his breathing as he repeated that fact over and over in his head. There'd been no identification on the body, and when he'd arrived on the scene, the bright red hair was the first thing he'd noticed. His stomach had dropped to his feet. Then he'd stumbled toward the woman on trembling legs, desperate for it not to be her.

I hoped we were getting a second chance, but now she's . . .

Rafe swallowed against the bile, threatening to rise up his throat, and tried to shake off the thoughts that had run through his head.

He inhaled, pulling in the scents of pine needles, moss, and damp earth from the rain they'd gotten the night before, but underneath those natural aromas, the scent of something heavier lingered—death. An unpleasant odor he'd smelled too many times before. Even in this wooded area, death permeated.

But the woman wasn't Tori.

Whoever this poor soul was, Rafe didn't know her. His eyes traveled past her face to the slit stretched across her pale throat. The sight was hauntingly familiar, and a strong sense of déjà vu washed over him. Multiple images of pallid necks marred by red slashes flashed through his mind.

"Captain?" The hand landing on his arm nearly made him flinch. He schooled his features back to impassivity before turning to see who wanted his attention.

He didn't know the uniformed officer in front of him. Lesco Drive extended outside of Rolling Brook, but the county had called in Rafe because of his experience as a detective in Chicago. A death like this wasn't something the sheriff's office dealt with often.

This wasn't an elderly woman who had passed peacefully in her bed. It was a life snuffed out much too soon.

Glancing around, he noticed half the team had turned some shade of green. Not even the detective from the neighboring district looked unaffected.

But Rafe had learned to set it aside. And he did so now,

smothering the rage, the turmoil, and initial panic that it could have been Tori.

"What is it, officer?"

The man glanced toward the body again, then rubbed the back of his hand over his mouth before answering, "The coroner just got here."

"All right." He didn't understand why the officer felt the need to inform him.

"He requested everyone give him some space."

Ah. Rafe nodded and followed the uniform as he led him about ten feet from the dump site.

From this distance, the woman's body became a stark white smear across the surface of verdant earth tones. She'd been stripped of her clothes, and what had been fair skin was made paler with its lack of life.

The coroner approached the corpse. Rafe hadn't met him before, and the overweight man lumbering to his knees beside the body didn't imbue him with confidence. Almost immediately, the coroner gagged and turned away.

After the man got himself under control, he started examining the woman. In under a minute, the coroner shoved to his feet and moved quickly to his vehicle.

He's going to barf.

The sound of heaving proved Rafe right as he headed for the coroner's car.

"Did you know her?"

"What?" The man coughed, gagged again, then turned to look at Rafe, though he didn't move from his bent-over position, one hand still resting on the trunk of his car.

"The victim. Did you know her?" It occurred to Rafe that

a man used to seeing death would only react by tossing the contents of his stomach if he knew the deceased.

"No"—the coroner shook his head and swiped a hand over his mouth before straightening—"first murder victim."

He couldn't help the incredulity in his tone. "Are you serious?"

How did this man get elected?

The coroner's light brown eyes narrowed as he pushed the wire-framed glasses he wore back up his nose. "Look . . . Detective," he guessed, "I don't know where you come from, but murder isn't commonplace here."

Rafe scowled. He found it hard to believe this could be the first homicide in Dale County, and the man in front of him had to be in his mid-to-late forties with the receding hairline and pronounced paunch he sported. "How long have you been coroner?"

The man stiffened and crossed his arms over his chest. "Less than a year."

Great. Rafe sighed inwardly. He hadn't been appointed lead on this case, but getting a real medical examiner to look at the remains would be his first priority if that happened.

He mirrored the coroner's posture and raised an eyebrow in challenge. "What can you tell me about the body then?"

The coroner blanched as he glanced toward the dead woman again. Then he cleared his throat and met Rafe's stare. "She's between 17 to 25 years of age, has been deceased between eight to twelve hours, and was killed off-site before being moved here."

Rafe had surmised most of that himself. About to ask if the county had a forensics lab, a commotion drew his attention.

The other detective stood behind two officers who had formed a wall with their arms outstretched. The distance made it too hard for him to hear, but from the detective's defensive stance, it wasn't good.

"Excuse me," he told the coroner without looking at him, then started toward the group.

After a few steps, a familiar voice turned his expression sour.

What the hell was *she* doing here?

The blood on simmer from his interaction with the coroner pounded in his veins as he stomped the last few feet.

"No press. You can't release this yet." The detective's voice pleaded when it should have been stern.

"But I'm not a reporter. I swear. I just—"

"What the hell are you doing here, Tori?" Rafe barked over the detective's shoulder.

The man glanced between them. "You know her?"

The scowl didn't leave his face. "Yeah."

Even though relief loosened something in his chest at the sight of her standing there with pleading eyes—alive— the rest of him was pissed that she would be here. The darkness always clinging to him had no place getting near her light.

The officers started to relax, and he tensed, not wanting Tori to see the body. "Do *not* let her through!"

She frowned at his tone, but he could see she didn't

understand why he wouldn't—*no, couldn't*—let her see the devastation behind him.

"Why not? I'm not press."

When his scowl deepened, she turned her attention to the detective. "He can vouch for that." She waved her hand at Rafe, and his anger climbed to the point of boiling over.

No way would he allow her a look at the corpse. "Can I? You studied journalism, didn't you?" He crossed his arms and gave her his most rigid stare. "How do I know you're not writing for a news outlet somewhere?"

Her eyes widened in surprise at his defensiveness before narrowing on him, the bright green as sharp as a laser. "I suppose you'd have to trust me."

His heart sank; the barb of her words hit home and drained the anger from him. He sighed, and the officers barricading Tori shifted uncomfortably.

When he asked the question this time, his tone was resigned. "What are you doing here?"

Her stare softened as if she knew she'd hurt him. "I got the alert, and I . . ."

He raised an eyebrow. "What? Thought you'd come take a look?" Rafe shook his head, unfazed by her curiosity, then looked skyward, asking for the help he needed to get through this before meeting her eyes again. "You don't want to see that, Tori."

She chewed her lip as she searched his face.

Damn, he used to love when she'd do that. It was a tell she felt uncomfortable, but it made him want to nibble on her lips himself.

"Can we talk?" She inclined her head and motioned

behind her.

He gave a slight nod, and she turned to walk away. Before he followed, he nudged the other detective. "Let's put up a perimeter. I don't know why the notification already went out, but since it has, she won't be the only one to come snooping."

The detective agreed and then instructed the other officers to tape the area off.

Tori waited by her car when he caught up to her. She was so beautiful. The last rays of sunlight peeking through the trees bounced off her bright hair like flames dancing in a fire. He hadn't gotten used to seeing her again—couldn't believe she'd come back into his life. But he wasn't sure she wanted a second chance the way he did. Not after her shot at him about trust.

At the thought, his scowl returned. "Why are you really here?"

She swallowed and tucked a strand of fire behind her ear. "I told you I'm working on a book. Well, my book is about a serial killer."

His whole body tensed uncomfortably. Every muscle constricted, bracing against the blow he knew was about to land.

"I'd like to interview you"—she chewed her lip—"about the Suit of Hearts Slasher."

All the air in his lungs disappeared. "No," he wheezed out, thoughts wheeling. How could she ask him that? And with another murder victim right behind him.

No way in hell am I talking to her about that sick bastard.

"Come on, Rafe. I need your insight as the detective who

worked the case. I real—"

"NO!" His shout surprised him as much as Tori, who stumbled back a step.

He shook his head, then softened his tone to hide the panic roiling in his gut. "Write about something else."

"What?" That one word sounded like he'd asked her to do something impossible instead of the simple task of changing what she wrote her book about.

"You heard me."

She crossed her arms over her chest, and he could see the temper she rarely showed brewing behind the sparks in her eyes. "I've already pitched the book."

"Write. About. Something. Else." His jaw clenched so tight it ached.

"I. Will. *Not.*"

Damned if the challenge in her voice didn't set his blood on fire. And *not* with anger. His gaze dropped to her mouth. Those wide lips were pressed into a firm line, and he had the urge to force them open.

Would she taste the same?

As he took a step toward her, her lips parted slightly.

"Captain?"

Rafe stopped on a groan and glanced over his shoulder. One of the uniforms gestured for his attention.

He waved a hand, then focused on the bright flame in front of him. He wanted to drink in her warmth, but he couldn't. Not yet. Not here.

"Go home, Tori."

She frowned slightly and glanced behind him. Undoubtedly, the officer stood there waiting.

When her eyes met his again, they were sharp like the gem they so clearly favored. "This isn't over."

Despite what she'd meant, her statement made him smile.

No, this is far from over.

She gave him one last glare before climbing into her car.

"Captain?"

"Yeah?" He watched Tori drive away with a mix of emotions that made him lighter and heavier all at once.

"Detective Gorsky found something."

Emotions he didn't have time to unpack right now.

Following the officer, Rafe pushed thoughts of her aside to focus on the job he had to do—a job he'd hoped never to do again.

* * * *

Rafe

Exhaustion dragged on Rafe. Dealing with a murder investigation was not how he'd planned to spend his Saturday night. His plans hadn't been very exciting—watching the latest James Bond film with a cold beer—but it was far more appealing than staring death in the face.

Another too-young, red-haired face.

Shaking the dead woman's image from his mind, Rafe unlocked his apartment. Without bothering to turn on the lights, he closed the door behind him and strode through the moonlight straight to the refrigerator. Even if his plans had changed, he could at least have a cold beer.

The beam from the refrigerator was almost blinding.

After he grabbed his Peroni and shut the door, he needed to blink the spots from his eyes. He popped the cap of his favorite beer—the red label, not the pale shit most people would think of when he told them he drank Peroni—then took a long swig.

As the malty amber beverage hit his palate, his tense muscles began to relax. They'd been tight since he'd gotten the call to come to the scene of a probable homicide.

After Detective Gorsky found a shoeprint, the sheriff's office sent a representative to the scene, which was fine with Rafe. He'd been happy to turn things over to the deputy and call it a night.

He'd hung up his detective hat months ago and had hoped by moving to such a small town, he'd never have to put it on again. But it seemed God, fate, or whoever the hell pulled the strings had other ideas.

The deputy had taken control and had the body prepared for transport to the regional lab, where a qualified medical examiner would take a look. Rafe hadn't been the only one unimpressed by the county coroner. Forensics, or what passed for it out here, had made a cast of the shoeprint Gorsky'd found. It was a lead, although, without a suspect, it was an ambiguous one at best.

But the M.E. should be able to give them an ID of the victim, and they could build a list of suspects from there. He worried about what else the M.E. might tell them. He hadn't been able to shake that sense of déjà vu, the similarities between the victims of the Suit of Hearts Slasher, despite knowing the bastard responsible for their murders was rotting in a jail cell.

Carrying what he had left of his beer, Rafe headed for the bathroom. More than anything, he wanted a shower to wash the stench of death from his nostrils. He navigated the dark hallway with familiar ease. When he reached his bedroom, he set his Peroni on a stack of boxes by the door before shedding his suit jacket.

He was working on kicking off his pants when he stumbled and fell into the stack of boxes, knocking them over. His beer toppled off, landing on the carpet of his bedroom floor.

Fuck! He was too tired to deal with this.

Kicking off the offending clothing, he slapped on the light. The beverage soaked into the plush beige carpet faster than he would be able to get it out.

He ran to the bathroom and grabbed a towel. As he knelt by the mess and tried to mop it up, the smell of malt replaced the lingering scent of death in his nose. Sighing at the small win, he mopped up what he could of the liquid.

With the beer situation managed, he reached for the boxes he'd tumbled. The smallest one from the top of the pile had come open. When he attempted to lift it, its contents spilled onto the floor. The sight of a little blue box paused the expletives about to drip from his lips.

Rafe knelt, his heart hammering as he picked up the tiny box. The velvet casing felt soft against his rough palm where he cradled it. He hadn't thought of it in years, and finding it now seemed . . .

He swallowed around the knot in his throat and drew in a much-needed breath. The company he'd hired to pack his home in Chicago had placed the small jeweler's container in a box labeled with high-value items. He supposed it was, though what it represented—its true value—was worth more to him than any dollar amount.

Unable to stop himself, Rafe opened the box. The emerald-cut diamond set on a thin gold band, accented on either side by square-cut emeralds, sent an ache from his heart all the way to the soles of his feet. The pain he'd dealt with before when he'd let Tori walk away hit him like a tsunami, and he fell on his ass.

Helpless against the onslaught, he shut his eyes and sank to the floor until he lay flat on his back. If he had one big regret in his life, it was never giving Tori that ring.

They'd both been young, her barely out of college and him only a few years on the force, but he'd been ready. From almost the first moment he'd met her, he'd known he wanted to spend the rest of his life with her. He hadn't cared when their plans had been thrown off course, not as long as she would be by his side. But life had a way of testing you when you thought you'd already weathered the worse, and he'd failed—severely. He'd let jealousy ruin what they had.

The memories assaulted him, and he groaned, squeezing his eyes tighter as if it would stop them. When a sharp stab of pain speared his chest, he winced, rubbing uselessly at the spot. It couldn't rub away the past. As much as he wanted a clean slate with her, Tori's earlier comment about trust meant that even if she'd forgiven him, she hadn't forgotten.

Back then, he'd thought it would be easier to let her go and move on. They'd both be better off with a fresh start.

He'd come to the conclusion that what they'd had couldn't be repaired. They'd gone through too much.

But how wrong he'd been.

He'd spent the last decade regretting his decision and wondered if he deserved a second chance with her now.

Would she give it to me?

He opened his eyes and sat up, staring at the engagement ring, which had never left its case. Rafe wasn't above begging for forgiveness, but he had to wonder if Tori still imagined a future with him. Had she done what he couldn't and gotten over him?

A new ache sprouted around his heart, and he slammed the lid closed.

This is pointless.

He pushed himself off the floor and shoved it back into the packing box. Reliving his screw-up was not how he wanted to spend the rest of his evening.

He shoved the boxes out of his path and headed for the shower. After flipping on the bathroom light, he frowned at his reflection in the mirror over the double sinks.

I look like shit.

The last few days had been rough. His battle with not letting the slasher case get to him hadn't been going so well. He needed a decent night's sleep and prayed the dreams wouldn't plague him tonight.

The only dream he *wanted* to have involved the kiss he'd missed with Tori. He'd back her up against her car, take that wide mouth, and fuse it to his. The fire of her temper had always burned hot, and some of his best memories of them together were of when they'd channeled that heat into the sheets.

Rafe shook his head. While the fantasy of kissing Tori appealed to him, he preferred making it a reality.

Turning from the mirror, he started the shower. Cold water blasted the black tiles of his walk-in. He let it warm up as he pondered how to approach her.

If he was going to have a future with her, he should probably start by giving her what she wanted in the present.

With an acquiescent sigh, he scrubbed his hands over his face, stepped into the shower, and let the warm water wash away the past.

He could do an interview—on his terms.

CHAPTER 4

Tori

Tori took a deep breath and stepped out of her car in front of the Rolling Brook Police Department. The building spoke of a bygone era, with its flat roof and cream stucco siding. Despite the morning sunshine warming everything around it, the police station appeared dull and far from inviting, making her apprehensive about what her reception would be.

Not ready to face it yet, she leaned against her car door to gather her thoughts. She'd come here to ask Rafe again about the interview, hoping his reaction on Saturday had been knee-jerk and with time to review it, he'd change his mind.

Though that was her hope, she knew better than to rely on it. She'd been working on a convincing argument for the past twenty-four hours—when she hadn't been lost in her book.

She sighed as her mind flashed back to their meeting at

the crime scene. She hadn't wanted to ask him that way, but why he'd gotten so defensive was beyond her. She rubbed at an ache in her head as regrets at letting her anger rise to meet his assaulted her temple.

Her lack of access to the crime scene had actually set the wheels in her mind turning, and she'd written the first three chapters of her book on Sunday. After she'd sent those off to her agent, she'd finally come up for air to take care of a poor, neglected Toby. He'd stayed so patient with her, though, lazily snoozing by her side until she'd been ready to do something other than write.

A stray thought made Tori pause. Maybe the anger had sparked her creative juices. In the past, Rafe had always been her muse. He was one of the few people who could bring out her temper. She was usually a hard one to rile and prided herself on being unflappable. But she'd been neither of those things on Saturday.

Memories of the times he'd angered her flooded her senses, and she shivered. They'd often ended up rolling around on the floor until she'd forgotten why she'd been mad to begin with. He had that effect on her, the ability to push any thoughts but the dance of their bodies together out of her mind.

She touched her lips as she remembered their encounter.

Had he been going to kiss me?

It had certainly seemed that way. Dropping her hand, she closed her eyes, remembering the passion they used to have.

Would it be the same?

No matter. It wasn't why she was here.

She shook her head at herself and opened her eyes. She didn't have time to get wrapped up in Rafe again, and she didn't think her heart could withstand another break like that.

Absently, she rubbed a hand over it. Putty and tape held the poor thing together as it was.

She was here for an interview—nothing more.

Tori pushed herself off the car and headed for the building. At least in turning in the first few chapters of her book, she'd bought herself some time on the rest of the story. Time she hoped wouldn't be needed to convince Rafe to grant her an interview.

* * * *

Tori

"Tori?"

She spun at the sound of her name, and her eyes widened before settling into a huge smile. "Jameson."

She hadn't seen the giant ginger since she and Rafe split, but he hadn't changed.

His expression became as unbelieving as hers had been. "I can't believe it." He blinked, and his face split into a grin. "Does Alonso know?"

Tori prayed her face wouldn't reveal her embarrassment as she struggled to answer.

Yes.

Is he happy about why?

Absolutely not.

She was worried enough that, for a second, she considered begging Jameson to help her convince Rafe to let her interview him. They had always been a good team when it came to getting him to do things he'd rather not. Like the time they'd cajoled him into trying out snowboarding, and he'd fallen flat on his ass.

She would've chuckled at the memory, but nerves were causing her stomach to cramp uncomfortably. She needed to get this over with.

"Um, yes. Can you tell me where to find him?"

"Even better"—Jameson's grin sharpened—"I'll walk you to his office."

"Thanks." She took a deep breath before following the redhead. So much rode on Rafe's interview that she felt uncharacteristically stressed.

Each step seemed to tighten the knots in her stomach. She'd been careless to not come up with a backup plan, never assuming he would disagree. He'd been so angry when she'd asked . . . but why?

You'd think the man would want to talk about solving the case of the decade.

Tori rolled her eyes, which helped settle some of the tension squeezing her insides. She could do this. She'd been on the debate team in high school and knew how to turn an argument. All she had to do was stay focused on the end goal, which meant not letting the past—or how hot Rafe looked in the present—distract her.

Yeah, because that's a piece of cake.

Her disgruntled sigh turned into a small gasp as Jameson stopped and knocked on Rafe's office door.

You can do this.

She smoothed her hair and her expression before stepping to Jameson's side. The man's broad shoulders had obscured her entirely from view.

Rafe opened the door with a scowl, but it quickly became a smile as his gaze landed on her. "Tori."

She took the smile as a good sign and returned it with one of her own. "Rafe. Can we talk?"

"Of course." He stepped aside for her to enter, but Jameson remained in the way, staring between the two of them.

Rafe glared at the big redhead. "Did you need something, Lieutenant?"

Jameson grinned widely, glancing from Tori to Rafe and back again. "Nope. All good."

When he made no move to leave, Rafe cleared his throat.

Jameson chuckled, then caught her attention. "It's good to see you again, Tori. I hope we'll all have a chance to catch up?"

She'd been staring at Rafe while he'd focused on his friend. Now, she looked at Jameson, whose eyes shone with mischief. "I'd like that."

The big ginger turned to go, whistling as he walked away.

"He hasn't changed."

Rafe grunted at her statement and motioned her inside his office. "In some ways, he has." He waved at one of the chairs in front of his desk. "He's married with a kid now."

"That's wonderful." She smiled, though the realization brought an ache to her chest. She was happy Jameson had settled down, but she envied the family he'd created. It was something she wondered if she'd ever have. "Boy or girl?"

"Girl."

"That's nice." Fearing rejection again, she glanced around his office, still not ready to ask.

He'd always kept things tidy. The carefully stacked folders and the dust-free filing cabinet didn't surprise her. The blinds were closed, and the low table below the double window appeared free of any personal items. No awards, no citations, though she knew he had them. Nothing marked the office as anything other than a temporary place of work.

"How long have you been here?"

"A month or so."

She hummed in disapproval and finally met his gaze. He stared so intently at her that she had to fight the urge to squirm. "What?"

He raised an eyebrow. "Did you come here to study my office, or was there something else you wanted?"

As he finished his question, his tone changed—softened, deepened—and she swallowed against the desire the timber of his voice and the promise behind it ignited within her.

Oh boy, was there.

A vivid picture of her prone across the desk while he hovered over her, those dark chocolate eyes laughing before his mouth crashed down on hers, nearly made her gasp aloud. She banished the image from her mind and tried to ignore the heat centering in her core.

What were they talking about?

Interview, Tori. Ask about the interview.

With a steadying breath, she looked away from his chocolate depths. "Yes."

"Yessss?" Rafe dragged the word out, and she fought a blush at how much he'd thrown her off balance.

When she had her emotions under control, she met his stare again, challenging him. "Yes, there's something else I wanted."

Why are his eyes so mesmerizing?

She could see past the bravado to a pain he usually kept hidden, and the sight of it—knowing an answering one lived in her—made her want to heal him any way she could.

What? Where did that *come from?*

He blinked, and she pulled her thoughts back to the reason she was there.

"Are you going to tell me what it is, or am I supposed to use my imagination?" He wiggled an eyebrow at her, the corner of his mouth twitching.

"Very funny." She rolled her eyes for effect but couldn't help the smile sneaking across her lips. The fact he was in a good enough mood to tease her gave her hope she'd get the answer she needed.

She took a deep breath against the nerves tap dancing in her belly and began softly, "I can't change the book, Rafe. And I can't write it without your help." She paused and pleaded with her eyes. "Please let me interview you. If there are certain . . . *things* you can't tell me, I understand, but please give me a chance to learn the rest." She chewed her lip, studying him as she waited for his response.

She didn't see any sign of the anger he'd shown on

Saturday, but the warmth that had been in his eyes moments ago fled. It sounded like he sighed as he pinched the bridge of his nose.

"All right."

Positive she'd misheard him, she was tempted to shake her head. "All right? As in, yes, I can interview you?" The tap dancing in her stomach crescendoed into a full-blown cabaret as giddiness washed over her.

He nodded, but when he met her gaze again, the teasing had returned to his expression. His eyes seemed to smirk at her as he said, "I have conditions."

Relieved and trying to hide it, Tori crossed her arms over her chest, then narrowed her eyes at him. "What kind of conditions?"

At this rate, she was desperate enough to promise him anything.

Rafe smiled, big and genuine, making her breath catch. She'd forgotten how powerful those were. Swallowing against the longing clawing at her throat, she waited.

"Have dinner with me."

A line of confusion marred her brow. "That's a condition?"

He chuckled, and the sound was rich and deep—and familiar. The hairs on the back of her neck stood at attention, and she fought a shiver of delight.

"No. It's a request." He leaned over his desk toward her, his smile returned, and any coherent thoughts leaked from her brain.

She could smell his cologne—cedar and smoke. The same he'd worn before, and the familiar scent shot arrows of heat straight to her ovaries.

"We can discuss the conditions then."

Mmm, I've got something I'd like to discuss with you, and it doesn't need words.

"Tori?" She was staring at a stray lock of hair that had fallen onto his forehead.

Would it feel the same? Her fingers twitched in her lap with the wish to find out.

"What do you say?" He waited for her answer.

"What?" She met his eyes and saw the laughter in them.

Oh, for Pete's sake! Clearly, it had been too long since she'd been with a man.

"Yes, fine." She cleared her throat. "When do you want to do dinner?"

"Seven o'clock at my place. Tonight?"

His place? A thought occurred to her, and she smiled. Fond memories flooded her and cooled the desire, heating her blood. "You still like to cook?"

Rafe grinned at her, a hint of wickedness in it. "I've gotten even better at it."

So much for her blood cooling . . .

She tried not to think about what he'd actually meant or how delicious his grin was as she made a show of gathering her things. "Well, that's . . . great."

When she stood, he followed suit and moved around his desk.

Ready to flee before she needed an ice bath, she told him, "Send me the address."

She stepped toward the door, then stopped in her tracks as an idea hit her. With a grin of her own, she turned and demanded, "I want *osso buco*."

It had been her favorite meal he'd made. She hadn't eaten it in years because every time she'd tried it at a restaurant, it hadn't tasted as good.

"Consider it done."

She could tell from his softened expression he remembered it was her favorite dish, and an ember of warmth sparked in her chest.

Desperate for air that didn't smell of him, she nodded. "See you at seven."

He walked her to the door. "Seven. And Tori?"

Cursing internally, she worked to smooth her features into impassivity before facing him.

She preferred the grumpy Rafe if she had any chance of keeping things purely professional between them. "Yes?"

"Bring your appetite." He winked, then gently closed the door in her face.

CHAPTER 5

Tori

"I need a drink." Tori huffed out a breath and glared at herself in the mirror. She'd touched up her makeup and styled her hair. It lay in loose waves around her shoulders. The result meant she looked . . . polished, but a little voice niggled she was trying too hard. And she didn't need Rafe thinking *that.*

Dinner started in less than an hour, and her nerves had been on edge all afternoon. A shot of whiskey would help calm those, but if this was work, and it *was*, she shouldn't have one. On a groan, she turned away from the mirror.

Where he lay on the bed next to the mountain of clothing she'd tried on and then discarded, Toby whined in response. She was no closer to figuring out what to wear than she had been an hour ago when she'd started.

Rubbing the top of the dog's head, she laid hers against his and sighed. "I need serious help."

Toby licked her neck, and she giggled. Lifting her head,

she scratched behind his ears. "Thanks, old man."

Some of the tension left her, and she glanced at the clothes on her bed again. Nothing seemed right. She wanted to strike a balance between date-cute and work-cute but had failed miserably.

As she turned to look through her closet again, the phone rang. She reached for it and answered as she searched through her options, "Hello."

"Hello, yourself, missy. What is this I hear about you being back in Illinois—not an hour away—and yet you haven't visited?" Tori's older sister Veronica had perfected the pouting tone, and hearing it now made her wince.

"Sorry, Ron. I've only just arrived, and I will visit—promise. I'm up against a deadline on this book, and I—"

"Don't use your book as an excuse! It's been months, and Auggie and Ali would love to see you. You know you're their favorite aunt."

The comment made her smile because it was true. Despite having two older brothers who'd married, her sister's children still loved her best. Even if she never had a child of her own, she felt grateful for her relationship with her niece and nephew. "I'd love to see them, too."

"Then come visit. I won't take no for an answer."

Tori sat on her bed and stared at her nearly empty closet. She would love to drop everything and drive up to see her family. They lived in Crystal Bend, a city about an hour north. The same one she'd grown up in. But right now, she had too much on her plate.

Like figuring out what to wear.

"Fine, but only if you help me first. I'm desperate, Ron."

She paused and took a deep breath, worried about her sister's response to what she was about to admit. "It has to do with Rafe."

Veronica gasped audibly at the mention of his name. "Is that why you're back here? I thought he was old news." Tori could imagine the frown and stern look she knew would be on her sister's face, but then Ron's voice softened. "What are you doing, Tor? You know how bad it ended last time."

Yes, I do. Her sister's words stung as they picked at the scab over her heart, threatening to uncover memories she'd rather leave in the past.

Maybe if she kept reminding herself of that, it would stop her hormones from going crazy every time she saw him—maybe.

She cleared her throat. "It's not like that. I'm interviewing him for my book."

Her sister gave a noncommittal hum, and Tori felt herself blushing. At least Veronica couldn't see her body's response to her half-truth. "We're having dinner tonight."

She didn't say anything, so Tori rushed on, "It's for the interview. Totally professional, um, I just—" She bit her lip before blurting, "I have no idea what to wear. Please help."

"If it's 'totally professional,' I'd think deciding on an outfit wouldn't be a problem."

She groaned at her sister's tone. There was a smirk in there and a raised eyebrow; she was sure of it. "Please don't 'mom' me right now. I need your advice—as a woman— friend to friend."

"Ohhh-kkkay,"—Veronica let out a long-suffering sigh—

"fine."

She would bet her sister rolled her eyes.

When Veronica spoke this time, Tori heard the grin in her voice. "Even if it's for work, it doesn't hurt to make him wish he had handled things differently . . . before."

She couldn't help her mischievous grin at the thought of making Rafe suffer a little bit.

"So, here's my advice—tight jeans and a low-cut blouse. Top it with a fitted blazer. That way, you're work casual with sex appeal without going date dressy."

Tori breathed a sigh of relief, and some of the gymnasts doing acrobatics in her stomach took a break from their routine. "Thanks. Oh, what about shoes?"

"Wedges. Heels are trying too hard, and you lose the point of the outfit."

She'd known Veronica would know exactly what to wear. She could've called her sister an hour ago and saved herself the anxiety. "Great! You're a lifesaver. Now, I really have to change and get out of here, or I'll be late."

"You're welcome, but don't think I forgot our deal. I'll be expecting a visit."

"You'll get it." Tori smiled, feeling lighter at the prospect of seeing her family. They were a big and rowdy bunch but never failed to fill her with joy. She turned to them whenever she felt the dark intruding, and their light always replenished hers.

"And call me after. I want to know how things go with him." Veronica's tone had returned to mothering.

"I will." In truth, Tori was grateful she had her sister to talk things over with. They were six years apart but as close as good friends who'd seen each other through hard times in the past.

"Tori?"

"Yeah? I got to go, Ron." She dug through the pile of clothes for the items her sister had suggested.

"I know, just . . . be careful."

Famous last words.

* * * *

Rafe

Dean Martin crooned softly in the background as Rafe chopped the shallot for his risotto. He'd grown up listening to Dino and hoped having the King of Cool's music playing from the speaker on his kitchen counter would set the right mood.

It was a calculated move—one he'd bet Tori picked up on. When they'd been a couple, cooking together had been a regular date-night activity, and Dino had always been part of the routine.

Rafe wanted to remind her of the good memories they'd shared. Then maybe she'd be open to making some new ones.

He moved the shallot to a prep bowl and started to grate the parmesan cheese. But he quickly stopped, realizing at this rate, everything would be finished before she arrived. He'd been so amped about her agreeing to dinner he'd started on it as soon as he'd gotten home. The *osso buco* was already cooking, and the risotto was nearly ready to start.

He glanced at the clock on the stove. It was almost seven. Picking up the small pile of cheese between his thumb and pointer finger, he dropped it into his mouth. As the salty flavor settled on his tongue, he set aside the box grater and parmesan. If this was going to be like old times, he had to leave something for Tori to do.

Smiling at the thought, he reached for his wine. The light red Chianti swished in his glass as he tilted it to his lips. Something else that had been her favorite. Notes of berry and smoke hit his palate, and he hummed in approval. He still preferred Peroni, but the wine tasted damned good. Hopefully, she'd like the bottle he'd bought specifically for her.

Setting his glass down, Rafe surveyed the kitchen. The Instant Pot held the *osso buco*. His mom gave it to him last Christmas after falling in love with the pressure cooker and insisted he have one. He'd only used the thing a couple of times, and the urge to check on the meal was strong, but to pop the seal would ruin it. The veal shanks had about thirty more minutes before they'd be ready to serve.

If all went according to plan.

He cleaned up the prep dishes, set out the rest of the ingredients for risotto next to his gas stovetop, and lit a few candles on his eat-in kitchen table.

He had good food, good music, good wine . . . all he needed now was Tori.

He couldn't help but glance at the clock again. It showed him ten after, but she'd never been one for punctuality. It used to drive him up the wall how she'd always be late whenever they went out.

I guess some things never change.

He chuckled and leaned against his granite countertop. But he quickly sobered. Despite the romantic atmosphere, he had a long way to go toward winning her back. A frown marred his full lips as he acknowledged the apology he owed her. If they were going to be able to start over, he had to get that out of the way first.

Eating crow sounded a lot less appealing than *osso buco.*

Not that he didn't want to apologize—he did. But to do so, he'd be bringing up past hurts, and he didn't know how they would affect her. She seemed so much like the bright star he'd fallen in love with all those years ago that he was afraid of watching her glow dim again.

An ache pulsed around his heart, and he stood to rub it as memories he'd rather leave in the past made their way to the present.

"I saw you with him." Rage had created a red haze hovering at the edge of Rafe's vision. He curled his hands into fists and clenched his teeth against the onslaught of Tori's tears.

"Of course you did. He's my counselor." Her body shook with a sob before she speared him with a look that made it hard to breathe. "Why are you being like this?"

He couldn't see the pain in her big green eyes, only deceit. "Then why were you meeting with him outside the office?" He opened and closed his fists, but the tidal wave of hurt he ran from kept creeping closer. The anger surged, and he yelled, "I SAW YOU!"

Without thought, he slammed his hand into the wall. The

gypsum board gave way under his fist, and Tori gasped.

When he turned to face her, she took a step back, her eyes as big as saucers. "You're scaring me, Rafe."

Not really aware of what she'd said, he advanced with a growl. "His hands were all over you."

"What? That's ridiculous! We were just having coffee." She shook her head at him, but he knew what he'd seen.

The man was fifteen years her senior, and he'd been leaning so close to her he'd practically been in her lap. Then the bastard had squeezed her shoulder. When he'd held her hand, right there, on top of the table, out in the open for anyone to see, the jeweler's box in Rafe's pant pocket had practically seared his leg.

Unable to look away, he'd stared, stricken by their intimate conversation. He'd finally gotten the ring and planned to propose to Tori that evening after picking her up from the counselor's office.

It sat next door to the coffee shop, and when he'd seen them through the window, he'd stopped in his tracks. A freight train had plowed into him, stealing his ability to breathe. Until the rage had burned through the shock freezing his limbs.

Rafe had been kindling it all the way home, and the blaze had built into an inferno by the time he'd unleashed it on Tori.

"THE FUCK YOU WERE!" He felt angry enough to want to grasp her shoulders and shake the truth out of her, but after she'd cleaved his heart in two, he was afraid if he touched her, he'd never let her go. Half of him wanted her to—to leave and let him lick his wounds in peace. But the

other half . . .

How could she do this? How could she cheat? After what they'd been through.

A snarl ripped from his throat as he backed Tori into the wall. While he towered over her, his vision turned inward, and he imagined letting loose on her counselor, pulverizing the fuck's face until it was unrecognizable.

I should be the one making her light up again, not that bastard!

His breathing became erratic, his body vibrating with anger as he fought for control. He'd almost done it. Had nearly let the rage take over, but the small part of his brain, which had remained sane, warned him it wouldn't have been worth it. A cop couldn't beat on some douchebag in the middle of a coffee shop. He'd never make detective with a strike like that on his record.

Tori's crying penetrated the pounding of blood in his ears, and Rafe brought himself back from that dangerous ledge.

His gut twisted as he stared down at her swimming eyes. He loved her more than anything and wanted to see her happy again. Like she had been . . . before. The ring was supposed to be the start of a new chapter for them. A reason to celebrate—enough to lift the gloom. But instead of looking forward with him, she'd looked elsewhere.

"How could you, Tori?"

Against the roar of his emotions, he nearly missed her soft reply, "You don't trust me."

The click of the door as she'd left still echoed in his head. Rafe blinked and realized the clicking was actually someone knocking on his door. He glanced at the clock,

7:17 p.m.

Shaking off the memory, he downed a gulp of wine and searched for the excitement he'd had all afternoon at the prospect of having dinner with Tori.

He couldn't rewrite the past, but he sure as hell wouldn't let her walk away again.

CHAPTER 6

Tori

When it felt like she'd been knocking for a ridiculous length of time, Tori glanced around the empty hall and wondered if she was in the right apartment building. This place looked brand new. The walls were painted a sleek light gray, bringing out the same shade in the abstract-patterned carpet. The modern atmosphere wasn't at all what she'd expected out of Rafe's home.

"You're late."

The amused tone had Tori whipping her head back to the door. Rafe smiled again, and it made her brain cells leak out. On the left corner of his mouth was a delicious crease.

What would he taste like there? Would it be different than before or as dark and spicy as she remembered?

Tearing her gaze away from his lips, she found his truffle eyes smirking at her. "I know. I'm sorry. Halfway here, I realized I forgot my phone. I would've left it, but I have all my notes and the questions I want to ask you on there."

He raised an eyebrow as he braced an arm against the doorway. The position made his bicep muscles strain against his white button-up shirt, and the veins in his forearm stood out because he'd rolled the sleeves up to his elbows. "I haven't given you my conditions yet."

Stop ogling him!

She brushed the comment off with a smile, hoping it hid the doubts playing with the tempo of her pulse. He better not back out on her. "Can I come in?"

He stepped to the side but barely far enough for her to pass by without touching him. Was he not sure he wanted to let her in?

She raised a brow this time as she squeezed through the opening he'd left her. Her arm brushed his, and despite the blazer, she felt a spark of electricity from the slight contact. Afraid to look at him, lest he see how off-kilter he made her, she glanced around his apartment. The ceilings were higher than she'd expected they'd be, and it made the box-like space less confining.

She'd walked into the "L" shaped kitchen with a large island in the center. Beyond it, a little eat-in area with a gorgeous live-edge table sat, currently covered in candles.

Candles? That was . . . unexpected.

Nibbling her lip, Tori moved to the island where a bottle of Chianti stood in invitation. This didn't seem like a professional dinner. Especially not when the music registered.

He was playing Dean Martin like old times.

Oh boy.

She was in trouble.

"For someone with questions to ask, you're awfully quiet." Rafe's voice sounded much too close.

She spun around and landed practically in his arms. Panic started to claw its way up her throat, and she gulped it down as she took a step back, hitting the island. "What is all this?"

Lines of confusion creased his brow. "Dinner."

"Uh, . . ." A nervous giggle escaped, and she turned crimson in mortification.

Kill me now.

She cleared her throat and willed the blood to leave her overly warm cheeks. "This is a bad idea, Rafe."

Looking into his eyes was a mistake. She chewed her lip as she stared at the dark chocolate swirling in turbulent eddies.

He stepped closer, boxing her in with an arm on either side of the island. "I disagree." His deep voice sounded amused, but the seduction in it made her knees weak.

When he bent his head toward her, the scent of his cologne replaced the delicious smells of tomato and garlic, sparking a different kind of hunger within her.

He lifted a hand and, with his thumb, pulled her bottom lip from between her teeth. A lightning rod of heat shot straight to her core and melted her resolve.

Rafe's mouth lowered to hers, and Tori closed her eyes, unsteady but uncaring, as she waited for his lips.

"When you chew your lip, it makes me hungry to do the same," he spoke so close to her mouth that his breath mingled with hers.

She stifled a groan.

What is he waiting on?

His hand cupped her face, his thumb brushing across her cheek and sending electric shocks all the way to her toes.

Kiss me, dammit!

"I never thought I'd have a chance to do this again." His breath tickled her ear, and she shuddered.

"Rafe," his name tore from her lips in a desperate plea, but instead of kissing her, he trailed his lips down her neck. Tori gasped.

"You smell the same." His nose brushed the hollow of her throat, and she shivered with need.

"So do you."

"I wonder . . ." he murmured as his hand came up to cup her face.

When she thought she couldn't take it anymore, his lips brushed hers—so soft, testing.

More!

As if he'd read her thoughts, he licked her lip where she'd been chewing it, then nibbled on the spot ever so gently.

Her mouth opened with a moan, and Rafe's tongue met hers. As they glided over one another, tasting and exploring, she gripped his shirt for grounding because her head swam with memories and sensations threatening to overwhelm her.

He tasted like wine and some other salty flavor—parmesan, maybe. The feel of him was familiar, and her body responded as though the years in between had never happened.

His hands slid up her back to pull her closer, and she wrapped a leg around him, the heat in her center searching for his. All the while, their tongues tangled in a well-known dance.

A voice in her head, which sounded remarkably like Veronica's, screeched at her to stop, but Tori ignored it. Reaching her arms around Rafe's neck, she pushed her chest as close to his as possible. She wanted to be skin-to-skin, to have those muscles she remembered under her hands.

Starving for more of him, she gripped his dark hair with her fingers and sucked on his tongue. He made a noise between a growl and a groan, then cupped her ass.

We're just as good together—maybe better.

His hand found her breast, and she mewled into his mouth. Arousal flooded her as he pinched her nipple through her bra. She was ready to beg him to take her to bed when a shrill beeping made him release her.

Rafe stared over her shoulder, but he didn't let her go.

Her head reeled, her chest heaving with each breath. "What is that?"

He met her gaze, and if she'd thought his eyes had been turbulent before, now a full-blown cyclone raged within them. "The timer for the *osso buco.*"

"Oh. Shouldn't you shut it off?" Her breathing returned to normal, but her thoughts hadn't caught up.

"Uh-huh. I should." Suddenly, he blinked, and a grin spread across his full lips. "How hungry are you?"

A blush warmed her cheeks as she realized what he was saying, and she swallowed another nervous giggle. She wanted to say, 'Not hungry at all,' but Ron's voice intruded again, admonishing her for kissing him in the first place.

What am I doing?

The desire fogging her brain cleared under the fear of having her heart broken again. She wasn't here for this.

Couldn't do this.

Not again.

* * * *

Rafe

Rafe had been grinning down at Tori, feeling lighter than he had in a year when he'd seen the mood in her eyes change.

His firebrand had retreated behind a wall of ice, then spent the entire dinner avoiding his gaze. He needed to see those emeralds—to know what she was thinking. Unfortunately, she'd steered the conversation away from anything too personal every time he'd tried to bring up their kiss.

He cursed himself for jumping the gun. He'd screwed up—again—by going too fast. He hadn't meant to practically consume her, but she'd been biting her lip, and he'd wanted—

No. He'd *needed* to kiss her. To know if their connection would be the same.

He'd gotten his answer, and it made him want to kiss her more.

Watching Tori now, he could tell by the determined gleam in her eye she was getting ready to ask him about the interview again, but he couldn't let her—not yet.

Not until he got the past off his chest.

Fuck, here goes.

"Tori, I'm sorry."

She finally looked at him fully, and the confusion on her face showed clearly in the crinkling of her nose. It was the cutest thing. "For kissing me?"

"What?" He shook his head, surprised she'd think that. "No." He rubbed a hand over the back of his neck. "Well, maybe for rushing things, but I meant sorry about . . . before."

He blew out a breath and reached for the hand fiddling with her wine glass. She'd barely drunk any of it.

When his fingers closed around hers and she didn't pull away, he took a deep breath and went for it, "After everything with the—"

Her hand tensed under his, and he heard her sharp intake of breath. Watching the turmoil cross her face, he decided not to say it.

In a soothing tone, he continued, "You stopped being you."

Now that he'd started, he had to get this out. "I felt like I was losing you, and then when I saw you with your counselor . . . I was jealous." Even remembering it brought back those feelings. He dropped her hand and scrubbed at his face. "I wasn't thinking straight."

Her expression darkened, her eyes going distant and pinched, but he had to finish.

"You looked happy again. I saw you smile for the first time in so long, and it cut me that he should be the one to make you smile again and not me. I . . . I failed you, Tori, and I let my jealousy ruin us. I'm so sorry. If I could go back . . ."

Rafe sighed and felt a weight slip from the pile on his chest as he said what he'd waited over a decade to say to her, "I wouldn't have let you go."

He knew he'd given her a lot to take in, but her vacant stare and lack of response worried him.

A few moments later, her hand on the table clenched. "I needed to go, Rafe."

He wasn't sure what to say in response.

"And you never came after me," she nearly whispered, her eyes flooding.

His heart squeezed uncomfortably in his chest, his instinct to reach for her. But she blinked the tears away and stood before he got the chance. "Tori—"

"Look"—she faced him with eyes hardened into gemstones—"I came here to interview you for my book. Not to dredge up the past. Are you going to let me do that or not?"

His shoulders drooped in disappointment as the weight from his chest settled in his stomach. "Of course, I said I would."

She gave a curt nod. "Great, then I'll be in touch tomorrow to schedule an appropriate time and place to conduct it. For now, I think we could both use some space from each other."

I'm losing her again.

"If that's what you want."

"It is." She made her way to the front door, and though his heart screamed at him to stop her, he knew he couldn't. "Goodnight, Rafe."

"Goodni—"

She stormed out the door before he even finished his response. He sank into the chair and poured the rest of the wine into his glass.

That hadn't gone as he'd hoped it would.

About to take a sip, Rafe's head popped up when the door opened. Tori's bright red hair appeared, and he jumped to his feet.

"This was at your door." She shoved a small manila envelope into his hand as the hope filling his chest deflated quickly.

"Thanks."

"Bye."

As quickly as she'd reappeared, she was gone. Rafe lowered into his chair, turning the envelope over, grateful for the welcome distraction from his sour thoughts.

No address.

Curious, he broke the seal and opened it. Upending the envelope, he shook out the contents. When a playing card hit his hand, he jerked back as if it had burned him, knocking his chair over during his scramble to his feet. His breathing accelerated in panic as the card drifted to the floor, landing face up.

It was the nine of hearts.

No fucking way.

CHAPTER 7

Tori

Tori drove home in a daze, her mind going in too many directions to focus on any one thing. They hadn't even talked about the interview, and that was the whole reason she'd gone to dinner in the first place.

Wasn't it?

How could she interview Rafe *now*? She'd thrown professionalism to the wind as soon as she'd let him kiss her. And sure, it had been amazing, but at what cost?

Her hands tightened on the wheel as she navigated blindly. What had he meant by apologizing to her now?

Over ten years too late.

Why would he bring up the . . .

She shook away the thought and the tears threatening to come with it. She couldn't go there. Revisiting the past was too risky. She didn't want to remember—to experience the loss all over again. Not when it could drag her back to that dark place. A place she'd crawled out of with painstakingly slow steps, vowing never to go to again.

Coming here was a mistake.

No, the whole book was a mistake. If she could toss it and start over, she would, but she'd already gone too far into the process . . . and the story. Even now, the characters tugged at her, begging to be heard. She was too tired to listen despite the distraction they offered from her problems.

Speaking of problems . . .

Tori blinked and finally focused on the road. She had no idea where she was. After slowing down, she turned on her high beams. The brighter light illuminated a wooded roadway devoid of any signs.

Great. Now I'm lost.

Grumbling at herself for not using the GPS to get home, she pulled onto the shoulder. Rafe lived on the outskirts of town in a newly developed area fifteen to twenty minutes from the house she rented, so she should have been home by now—*if* she'd been paying attention to where she'd been going.

After she parked, she retrieved her phone from her purse to open the map application. She was beyond ready to end this disastrous evening.

No service. *Fan-tastic.*

The tears she'd been swallowing back filled her eyes as she stared at the lack of bars on her phone. Doubts bombarded her—about the book, the kiss, what she was doing in Rolling Brook. When her stomach cramped, she closed her eyes and leaned her head against the seat. Tonight had not gone at all as she'd planned.

She hadn't been able to enjoy her favorite dish because of agonizing over the kiss. It had been hot enough to burn away any qualms she'd had about the past. Well . . . almost. The heat of it still simmered low in her belly, but it wasn't enough to burn down the barricade around her heart.

Then Rafe's apology . . . of course, a part of her had wanted to accept it, but fear had stayed her words. She could be hurt if she accepted and they started seeing each other. The possibility they wouldn't last, that they'd fall apart again . . .

She wouldn't risk it.

With a sigh, Tori opened her eyes to stare out at the night. The stars seemed so much closer than in L.A. as if she could reach up and pluck one from the sky. A gust made the tree branches sway, distracting her from the twinkling lights. She thought they seemed peaceful when it settled, gently dancing with the wind.

A flash of something moving through the woods had her squinting, but her eyes were still watery.

Is that a person?

When she blinked the tears free, it had disappeared. Shaking her head at herself, she reached for her purse to grab a tissue. As she stretched for it, she knocked her phone with her thigh, causing it to slide between the center console and her seat.

Cursing as her night continued to spiral, she twisted, reaching her hand as far as it would go down the crack, but the phone had fallen too far to grasp.

Dammit, dammit, dammit.

A knock on her window made her jump, and she whirled in her seat with wide eyes. Adrenaline had flooded her veins, and her heart beat wildly. She was ready to slam her foot on the accelerator when recognition dawned.

The detective from last Saturday.

She took a deep breath and rolled her window down, scolding herself for being so engrossed in her predicament that she hadn't noticed the lights of the vehicle pulled up behind her. "Detective?"

He bent his tall frame, leaning so that she could see his angular face. The worried expression left, and a hesitant smile appeared. "Tori, right? Are you having car trouble?"

"Ah, no, but . . ."—she let out an embarrassed laugh— "I *am* lost. Can you tell me how to get to Rolling Brook? I think I must've taken a wrong turn."

He chuckled. "I'd say so. You're almost twenty minutes in the opposite direction. Rolling Brook's east of here."

"East, right." What was it with men and using cardinal directions? How in the world was she supposed to know which way was east? "So, um, how do I get back?"

He grinned, and it lit up his light green eyes. "If you keep going the direction you're headed, you'll go farther away. Make a U-turn here, then follow this road until you reach an intersection. You should see the sign for Route 30. Follow that to get back into town."

Okay, that sounded simple enough. Tori smiled in relief. "Thank you so much—" She frowned slightly. "I just realized I don't know your name."

He offered his hand, and she accepted on instinct. "Ben. Ben Gorsky." She shook it, his palm warm, almost comforting against hers. But he didn't release her right away. "Can I ask . . . what were you doing at the crime scene on Saturday?"

She tugged, and thankfully, he freed her hand. She wasn't sure if he'd held onto it as an intimidation tactic or something else. She arched a brow at him, refusing to be daunted. "Research. I'm a writer."

"Really?" He seemed genuinely interested. "What do you write that has you wanting to look at murder victims?"

She wasn't in the mood for this conversation but figured she owed the man after he'd helped her. "I'm a crime fiction author." Sighing, she admitted, "T. E. Graham."

His eyes widened. "No way!" He grinned. "My aunt loves your books. Meg's always pushing me to read them."

"Oh, that's sweet . . ." Tori answered automatically, but then the name registered. "Is Meg a librarian?"

"Yes"—a line of confusion wrinkled his brow—"you know her?"

This time, her smile came easy. "Yes, we've met. She seems like a wonderful person."

"She is, well"—he smirked—"when she's not badgering. I bet next time you run into her, she has a book for you to sign."

Tori laughed. "I'd be happy to sign it." He stared at her, assessing, so she nodded, trying to steer the conversation to an end. "I should really get home. Thank you for the directions."

"No problem. I'll have to tell Meg we met." He smiled and stepped back with a wave.

After returning it, she put the car in drive. Making sure

there wasn't any traffic, she pulled around and headed home. As she drove away, she glanced in her rearview mirror.

Detective Gorsky watched her leave. It's not like she would get lost again *that* quickly. Tori shook her head. People were so different in small towns.

And apparently, they all knew each other.

She smiled, thinking she'd tell Meg about meeting her nephew the next time she saw her.

As she drove toward Route 30, a thought niggled at the back of her mind.

I wonder what the detective was doing out there?

* * * *

Rafe

Rafe had picked up the card gingerly, though his prints were already on it. It was currently lying with the envelope on his kitchen table. The initial fear that had shaken him had dissipated, and a rage so strong it threatened to burn out reason replaced it.

"I don't give a shit. I want to talk to the son of a bitch," he barked into the phone. Calling the prison where the Suit of Hearts Slasher was incarcerated might not be the most brilliant move, but he wasn't thinking smart at the moment.

"Look, officer—

"Captain," Rafe corrected with a growl. He'd already explained who he was, but the fucking imbecile on the line couldn't bother to remember.

"Captain then. No matter how many times you yell at me, I can't let you speak to him. One—you're not on his approved call list. Two—it's outside call hours."

"I don't give a flying fuck what time it—"

"Sir! I'm just a corrections officer. You got a problem with the rules; take it up with the warden."

"I will, you—"

The fucker hung up on him.

Dammit! Rafe slammed his phone on the table, then winced at the sound of an ominous crack. Turning it over, he found the screen marred with a spiderweb pattern.

Great. Just fucking great.

He reared his arm back, ready to sling the aggravating thing at the wall when it started to ring. He glanced at the caller ID. It was the sheriff's office.

News travels fast in a small town.

He'd called the chief to inform him about the nine of hearts, but he hadn't expected to hear from the county until the morning at the earliest.

Tempering the rage, making him want to crinkle the playing card into nothing, he stared at it as he answered the phone, "Alonso."

"Captain, this is Deputy Sorenson. Sorry to call at this hour, but we got news from the M.E.; I thought you'd want to hear it."

So, they weren't calling about his special delivery.

Rafe pinched the bridge of his nose, but the headache had already started. Judging by how this night was going, it wouldn't likely recede any time soon. "Yeah? What did they find?"

He heard the deputy blow out a breath. "We got a positive ID on the victim. Her name was Tegan Powell. She was a student at Loyola in Chicago."

When the deputy paused, the hesitation evident, Rafe swallowed. The implications of what he suspected made his gut quiver. "ID is good. But that's not what you called to tell me."

"No, it's not. Look . . . I know you worked the slasher case."

His knuckles turned white, where he gripped the edge of the table for balance. He blew out a breath, but it didn't ease the tension gripping him.

"There was evidence of sexual assault postmortem."

Not again. This couldn't be fucking happening again.

The blood drained from his face. When the room started to spin, he sat down before he fell. He'd hoped receiving the playing card had been a sick joke, but now . . .

When Rafe said nothing, the deputy continued, "She's the same type, same wounds. I know the Suit of Hearts Slasher is in prison, but—"

"It could be a copycat," he forced out through a constricted throat. Closing his eyes, he leaned over with his elbows on his knees as he tried to breathe normally.

"It could. The sheriff wants you on this case. If it's—"

"I have more evidence. Someone sent a card from the suit of hearts to my apartment. Found it this evening."

The deputy swore, and Rafe explained, "It's the nine. We stopped the Suit of Hearts Slasher at eight."

"You think someone's picking up where he left off?"

He wished like hell he was wrong, but too many signs

pointed to yes. "I hate to say it, but it's starting to look like it."

"I'll brief the sheriff, and your chief will get word, too. This has priority, Captain. Whoever this sick bastard is, we need to stop him before he goes for number ten."

"Agreed."

After he hung up with the deputy, Rafe brewed a pot of coffee. He wasn't getting to sleep anytime soon, and he worried that the nightmares would plague him when he did. Seven women, all young, all with bright red hair like Tori. They haunted him as much as the Suit of Hearts Slasher.

He may not have killed them, but he hadn't saved them either.

CHAPTER 8

Tori

Restless, Tori fidgeted with the strap on her oversized bag as her stride ate up the sidewalk. It was barely nine a.m., but she'd already taken Toby on a walk and gone for a run in the park. Unable to sit still, she'd decided to head to the coffee shop she'd noticed a few days ago with the hope that the change of scenery would settle her thoughts. They'd been going nonstop since last night's catastrophe, and what little sleep she'd gotten had been plagued by dreams—or memories—of her and Rafe together. Both the good and the bad.

She needed to contact him about the interview, but she wanted . . .

Breathing room.

As if time or distance would make her less attracted to him and less affected by their past. The knot she'd woken up with in her chest squeezed tighter. No matter how hard she denied it, a piece of her soul still belonged to Rafe.

Seeing him again . . . kissing him again had woken that dormant part of her, and it scared the bejeebers out of her. Maybe she *should* go to Crystal Bend to visit family for a while.

She sighed and lifted her face to the morning sunshine. That felt too much like running away. Besides, she had a job to do, and she wouldn't let Rafe keep her from doing it. With how distracted she'd been by him last night, she hadn't picked up on Detective Gorsky calling the remains they'd found on Saturday, a murder victim. But she'd realized it this morning, and now she was near to bursting with curiosity.

Who was the victim? How were they killed?

Though she knew Rafe had those answers, she wasn't ready to ask him yet.

If she'd been in a better mood, she'd have smiled as, up ahead, she saw the sign for Common Grounds. It *was* a cute name for a coffee shop, but in her current state, all she could think of was how far from common ground she and Rafe were. Which meant asking him about the murder victim wasn't going to happen. At least not until she'd figured out what to do with his apology.

Running as far away from those thoughts as she could, she focused on the brick building with its bright red awning. The sign hung over the door from a wrought iron mounting bracket. It had curlicues fitting for this downtown area's Victorian vibe.

The shop looked like the type to hold poetry readings and open mic nights. Places like that always seemed to have good coffee, and she hoped this one wasn't an exception to the rule.

She would admit to being a bit of a snob regarding the stuff. After too many semesters of watery sludge brewed by her roommates in college, she'd resorted to drinking flavored lattes heavy on the cream and light on the coffee. But after she'd hit thirty, she'd needed a change and had started brewing coffee herself. Not one to do anything without researching it first, she'd learned about the different types and how they were produced and tried cup after cup until she'd settled on what she liked—arabica beans, medium roast.

As she neared the shop, she was admiring the hand-painted coffee cup with steam emitting from its rim on the window when her toe caught on the uneven sidewalk, and she stumbled, nearly face-planting into the offending concrete.

A meaty hand stopped her fall and righted her. "Whoa, steady there."

Crimson with mortification, Tori shoved away the hair falling into her face so she could see her savior. He looked to be in his forties. His shirt strained against its buttons, and his comb-over had blown out of its part. "Thanks for that."

He pushed his glasses further up his nose, his light brown eyes blinking at her. "No need to thank me. Just be careful. Wouldn't want you to damage your pretty face."

Ugh. Please don't be hitting on me.

He'd smiled at the comment, and she didn't want to be mean, but this was the *last* thing she needed. "Right. Well, I've got to go. Thank you again."

She spun away and opened the door to Common Grounds before Combover had a chance to respond.

The scent of freshly ground beans met her nose and banished the uneasiness of the encounter, especially as she saw through the window that the man was leaving.

Not only did the shop smell amazing, but its noise relaxed her. She'd spent many days huddled over her laptop in a bustling café, writing furiously. Hearing the beat of popular music from overhead speakers, the roar of a grinder, and the whir of a milk frother gave her the sense of peace she'd been searching for since she'd woken up.

Feeling the knot in her chest loosen a little, she smiled and stepped into line. A few people were in front of her, but she didn't mind. It would give her time to deci—

Her thoughts stuttered as she recognized the man giving his order. Moving slowly so as not to draw attention, she rotated and headed for the door.

"Tori?" She'd almost reached it when Rafe's voice stopped her.

Shit! Her shoulders gave a tiny flinch before she braced them and turned around. "Oh, Rafe, hi." She smiled and hoped it didn't look as fake as it felt. "I didn't see you. I forgot my wallet and was going to get it."

Real smooth, Tor. She mentally rolled her eyes at her lame excuse, knowing he wouldn't buy it.

He didn't return her smile. Instead, his stare bore into her, intense enough that she wondered if she'd gotten something on her face. The muffin she'd eaten for breakfast had been rather crumbly. Fighting the urge to swipe at her mouth, she returned his gaze.

He looked tired, the shadows under his eyes telling her he hadn't slept much either. Had her rebuff been sharper than she'd intended last night? There were a lot of emotions swimming in those dark pools, but the regret she glimpsed yanked harder on the knot she'd been trying to loosen all morning.

"Raffaello?" The barista called, setting a large paper cup on the counter.

Rafe didn't acknowledge the girl, and at the use of his full name, Tori raised a brow.

He shrugged. "She took it from my card."

The Rafe she'd known would do practically anything to keep his full name a secret.

Tori frowned. "Are you okay? You seem . . ."

Not yourself? Worn down?

But how could she say that without sounding offensive? "Different."

"Yeah, just tired." Even his voice sounded listless. "Didn't sleep."

Well, his not sleeping made her feel ten times worse. She opened her mouth to apologize—for what exactly, she wasn't sure—but he stopped her.

"Not you. I mean, not because of . . . dinner. It's work."

"Oh." And why didn't *that* make her feel better?

She'd turned into a basket case. Despite how tired Rafe looked, he was still the most attractive man she'd ever met. His full lips tempted her, knowing they'd taste as dark and delicious as the chocolate of his eyes. More than the usual stubble peppered his face, and her fingers itched to rub it.

Something about him tugged at her. Deep in her belly.

Regardless of how she felt about him emotionally, physically she was ready to drag him into the bathroom with her and lock the door.

Don't go there.

Blinking the fantasy free, she saw the barista waving the cup in their direction.

"You should probably get your coffee." Her cheeks burned as she gestured toward the counter, and he finally stopped x-raying her with his eyes to turn around.

She intended to use the distraction as a means of escape when his head whipped back to her. "I'll buy yours. Least I can do after . . ." His whole expression went rigid as if he couldn't bear to finish.

So much for leaving.

This was a problem. She had her wallet, but if she revealed that, he would know she'd been lying. But she also didn't want him to think he needed to pay for her.

Unsure of what to say, Tori chewed her lip. His gaze tracked the movement, and she stopped, realizing what she was doing and remembering what it had led to the last time.

"Raffaello!" The barista saved her from further embarrassment.

As he finally went to pick up his coffee, she tried to relax her tense muscles and slow her racing heart at the thought of kissing him again.

That was so not *a good idea.*

Rafe returned with his coffee, and she had a decision to make. "What would you like?"

Since avoiding him hadn't worked, she may as well use

running into him to her advantage for the book. "Can we talk?"

His hand tightened around his coffee cup, but he nodded. "Yeah. Grab us a seat, and I'll get you . . . do you still drink those overly sweet caramel vanilla lattes?" He raised an eyebrow, his mouth twitching like he wanted to smirk at her, but his lips didn't quite make it.

Ridiculously touched that he remembered what she used to drink, Tori smiled, and her heart warmed despite the wall of ice she'd tried to put between them. A wall she needed intact to get through this interview.

Her smile faltered, and he shifted, sensing her unease. The Tori who'd drunk caramel vanilla lattes existed in the past. Her tastes weren't the only thing that had changed. "I'll have a small of whatever their medium roast is."

When he returned to the counter to order for her, she settled at a table in the back corner of the coffee shop. With no one seated next to them, it provided a measure of privacy, though the noise meant she wasn't worried about their conversation being overheard.

She scooted the black metal chair closer to the wooden table, then pulled her phone out of her bag. He wouldn't distract her from interviewing him this time. The one thing she felt comfortable talking to him about was her book. Everything else . . . she'd avoid at all costs.

Scrolling through the notes on her phone, she glanced up when she heard "Raffaello" called again. He grabbed the cup and paused as he scanned for her. She gave a wave to get his attention.

While Rafe approached the table, she couldn't help but

notice he looked vulnerable. As if the armor usually covering him had slipped. The shadows on his face and the drooping of his shoulders made the rope around her chest pull tauter. Glancing away, she took a deep breath and steered her thoughts to a safer topic.

When he sat, she forced a smile. Her insides were so confused from the mixed signals that caffeine wasn't likely to help the situation. "Thank you for the coffee."

He nodded but didn't say anything. Though his eyes were tired, she could see the heat simmering in them. Not ready for another stare-off, she led with what she knew would cool his blood. "Do you have time now for me to interview you about the slasher case?"

If she hadn't been watching him closely, she might not have seen his posture go stiff before he leaned back in his chair, trying to appear relaxed. "I'm sorry, but I can't."

She refused to let him deter her. Hiding her curiosity about his reaction, she told him, "Well, okay, tell me when *is* a good time for you."

"No, Tori"—his voice softened, but it didn't lessen the blow of his words—"I can't do the interview."

He could *not* be serious. She needed his help, and he'd already offered it. Her anger stirred in her belly, coiling like a snake preparing to strike.

How could he go back on his word like this?

The anger quickly morphed into outrage, rising up her throat in a spew of words she would likely regret. "Is this because I didn't want to jump into bed with you?"

His eyes widened before he slapped his cup on the table hard enough to have coffee spewing out of the lid. "It pisses me off you would even think that," he growled.

Great. Now we're both angry.

"Well, what am I supposed to think, Rafe? Why else would you go back on your word, hmm?" She crossed her arms over her chest and glared at him.

He scrubbed his hands over his face. When he looked at her, the defeat in his gaze cut through her glare. "Because it's an open case again."

"What's an open case? What does tha—" The blood drained from her face, shock replacing her anger. "You mean he's back." She swallowed as certain things became clear. "Saturday, the homicide . . ."

Rafe pinched the bridge of his nose before confirming what she already knew, "Yeah. A young woman."

As she recovered, her thoughts started racing, searching for answers. "But how is that possible? How do you know it was the slasher?"

He sighed, and the worry in his eyes made her stomach drop. "The envelope you handed me last night? It had his calling card in it."

She hadn't worn her journalist hat in a long time, but a part of her itched to break this news. What a coup the story would be when it *did* break.

Then the implications of what he'd said hit her, and she gasped, slumping in her chair. "My prints are on it. Am I . . ." This situation had gone from bad to worse. Tori shook her head. "Is that why you can't tell me about it? I'm a suspect?"

"You're not a suspect," he paused, his body visibly stiffening as fury flashed in his eyes. She didn't understand why, and he hid it before she had a chance to ask. "But you are a witness." His hand tightened on his cup, and she worried he'd crush it. "I need you to tell me about finding the envelope."

She drew a deep breath, calming the rising wave of panic trying to overtake her at the thought of being caught up in this. "All right."

He observed her as he asked, "How did you find it—exactly?"

"It was lying on the carpet right outside your door."

"Okay,"—he nodded encouragement—"did you see anyone around when you found it? Was anyone in the hall?"

Tori recalled finding the envelope. Her thoughts at the time had been swirling around her head like tornados, but she didn't *think* anyone had been around. "I don't think so."

"Did anything else stand out to you? Things you saw that seemed out of place or suspicious?" his voice soothed as he tried to coax more information from her.

Closing her eyes, she let it wash over her as she transported herself to that moment outside his door.

She'd paused, unsure she'd wanted to leave things like that with him—so unresolved—but as soon as she'd started to change her mind, her conscience had been there to remind her dredging up the past wasn't worth the risk. After taking a step, she'd heard the manila paper slide when her foot kicked it. Too distracted to care what had been in it, she'd debated sliding it under his door but had decided that doing so would be the cowardly move. The least she could've done was to make sure he received it, so she'd faced him again, even though every cell in her body had demanded she make her escape. Apart from her emotional state, nothing about the scene struck her as 'off.'

Tori opened her eyes to find Rafe's gaze patiently trained on her. "No, I'm sorry."

He shrugged as though the lack of information didn't matter, but the tension in his frame didn't escape her notice.

"What now?"

He sighed, and his shoulders drooped again. "I go back to the crime scene."

She instantly perked up, still itching to see it. "Let me go with you."

He raised an eyebrow, but the fact that he didn't automatically deny her was promising.

"A fresh set of eyes could be good. Plus, you owe me." His hand on the table clenched into a fist, so she quickly added, "For not doing the interview." She didn't want him to think she'd meant about their past. That subject she wasn't ready to revisit with him.

His hand relaxed, and he took a sip of his remaining coffee. "Fine. But I'm on my way there now."

"Now works for me." Tori smiled and slid her chair back. If his plan had been to shake her loose, she'd show him she wouldn't be so easy to get rid of. Picking up the coffee she hadn't tasted, she grabbed her bag. "Let's go."

Rafe didn't move. His eyes raged with indecision, but she wasn't backing down.

"If you don't let me go with you, I'll go on my own." It

wasn't a bluff, especially now that she knew the crime scene was connected to the slasher. Visiting it would be prime research for her, but she preferred to do it with his help.

He scowled at her, no doubt aware she'd meant what she'd said. "This is a bad idea."

Her smile turned into a grin. Reaching for his arm, she tugged him to his feet. "I disagree."

CHAPTER 9

Rafe

What the hell am I doing?

Rafe wished he had an answer for that as he drove out to Lesco Drive—Tori in tow. She sat quietly beside him, though her fingers furiously typed on her phone. Her sultry floral scent proved inescapable inside the department SUV, and her warm smell made him angrier. Bright ray-of-sunshine Tori was involved in a murder investigation. And not just any investigation but another fucking slasher case.

And it was all his fault.

A scowl marred Rafe's face, and he had to consciously relax his hands, or they'd be clenched around the wheel. If he hadn't invited her to dinner, she wouldn't have found the card in the first place. She wasn't a suspect in his mind but someone who—because of him—had been in the wrong place at the wrong time.

He'd planned to call her this morning to ask her about finding the envelope, but running into her had been a stroke of luck.

Or so he'd thought.

He'd already canvassed the residents on his floor, and none of them had seen anyone deliver the envelope. That had been disappointing news, but even worse was finding out when the prints had come back that only his and Tori's were on it. Because it had meant he'd be forced to question her—to drag her into the investigation.

But to take her out to the crime scene?

This is insanity.

A growl left his throat as he stared daggers out the windshield. Out of the corner of his eye, he saw her shift in the seat beside him, causing her scent to float over him like a caress. It teased him and left him wanting more—so much more.

"Something you want to say?" she asked gently, even encouragingly, but he knew underneath the tone she smirked at him.

Why had he given in to this madness?

Probably because he'd known if he hadn't agreed to take her, she *would* have come out to the scene on her own . . . and because he was desperate enough to spend time with her that he'd take it any way he could.

But this book made her reckless. He wanted to send her back to where she came from—far, far, away from here.

Where she'd be safe.

An image of her face on the dead woman from Saturday flashed in his head, and his stomach roiled. The possibility of that happening terrified him.

A wave of panic seized him as the dreams he'd had the night before replayed in his mind. More than once, he'd been jolted awake in cold sweats, his heart racing, his muscles constricted because Tori had been in the hands of that sick bastard.

If only he could strap her to his side like the firearm attached to his hip. At least, that way, he'd be able to protect her.

"I guess not, then," she hummed and returned to fiddling with her phone. She must take notes on there or something, the way her fingers dashed over the screen.

"What are you typing?"

"Ah, so he *does* speak."

Yeah, she was definitely smirking. Too bad he felt too tired to challenge her. Tori had always hated the silent treatment, though, and he knew he could win that game. So, he said nothing and waited for her to respond.

As he made the turn onto Lesco Drive, he heard her sigh. "An idea for a scene in my book. I'll lose it if I don't get it down now."

He enjoyed her books, but he didn't like the idea of this one. Her writing about a villain based on the Suit of Hearts Slasher made his skin crawl. "What's the plot anyway? Apart from the serial killer?"

She faced him, and palpable excitement vibrated off her. "The heroine is a female detective who gets drawn into a serial killer case because of her background. But!" He heard the smile in her voice when she continued, "As she starts investigating, she falls for the main suspect. Then things get interesting when the killer comes after her."

"Interesting is one way of putting it," he muttered.

He had to admit, it did sound like a captivating read, but he still wasn't on board with this. Not when it meant Tori would be delving into the dark parts of society he'd always tried to shield her from.

"You could've researched any serial killer. Why the Suit of Hearts Slasher?"

A small part of him held out hope it had to do with his involvement as the detective on the case. Had she followed his career as he'd followed hers?

Instead of answering, she dropped her phone in her bag and waved at the window. "Oh look, we're here!"

* * * *

Rafe

Rafe glanced up from his squatted position as he heard tires crunching over twigs and fallen leaves. A police cruiser parked next to his SUV. It had to be Gorsky. The detective had been trying to get ahold of him all morning, judging by the handful of missed calls he'd yet to return.

With a sigh, Rafe stood, brushing at his slacks as he waited for the man. Tori stood across the small clearing, typing again on her phone. They'd been here for about half an hour, and she'd managed to avoid him the entire time. Flames danced in her hair as the sun hit it. Seeing the literal light shining around her punched him in the gut.

She was his fire; her glow warmed his soul and chased out the shadows.

Despite the years in between, his heart hadn't forgotten her.

Not in the least.

He didn't question how she'd affected him again so quickly. He needed her like he needed air.

But he also wanted her safe.

Ignoring the need pouring through his veins, he forced himself to look away. He glanced around the scene again, but it had given him no new information. A variety of trees made this area heavily wooded, though it would change soon. Some of the leaves were already dropping. But most branches were full of green foliage, blocking nearly everything from view. It was secluded but not so far from the road you'd get lost if you were unfamiliar with the location.

Lesco Drive bordered a residential neighborhood that was popular as a local summer vacation spot. A lake with cabins brought in families a few miles north. Had the victim been out here for a weekend getaway? Since she'd been a student in the city, he needed to get in touch with Chicago P.D.

That should go smoothly enough.

Having left there such a short time ago, he had his share of contacts.

Turning in a circle, he scanned for anything he might've missed the last time he'd been here. Then, his thoughts had been torn between the job and Tori.

Now, he couldn't even separate the two.

Fucked up any chance of that last night.

"Hey, Captain." Gorsky waved as he entered the

clearing.

Rafe acknowledged the detective, but the greeting he'd been about to give died on his lips as Gorsky's face broke into a grin.

"Tori," the detective called out. "Fancy meeting you here," he added with a wink as she walked over.

When the fuck did these two get better acquainted?

His hands clenched into fists as she spoke to Gorsky like they were old friends. Fighting a primal urge that made him want to grab her and drag her away from this upshot, Rafe took a deep breath to calm down. He had no claim on her, and letting jealousy take over wasn't an option. Still, he wanted to punch the fucker in the face for smiling at her like that.

She's not yours. She's mine.

"We matched the shoeprint."

He stared hard at Gorsky when the man's words finally sank in. Unclenching his jaw, he smothered the possessiveness gripping him so he could focus on the case.

"That was faster work than I expected," the words were like acid as he forced them out.

A rueful smile crossed the detective's face. "Well, it was Ian's."

Not understanding, Rafe's brow furrowed. "Ian who?"

Gorsky scrubbed at the back of his neck. "Ian Dundy, the coroner."

"Dammit! I thought you said it wasn't one of ours." His jaw clenched again, and he gripped his hair in frustration.

The detective shrugged as if losing the one lead they'd had wasn't a big fucking deal. "I was wrong."

"Great, another dead end," his voice came out in a snarl, but he didn't have the capacity to care if he pissed the man off or not. He needed to figure this out before anyone else got hurt.

To his credit, Gorsky didn't take offense. "Another?" His brow furrowed in confusion.

"Yeah, no prints on the envelope or card," Rafe bit out through a throat that had gone raw.

The detective scratched at his jaw. "How do you know the two are connected?"

Tori opened her mouth like she wanted to say something, but he wanted her out of this. "I just do."

He felt it through to his bones. Knowing was an itch he couldn't scratch, and it clawed at him incessantly. Either a new slasher had emerged, or the man he'd sent to prison had found a way to get back at him. The sick fuck had promised retribution until the gates had closed on his demented smile.

This whole past year, he'd been trying to put the case behind him, but that promise and the faces of the dead women continued to haunt his dreams.

"All right, well, we've started canvasing the closest residences. Maybe someone will have seen something," Gorsky broke into his gloomy thoughts.

"Yeah, good." It was always a long shot but one they needed to take.

"Can I interject?" Tori raised a brow as if she expected him to refuse.

"What are you thinking, Sunshine?" The nickname slipped unbidden from his lips. He hadn't called her that since they'd split, but he was too tired to keep his guard up.

Her eyes flashed with surprise before she looked away, gesturing around the clearing. "Why are there no signs of a struggle? If he killed her here, the—"

"He didn't." Rafe sighed and scrubbed his hands down his face. He needed a nap, not to rehash the details of the homicide with her.

"She was dumped here after the fact," Gorsky supplied when he didn't elaborate.

"Hmm." Tori tapped her finger to her lip as the wheels in her brain turned. "So that's the same as the other slasher murders. I wonder why he mailed the card then instead of leaving it with the body?"

The detective nodded, making Rafe want to punch him. *Could they* be *any chummier?*

"Yeah, that's a good question. It's why I'm wondering if the two really are related."

Rafe's fists clenched at Gorsky's statement, and his pulse sped as a fit of irrational anger overtook him. If he didn't get himself under control, he might do or say something he'd regret, like forcefully wiping the smirk off this idiot's face.

She glanced his way, her eyes widening before she laid a hand on his arm. "Either way, you'll figure it out." Her voice and touch were meant to soothe.

Rafe focused on that, staring into her dark green depths as he pushed everything he felt into a box, stuffing it down where it wouldn't affect his ability to do his job. When he felt like he had it closed off, he blinked, freeing himself from her gaze.

He cleared his throat and turned to Gorsky with a new sense of calm. "It's a message—the body and the card. Both were meant for me to find."

The detective still looked skeptical, so he continued, "Why dump her here unless getting my attention was the goal?"

Gorsky scratched at his chin. "I don't know. Maybe the killer's from Chicago, and they drove out here, dumped the body, hoping it'd keep the murder from coming back on them?"

He frowned at the possibility. "I'm going to talk to Chicago and find out more. We don't know if the woman was already out here or if she went missing from the city." Shaking his head—those questions should already have been asked—he focused on Gorsky. "What else did the M.E. find?"

The detective perked up at the mention of the medical examiner. "Actually, I'm glad you asked. I forgot to mention they found trace particulates on the body, but they haven't been able to identify them yet. And evidence of barbiturates in her system."

He wasn't surprised to hear they'd found a sedative in the woman's blood. The slasher had used them on his victims. "What kind?" He wanted to know if it was the same one.

Gorsky frowned, then reached into his shirt pocket for a small notebook. Rafe waited while he flipped through the pages until he found what he sought. "Pentobarbital. It's used for MRIs and—"

"I know. Thanks," he cut the man off as his stomach knotted. "It's the same sedative the Suit of Hearts Slasher favored." It started to work quickly but didn't last long unless someone was given an above-normal dose.

Tori hummed, but Gorsky only shrugged. "The M.E. said it's fairly easy to get. Medical professionals, even vets, use it, and people with insomnia or seizures are sometimes prescribed it."

He knew all this, but hearing it repeated made the weight on his shoulders that much heavier. "Yeah, it'll be hard to trace."

"Do you think he kills them while they're sedated?" she asked, typing on her phone. Back to making notes for her book, Rafe figured.

"Yeah, he doesn't want to deal with them fighting back." The Suit of Hearts Slasher had been a coward, and he doubted this killer was any different.

"Small mercies." Gorsky shook his head. "At least they're already dead when he rapes them."

Fucking idiot!

Livid over the detective bringing that up, Rafe's teeth ground together. The blood he'd worked earlier to calm pounded at his temples.

Tori hadn't needed to know that detail, and she'd frozen at the news, her face turning pale. Her eyes were huge when she exclaimed, "That's horrible!"

It was time to get her out of here. He didn't want her contemplating how the slasher abused the poor women he murdered. He hadn't told her about the sexual assault on the current victim's body, and he had been hoping she wouldn't find out.

"I think we've seen all we can here." He reached for her arm, and she didn't protest when he started to steer her away from the crime scene.

Calling over his shoulder, he told Gorsky, "Contact me if you find anything new."

She hadn't said anything else, and he started to worry by the time they'd reached the SUV. He released her arm, and when she made no move to get in, he turned her to face him.

Her eyes were brimming. The sadness there squeezed at his heart. "I'm sorry, Rafe."

Confusion wrinkled his brow. What was she apologizing for?

A tear spilled over, and he wiped it away with his thumb. Her cheek felt impossibly soft under the rough skin of his palm. He shook his head, hating that she was here and that being caught up in this made her cry. "Don't cry, Sunshine."

Tori hiccupped and reached for him, burying her head in his chest. He hugged her close but wasn't sure who needed the comfort more. To have her in his arms was torture, yet he'd endure it any day to feel her warmth seep into him. With her perfect breasts molded to his chest and the smell of her floral shampoo filling his nostrils, the weight dragging him down eased. As her soft waves brushed his chin, he thought, if he could have her back, this would suck a little less.

But he couldn't have her.

If he was going to keep her safe, he needed her to stay

far away from him and the darkness that wouldn't seem to let go.

Rafe closed his eyes and committed the moment to memory. He took a deep breath of her scent, kissed the top of her head, and then, despite the burning in his gut, he pushed her away. "You should go home."

CHAPTER 10

Tori

The temperature hovered in the 60s, making Tori feel like she could run forever. Running in the heat in L.A. had been brutal in comparison. She'd lost track of her mileage as her mind wandered, but she had to be getting close to five. The distance was longer than her usual run and her second of the day.

After leaving the crime scene with Rafe, she'd spent the afternoon writing until she could no longer contain the tempest of her thoughts about him. The story her characters were enthralled in had kept it at bay for as long as possible, but she'd felt the tide rising and had put on her running shoes.

Not to escape the storm. But to confront it.

Running always helped her work through problems; right now, she had more than her share.

Thanks to Rafe Alonso.

She frowned, picking up her pace as she huffed her way

through the winding park trail. Stray pine needles crunched under her feet as her tennis shoes landed on the asphalt path. Pine, oak, and ash trees loomed overhead, scenting the air with their earthy smell as fall teased the wind, announcing its imminent arrival.

Typically, that would have made her smile, but Rafe had her all kinds of confused. First, he'd apologized. Next, he'd been grumpy with her, then he'd comforted her when she'd fallen apart, calling her by her old nickname, and when she'd been—almost—ready to lower her guard, he'd pushed her away.

And I thought women were complicated.

Tori rolled her eyes, wishing she could figure him out. She knew he was stressing over the case, and if the slasher had resurfaced . . .

She shuddered, thinking about the possibility. She'd known the Suit of Hearts Slasher had abused his victims, but it was one thing to read about it in the news. Realizing it could've happened right where she'd been standing had been another thing entirely. Then there were the memories it stirred up.

Of Aimee.

Thinking about her best friend from college always brought a pang of sorrow to her heart. She hadn't been with her friend when it happened, and Aimee had been too embarrassed to tell her about the rape.

After she found Aimee unconscious on their bathroom floor from an overdose, the truth finally came out.

Tears flooded Tori's eyes, and she blinked them away. She'd already fallen apart in Rafe's arms. There was no use doing it again. She'd apologized, sorry she'd needed his comfort in the first place when she wasn't sure he'd wanted to offer it.

Shaking that off, she widened her stride. She'd made it past the pain then. She would do so now. Just like Aimee. It had been a long year of recovery for her friend, but they'd pushed through—together.

And then she'd found Rafe.

They'd met her sophomore year in college. She smiled, remembering how their meeting had gone down, her steps unconsciously lighter. He'd been the officer on duty who'd received the call of a noise complaint about the party she'd been at. It had gotten out of control, and he'd busted it up. She'd been trying to sneak out unnoticed because she'd been drinking, even though she hadn't turned 21 yet.

Rafe had stopped her before she could squeeze through the door. Her red hair made her too easy of a target, and it caught his eye.

Warmth not merely from the exercise bloomed in her chest as she thought about that night.

He'd insisted on giving her a ride home. Because she'd been too afraid of getting in trouble to argue, she'd had the best ride of her life. They'd circled the block too many times to remember, lost in conversation. There'd been no mixed signals then. When he'd finally dropped her off, he'd taken her number *and* her heart.

And as hard as she'd tried, she'd never fully gotten it back.

Her smile faded, and the sixty-degree air turned chilly. After all Rafe had to deal with . . . perhaps she *should* cut him some slack. The open slasher case had to be a thousand times worse for him.

To think he'd finally stopped the murderer only to have him strike again.

A cramp seized her left side, and she slackened her pace, unsure if it came from the exertion or her mixed feelings over Rafe. He certainly had the ability to tie her up in knots.

She slowed to a walk, massaging the stitch in her side as her thoughts revolved around him. His question from this morning taunted her.

Why the Suit of Hearts Slasher?

She'd known it would come eventually, but she still hadn't been prepared to answer. The idea of writing about a serial killer occurred to her *because* of Rafe.

If the Suit of Hearts Slasher hadn't made headlines, and if he hadn't been the detective on the case, she didn't know when she would have seen him again. She'd spent years being mad at him—despondent even—but at some point, she'd forgiven him, though she'd refused to acknowledge it.

She'd wasted years lying to herself—telling herself she'd moved on—when, in reality, she'd feared Rafe's reaction to seeing her again. The fear had kept her from trying until the opportunity her book presented had given her the perfect opening.

She sighed and wiped the beads of sweat from her forehead with the back of her arm. Running had helped her work out one thing—writing about a serial killer was an excuse to get close to Rafe. If she could admit that to herself, maybe she could admit it to him, too.

The sound of a snapping twig broke into her thoughts. Tori glanced around but didn't see anyone. Regardless, she started running.

The noise could've been an animal instead of a person, but she had no desire to meet a coyote, a bear, or whatever lived in these woods. Chiding herself for letting the Hallmark-like quality of the town lure her into a false sense of security, she vowed to be more mindful of the hour next time she went for a run. The sun had started to set, and she didn't want to be here when it turned dark. This might not be Chicago or L.A., but a woman running alone at night was easy prey.

Though her eyes continued to scan, they didn't land on anything except trees. Even so, the hairs on the back of her neck stood up. Ignoring the stitch, which hadn't gone away, she picked up her pace, unable to shake the sense of being watched. Out of habit, she reached for the keychain-sized mace bottle she always kept with her.

With the small black cartridge clutched in her right hand, Tori hoped she didn't have occasion to break it in. Her lungs hammered against her chest at the possibility as she pushed herself hard on tired legs. The end of the trail loomed closer and closer.

Only a quarter mile left!

When she broke out of the tree line, her breath rasped out in relief, but her legs didn't stop until she'd reached the steps of the house she rented. Gasping, she let herself inside as quickly as possible. Her eyes searched the street and the park's edge again, but she saw no one following her.

I'm losing my mind.

Mad because she'd managed to freak herself out, Tori worked on steadying her breathing as she closed the front door.

She'd barely gotten her breaths under control when something barreled into her back, and she fell against the door with an "oomph." When she righted herself, excited barking met her ears.

Turning, she bent and reached for Toby with a laugh. Rustling his fur, she told him, "Sorry, bud. I know I cut it close to dinner time."

He licked from her chin to her hairline in response.

Tori squealed and pushed the dog off her. He sat on his haunches, clearly pleased with himself, his tongue lolling out in a silly grin.

"You know I hate that," she scolded, even though it made her smile.

Chuckling to herself, she stood and headed for the kitchen. A hungry Toby followed right on her heels.

* * * *

Tori

Tori huddled in the corner of the library at what she'd come to think of as 'her desk' when a prickle bristled her scalp. She paused, forgetting the stream of words she'd been about to type as she glanced up from her laptop.

Yet, no one was visible.

That's weird.

She'd come several times to the desk Meg had shown

her on her first visit because of the privacy it offered. It wasn't unusual for people to wander back here, but, more often, it remained quiet.

Tori liked it that way. Just her and her typing—the sound of progress. Over the last week, she'd come to work on her book every afternoon.

Better than worrying about Rafe.

She hadn't heard from him since they'd visited the crime scene—days ago. Not that she'd expected to, but she'd—

Tori winced at the strike of a stomach spasm. Rubbing the spot with her palm, she admitted she'd hoped he *would* call.

But then *she* had been the one to ask for space, so could she really be mad if he gave it to her?

Frustrated with herself, Tori huffed out a breath and flexed her fingers. At least she had the book to keep her thoughts busy. Shrugging off the lingering feeling of being watched, she tried to pick up where she'd left off. Her hands had barely touched the keys again when Meg came around the closest stack.

The older woman started, her free hand flying to her chest. "Tori!"

As she recovered from the fright, she chuckled at herself. "You surprised me. I didn't see you come in, and no one seems to sit back here but you." Meg's face crinkled in a smile as she adjusted her glasses. Her short, gray-streaked hair curled around her face today, accenting its angles.

She returned Meg's smile. "You weren't at Circulation when I came in, but I would've stopped by before I left."

Meg nodded, then reshelved the book she'd been carrying. "I heard from Ben. He's started on your latest release."

She laughed, knowing Meg had been trying to get her nephew to read Tori's books for years. When she'd first returned to the library, she'd started to tell Meg about meeting Detective Gorsky, only to find out he'd beaten her to the punch. "Well, I hope he enjoys it."

Meg made a noise that sounded suspiciously like a snort. "I'm sure he will."

Her nose scrunched up as she watched the librarian. "What aren't you saying?"

"He's family . . . and I love him." The older woman sighed, then fiddled with her glasses.

"There's a 'but' in there." Tori leaned forward in her chair and lowered her voice. "Lay it on me, Meg. I only like suspense in novels."

"Well, I just feel I should warn you that he's a bit of a flirt."

Tori blinked. She wasn't sure what she'd expected, but it wouldn't have been *that.* "Okay." Her thoughts tumbled over one another, unsure how she'd come to be in this situation.

Meg shook her head. "He's always had a thing for redheads."

A flush crept up her neck. "Are you saying . . . I mean." She was full on blushing now.

Dammit!

"He's interested in me?"

Why did she suddenly feel like she'd returned to high

school?

Tori cleared her throat before Meg could answer. "Never mind. That is *so* not in the cards for me right now."

And she was *so* not interested in Ben. Sure, he was good-looking, but he wasn't . . .

He isn't Rafe.

"Oh, now, I've made you uncomfortable." Meg tsked at herself before patting Tori on the shoulder. "I'm sorry I brought it up."

"No, it's fine." She tried and failed to laugh off the embarrassment. At least her cheeks felt less hot when she started to explain, "There's, um . . ."

How could she say this?

The older woman grinned. "You already have a beau."

Not exactly. "I'm not available."

Because I've been pining for the same man for over a decade.

Geesh, she was pathetic.

"That's great. I'm happy for you."

That makes one of us.

She wished for something to be happy about. Despite how much of a fraud she felt, she thanked Meg.

When the librarian left, Tori slumped in her chair and lowered her head in her hands. Exasperated with herself, the situation, and Rafe, she tugged at her hair.

How did I get here?

On a groan, she lifted her head.

It was the nickname.

He hadn't called her Sunshine since they'd split; hearing him use it had been salve on a wound. It smoothed over the hurts he'd dealt her and made her want to try again. The chemistry had endured between them. It burned just as hot, maybe hotter. The feelings . . .

She *thought* he still had feelings for her. And hers had certainly not diminished.

But now he ignored her.

Gah! Do I really want to do this again?

Tori slammed her laptop lid shut. *How* she'd gotten herself in such a mess wasn't important at the moment.

But how she'd get out of it *was*.

CHAPTER 11

Rafe

Two weeks.

That's how long it had been since Rafe last held Tori in his arms. He wasn't sure why it felt like an eternity when he'd previously spent over a decade without seeing her.

But it did.

Knowing she was so close but he couldn't touch her . . .

It was slowly driving him insane.

A scowl crossed his face, and he clenched his fist around the paper in his hand, crinkling the report he'd just read. The sound of it shattered the quiet that had crept over his office like a heavy fog. Laying the assaulted paper on his desk, he let out an irritated exhale, attempting to smooth it out.

Chicago P.D. had sent him the report. He'd gotten in touch with contacts at the district he'd left. They'd looked into the case of Tegan Powell, the murdered student. She'd gone missing from the city, not locally. Her friends had reported it the next day after she'd never made it home the night before. The students had been out at a club, but Tegan had left early, which told Rafe the slasher had grabbed her when she'd been walking home alone.

And she'd been dumped in Dale County on purpose.

But he wasn't sure whether that purpose intended to send him a message or merely to throw off suspicion as Gorsky had suggested.

They'd had no luck identifying the particulates the medical examiner had found. On top of that, they had no murder weapon. Before, the Suit of Hearts Slasher had used disposable scalpels from his embalming toolkit, something he'd had easy access to as a mortician. All the M.E. had confirmed was the weapon had a smooth, thin edge, so he had people chasing down medical supply companies without real evidence to back him up.

Rafe groaned and dropped his head in his hands, propping his elbows on his desk.

There'd been no more slasher murders, and while that should have brought relief, it actually made him restless. He'd begun questioning if someone had been toying with him—sending the girl *and* the card.

Were they dealing with a copycat, or was this something else? Was someone trying to hide behind a notorious serial killer?

Maybe it was a last jab from the bastard he'd put away?

Or—and this proved the hardest question to ask—*Did I fuck up and send the wrong man to prison?*

Which would mean the real slasher was still out there.

The unanswered questions turned endlessly in Rafe's head. He grew grumpier daily, his stomach burning with enough anger over the lack of new information that he was popping antacids like candy.

Is staying away from Tori worth it?

It didn't feel like it when they were getting nowhere and had no real clue whom they were dealing with.

Pushing back from his desk, he stood. His hands clenched at his sides before he consciously relaxed them. Taking a deep breath, he walked to the window and cracked the blinds. If he couldn't have *his* Sunshine, the afternoon's rays were better than nothing.

With a sigh, barely hinting at the frustration making his muscles tense, he stared at the empty table below his window.

She'd been right. He'd yet to move in.

Not being one to show off, he wasn't interested in putting his awards and accomplishments on display. But there had been a few personal items on his desk in Chicago—a picture of his mother and the mug Tori had bought him when he'd gotten his first promotion—ones he hadn't set up here. Because he hadn't been sure he would stay.

But with her here, he wasn't going anywhere.

His chest squeezed, and he coughed out a breath. Trying to keep his distance to keep her off the slasher's radar wasn't an easy task. Not when he wanted to plunge his hands into the fire of her hair and pull her close, capturing those soft pink lips with his own. To remind her that she belonged to him—body and soul.

To show her they could make it work this time.

Placing an arm on the wall, he leaned into it as he stared out the window in thought. The light shone on his bare forearms, having folded his sleeves up hours ago. He rarely made it through a full day with them down. Maybe he rolled them for comfort, or maybe it was a useless attempt to eliminate at least one of the constraints hanging so heavy on him. Ridding himself of that layer of clothing rarely eased the load weighing on his mind. His olive skin glowed in the light, but he didn't feel the sun's warmth. A cloud hung over him, and it cast only shade.

Fate had given them a second chance, but Rafe worried he was squandering it. Or perhaps fate was merely a cruel mistress who'd dangled Tori in front of him, knowing he would push her away to protect her from the darkness that came with his job.

Maybe I was never meant to have her.

The thought pierced him like a bullet, puncturing his heart. He winced as the pain spread. A headache brewed, and he pinched the bridge of his nose to ease the tension there.

Thinking led to more questions; what he needed was action. Turning from the window, he grabbed his suit jacket. When his phone rang, he'd shrugged one arm in, determined to hunt down answers.

Annoyed at the halt in his progress, he grabbed it off his desk with the arm not yet through the sleeve. "Alonso."

"Captain," Detective Gorsky's voice brought a scowl to his face. He'd been avoiding the man since their last encounter.

He remained pissed at him. Part of the reason was jealousy over the man's familiarity with Tori. He recognized that, but it didn't change the way he felt. Thinking about Gorsky with her made the blood drum in his veins.

"We've got another body."

Well, fuck.

* * * *

Rafe

"For fuck's sake!" Rafe roared when the branch he'd thought he'd pushed out of the way managed to come back and slap him in the face.

Thankfully, he hadn't gotten stabbed in the eye, but his cheek smarted as he followed Detective Gorsky to where the second body had been found. This dump site appeared more wooded than the area off Lesco Drive had been. The fact that Gorsky climbed over brush and ducked under branches with ease only served to anger him more. He drilled holes in the detective's back, which might be why he'd missed the branch in the first place.

Not that he'd admit it.

A snarl tickled Rafe's throat, but he swallowed it down. He needed to focus on why they were out here instead of stoking his annoyance toward Gorsky.

Someone else had been murdered.

The detective had told him very few details over the phone, and he was anxious to see the scene for himself.

As they drew closer, Rafe heard the voices of the uniformed officers already on site. The sheriff's office had sent deputies, and the coroner had arrived before him.

"Seems I'm the last one who got the call," he kept his voice level despite the note of bitterness souring his tongue as he remarked to Gorsky. They'd stopped at the perimeter, the yellow tape already cordoning the body off.

The detective rubbed at his neck before he glanced over. "Sorry, that's my fault. I didn't think . . ." Gorsky trailed off, searching for the right words, but he wasn't going to wait for the man to find them.

"You didn't think?" Rafe's tone probably came out sharper than it needed to be.

"No, I meant—" the detective shook his head, then lifted the tape for Rafe to step under. "Just see for yourself."

More than ready to, he sent Gorsky a glare as he stepped past the barrier. Not two steps in, the stench reached his nose. This body smelled far from fresh. He paused, swallowing down the contents of his stomach, trying to come back up at the rancid scent of decay.

Dumpster and shit.

There wasn't a worse odor in the world. He felt Gorsky's smirk from where he'd stayed beyond the tape.

Fucker could've warned me.

When he had his gag reflex under control, Rafe edged closer. If the officers who'd responded had thought the young redhead had been bad, he was willing to bet many of them had already lost their lunch over this scene.

The victim's bare skin had been exposed long enough to collect a covering of leaves, but the colorful fallen flora couldn't diminish the grotesque sight of the rotting corpse.

He was surprised at how intact this one remained,

considering its location. But even though animals had left it alone, the insects hadn't. They'd taken up residence amid the blackened flesh. Perhaps it had been pale at one time, but he couldn't be sure.

Covering his nose, he dared to crouch next to the body for a closer look. When he did, surprise echoed through him.

Male?

His head whipped to Gorsky, who nodded. So that's why the detective had hesitated to call him. Was this even a slasher murder? All the victims prior to this had been female—redheads.

Rafe focused on the corpse again. Though maggots had completely filled the slice, a tell-tale cut spread across the throat. They wiggled and squirmed as they feasted, and he had to look away as his stomach attempted to revolt. His eyes drifted to the scalp. What remained of the man's hair had shifted from his head, along with the skin that had held it. Dirt, leaves, and insects mixed with the strands. It might have once been red or light brown, but he couldn't be sure now.

The wind blew the putrid odor into his face, and he had to stand to distance himself from the decomposition. Breathing through his mouth provided barely any relief. No doubt the smell would cling to his nostrils after he left the scene. That was the problem with death. Not only did it relish in making its presence known, but it liked to linger—to remain an ever-present reminder for the living of how fragile life was.

Rafe stared past the deceased, and his eyes fell on the

coroner. Would the man be more or less helpful this time?

Determined to find out, he took a step toward the county official, but Gorsky stopped him. "So, what's your take?"

He turned to address the detective, answering his question with one of his own, "What did Dundy say about this victim?" He glanced toward the man whose balding head glistened with perspiration despite the cooler temperatures.

The coroner ought to take better care of himself. Sweat soaked the armpits of his button-up shirt, and Rafe figured the trek through the woods had been more exercise than the man had gotten in a while. At least this time, he didn't look like he would puke.

"How long's it been here?"

"He estimates a couple of weeks. Said there's too much damage from the insects to tell for sure if the wound is the same, but the width and placement are similar. We don't *know* if it's a slasher murder." Gorsky eyed him for his reaction. "Did you get another playing card? If the body's been here for weeks . . ."

Then I should've already received one.

Though the detective didn't say it, Rafe understood what he implied. "I haven't."

Gorksy nodded as though he'd already known the answer. "There is something . . ." He scratched at his neck before meeting Rafe's eyes. The almost sheepish expression churned his stomach with worry over what the man was about to say.

"What is it?" His fists clenched as he braced himself for

the blow he felt coming.

The detective cleared his throat. "It's probably not connected, but it just . . . makes you wonder."

Rafe's teeth ground together, his patience wearing thin. "Spit it out, Gorsky."

"A couple weeks ago, Tori was out this way. I found her parked on the road near here at night. It's probably nothing, but I should talk to—"

"No!" His pulse pounded in his ears at the mention of her name. His face twisted into a mask of fury. "I'll handle it." No fucking way would he let Gorsky drag Tori further into this.

"Whoa"—the detective held both hands up and stepped back—"I'm fine with that. Just thought you should know."

Reining in his glower, Rafe flexed his fingers, but it didn't loosen the tension taking over his muscles. His pulse never settled, pounding so hard in his head that it felt like each beat was a strike.

"Thanks," his growled response showcased more anger than gratitude, but he didn't care.

He needed to talk to Tori.

Now.

CHAPTER 12

Tori

Tori blinked when the screen of her phone lit up, breaking her out of the veritable trance she'd been in while working on her book. Her eyes smarted, and she groaned, rubbing them in a useless attempt to relieve the tension. She'd been staring, unblinking, at her computer screen for far too long, and now they were making their protest known.

When her phone buzzed, vibrating the desk, she picked it up and saw another alert from the county. Ever curious, she opened the message, and her stomach cramped.

Another body.

She wondered who it would be this time and if the slasher had caught another victim. Despite the dread she felt over this loss of life, part of her wondered if she could use it as an excuse to contact Rafe, sparking an ember of hope in her chest.

Wow, I'm pathetic.

She was actually thinking of capitalizing off of someone

else's misfortune. A dark, slimy feeling started in her toes and slithered up her back. If she hadn't hit rock bottom before, she might have thought she'd found herself there now, but she knew better. Disgust and the hint of loathing were far less frightening emotions than those she'd already faced.

Not that Rafe would tell her anything if she asked. His two weeks of the silent treatment had shown her as much. It managed to make her hurt all over again. Her stomach burned as she frowned, deep in thought, out the window at the sunset coloring the sky.

He's avoiding me.

She wished she knew why. His ignoring her threatened to drive her crazy. It was a plot twist she couldn't figure out, and it kept needling her despite how much she wanted to forget about it.

When Toby laid his head in her lap, she jumped. On a relieving breath, she smiled at him as she stroked his shaggy face. He must've sensed her mood. "You may not be much of a hunter, but you're a pretty good emotional support animal."

His mouth opened with a smile as if he understood, panting at her. The easy comfort he offered already lifted her spirit. She scratched behind his ears, and his tongue lolled out. "Yeah, I bet that fee—Oh!"

The dog jerked around so quickly that he rocked into her chair, nearly sending her toppling over. She grabbed the desk just in time to keep that from happening. "Toby!"

But he'd already raced to the front door, barking so loudly she raised her arms, tempted to cover her ears.

When she neared the spot he'd taken up as sentry, she understood why the dog had gone crazy. Whoever her visitor might be, they were pounding on her door like they wanted to break it down.

"What in the world," Tori muttered, then she checked out the peephole.

Rafe.

Her stomach jumped, then dropped like a stone at her feet. Her initial excitement waned as she could see the anger coming off of him in waves, even through the distorted image.

Well, this will be interesting . . .

She pulled the door open quickly to stop his assault and almost got hit in the face with a fist.

He jerked his arm back, his eyes widening for a second before the glower returned. "Dammit, Tori. Be careful!"

She lifted a red brow at him. "*Me,* be careful? You're the one trying to break down my door."

He gave her a deeper scowl in reply. "Can I come in?"

Toby had stopped barking as soon as she'd opened the door, and she glanced at him now. "Should we let him in?"

Before she had a chance to, Rafe pushed the door open with a growl, forcing his way inside. "Who's here with you?"

His answer was excited barking as Toby pounced. "What the—" The dog's paws landed squarely on Rafe's chest, pushing him into the door, which slammed shut with the force of their combined weight. At nearly 70 pounds, Toby's jumps packed a punch. He'd knocked her into the door on more than one occasion.

She stared, amused, as Toby licked Rafe's face. "Some

guard dog you are," she chided without any heat.

"Hey, now, who's this?" He ruffled the dog's fur as a smile transformed his expression.

Surprised, she could only blink at him. His anger seemed to have vanished. She watched Toby prance under Rafe's attention and shook her head. Maybe she *should* train him as a therapy dog.

"This is Toby. My fierce protector." She rolled her eyes when the dog yipped and nudged at Rafe with his head. "Clearly," she added, her voice dry, and he chuckled. Though truthfully, relief had flooded her tense nerves, seeing him in a better mood.

He kept petting the dog as he asked, "Toby? As in the dog from Sherlock Holmes?"

Another surprise. Not many people understood the reference. "The very same." Her smile was tentative. "You might be the only person who's gotten that."

"I know how much you love Arthur Conan Doyle."

"*Sir* Arthur"—she smirked at him—"but yes, his work inspired me. I'm surprised you . . ." She trailed off, unsure of the ground under her feet. She worried bringing up their past would cause the scale of his emotions to tip back into dangerous territory. Nervous jitters started in her stomach and spread. "Never mind. Do you want to sit down?"

Before she could turn away and flee to the living room, he stopped her with a hand on her arm. The contact shouldn't have sent shockwaves rolling through her, but it did. Electricity sparked from the spot, firing along her nerve endings and heating everything in its path.

When she met his eyes, she gulped—in them swirled too

many emotions to decipher, darkening the chocolate to rich coal that stoked the fire burning within her.

"I remember everything about you, Tori."

His hand went from gripping her arm to trailing slowly up her cheek. "What you feel like."

His thumb brushed across her lips, and the heat arcing through her settled in her core.

Uh-oh.

"What you taste like."

When he bent his head toward her, she nearly melted against him as his words and touch clouded her senses. But it wasn't right for him to avoid her for two weeks and then—

His nose brushed her collarbone, and she swallowed a moan.

"What you smell like." His voice was a smooth whisper, weakening her knees.

And her resolve hung on by a thread.

"Rafe," she practically gasped his name as his nose trailed across her jaw. But before his lips could land on hers, Tori stopped him. They'd end up naked on her floor if he kissed her, and she wasn't ready for that. "Why were you angry before?"

She felt his sigh against her neck. Then he pulled back, looking her in the eyes. "Maybe we should sit."

She searched their depths but came up with more questions as the shield he sometimes wore slammed into place. With a sigh of her own, she led him to the living room.

Toby had calmed down and followed dutifully, jumping

on the plush gold couch. She settled next to him, gripping his fur for comfort, while Rafe took the seat adjacent in a black wingback chair.

Dressed in a black suit, he blended with the furniture, looking all the more imposing. His eyes, hair, and skin were dark compared to hers. She wasn't sure why she found the contrast so alluring, but she did.

Biting her lip, she tried to bring her thoughts around to something other than how much she wanted to kiss his full mouth. She'd always been a little envious of Rafe's lips. Hers weren't nearly as . . . juicy-looking.

"The night we had dinner . . . where did you go after?"

"What?" She blinked and met his eyes. It was much better to look there than at his—

Focus, Tori.

She replayed what he'd asked, her nose scrunched, and a line creased her brow. "Nowhere. Back here. Why?"

His eyes flashed with anger before his shield came up again. "Were you near Forest Grove?"

Truly perplexed now, she frowned. "I don't know where that is."

"It's a town about twenty minutes west of here."

Again, with the cardinal directions. She had no idea what was west of here. She wanted to roll her eyes, but then realization hit.

Ohhhh. She nodded at herself. "I did get turned around on the way home and went in the wrong direction. But then I ran into Detective Gorsky, and he set me straight." Rafe's hands fisted on the chair, but she kept going, "Is that where I was? Near that town?"

When he didn't respond right away, she studied him as she waited. His jaw clenched, as tight as his rigid posture. In the dramatic chair, he looked like a king on his throne—a dark one whose eyes burned with hellfire.

Wow, she was in a strange mood.

She would've laughed if it wasn't clear his anger had returned. She could practically see it crawling under his skin as he tried to contain it. Blinking that visual away, she blamed her sister for the direction of her thoughts. They must've been prompted by the call she'd received earlier from Veronica, who'd asked her to visit for Halloween.

October had barely started, but Tori knew the holiday would be here all too soon. Her niece and nephew had put the pressure on, begging her to go trick-or-treating with them. But with the book and everything going on—or *not* going on—with Rafe, she'd put them off, promising to come for Thanksgiving instead.

She was wise to her sister and knew Veronica wanted to dig for information about him. She'd heard the lecture waiting for her in the tone of her sister's voice.

The weight of the past settled on Tori's shoulders, and she suddenly felt weary. "Tell me why you're asking about this." She searched his eyes, but they gave nothing away.

"There's been another murder."

She didn't gasp; she didn't go pale with shock, but not because of the reason he might've thought. No, she'd known already because of the alert. "I know."

"You know?" He raised an eyebrow at her, but whatever guard he had on his emotions didn't slip.

Getting peeved at his coldness after he'd almost kissed her mere minutes before, she crossed her arms over her chest. "Yes, I got the notification right before you arrived."

Rafe didn't react, and his use of the silent treatment made her twitchy. Was she under suspicion for something? It proved hard to tell when the man sent more mixed signals than an antenna on a cell tower.

Lifting her chin, Tori challenged, "What does the murder have to do with where I got lost?"

He steepled his fingers and stared at her over them. "You don't know?"

She resisted—barely—rolling her eyes at him. "No. That's why I'm asking."

Get a clue, Raffaello.

In her mind, she sneered at his full name. She wasn't sure, but she thought he might be acting deliberately obtuse. It was getting on her nerves. If he didn't say something in the next three seconds, she—

Rafe clapped his hands, and the noise made her jump. "Good, then." He had the nerve to smile at her, though it had an edge to it. "It's where the body was found, and Detective Gorsky saw you there . . ." He shrugged like it wasn't a big deal, his smile still carefully in place, but she didn't trust it.

Whatever Dr. Jekyll said, Mr. Hyde was still in there.

As what he told her sank in, she had a near-hysterical moment where she wanted to laugh because her life mirrored fiction. Not an hour ago, she'd written the first signs in her book that made the hero seem suspicious in the heroine's eyes.

"So, I'm a suspect?" Though she kept her voice light, it couldn't hide the nerves underneath. She wove her fingers together to keep from fidgeting.

Sensing the tension in her, Toby shifted, laying his head in her lap. She unwound her fingers and stroked his fur, staring Rafe down. There was nothing for her to be worried about. She was innocent, after all. But she wasn't sure what he thought, not now when he did such a good job hiding behind his badge.

His smile disappeared. She glimpsed the anger simmering in his eyes for a moment, but then he shook his head. When he spoke, it was gone, his expression once again neutral. "This isn't solely my investigation. You being near where a body shows up, around the same time it was dumped . . ."

She swallowed, the bile burning her stomach and making its way up her throat.

I've got nothing to worry about.

If only her body believed her head.

"I'll do what I can, but there's bound to be questions, people wondering. Hopefully, we can clear you when the M.E. gives us the time of death."

Hopefully?

Struggling to nod, she stared through him as visions of being brought in for questioning over a murder investigation started playing through her mind. What if they couldn't clear her, and this dragged on? Would Rafe begin to doubt her?

Or would he even care?

Pain sliced at her heart like the quick sting from pulling

off a scab.

"Dammit, Tori!"

"Wha—" He pulled her into his chest, cutting off the rest of her question. Toby yelped in protest at the sudden movement. She'd been so absorbed she hadn't noticed Rafe move. He'd grabbed her so quickly she was dazed enough not to resist as he crushed her against him.

One arm cradled her head, and the other hugged her back as his anger unleashed in a fury of words. "I was *trying* to keep you out of this, but you keep *putting yourself* in harm's way!"

She was about to complain it wasn't her fault when he gripped her shoulders and pushed them apart to look into her face.

"Do you think it's been easy? Staying away from you?" he yelled at her now, "It's not what I want, that's for damn sure!" His eyes burned with a different kind of heat, but she was too perplexed by his words to feel the burn.

Her head reeled at the news. As the look in his eyes penetrated, her stomach tightened with nerves, her voice coming out in a breathy whisper, "It's not?"

"No!" Despite the harshness of his words, his hand was gentle when it cupped her cheek. "But you're his type. Don't you see it?"

Now, she struggled to keep up. Her brow pinched, her gaze narrowing. "Whose type? What are you talking about?"

Rafe's eyes flashed with rage, his hand clenching into a fist on her shoulder. "The slasher!"

She gulped. It's not that she hadn't made the

connection. She'd known the slasher's victims had been redheads. But to think she was in danger because of her hair color seemed a bit of a stretch.

Gathering her courage, she gripped his fisted hand and held it between hers, urging him to calm down. "I'll be careful."

His knuckles were rough against hers. Staring at his olive skin, she traced her finger across the callouses.

"I want you to leave."

Tori's head jerked up at his gruff demand. She would've dropped his hand, but he turned it over, gripping hers.

Always slow to anger, she felt it building, stirring the emotions swirling in her belly. "I live here. *You leave.*" She lifted her chin on the challenge, her eyes flashing with their own heat.

"No," his voice gentled, his free hand coming up to cup her face, but she jerked from his grip. "I mean, leave town. I want you safe."

The retort she'd been about to fire back with died on her lips as she saw the anguish in Rafe's eyes. But she wouldn't give in to it. "I'm not running away out of fear."

Not this time.

"Please, Sunshine. All those women . . ." He looked away, and his jaw muscles flexed.

She fought the urge to soothe him, especially when he met her gaze again. A soft gasp escaped at the pain shining in it.

"I saw you. Each time, I thought, what if it's Tori? I still see them"—his voice cracked, squeezing her heart—"in my dreams." The weight he'd been carrying around made itself clear. "I can't let it happen to you. Please leave. Go back to California or go on vacation. Just somewhere far away from here."

The turmoil in his eyes, in his voice, resonated within her. Wanting to soothe them both, she cupped his face and pulled his mouth to hers.

As their lips connected, the electricity she'd felt earlier charged through her, and she wrapped her arms around his neck, digging her fingers into his dark hair. She gripped it as though it could ground her, but the current ripping through her coursed harder and faster on its way to her core.

She opened her lips, and their tongues met and dueled. His taste—coffee and spice—flooded her senses. The familiar flavor instinctively enticed her to respond to it.

His hands found their way to her back, where they lowered and gripped her behind. When he lifted her, Tori was ready, wrapping her legs around his waist.

He walked her backward, lowering them to the couch, still exploring each other with their tongues. When their centers connected, heat matching heat, she moaned, and Rafe swallowed it.

His length strained against his pants.

So hard. So ready.

She wanted him, but . . . there was a reason she'd wanted to wait. When his hand found her breast, her thoughts scattered. He played with her nipple as he kissed his way down her neck.

The reason eluded her. All she could think was it had been too long since she'd done this, had this. When his other hand moved between her thighs, she groaned and succumbed to the wave of desire threatening to overtake her.

"Rafe," she wanted to tell him she didn't care about tomorrow. She wanted this. She wanted *now*. Regrets were for later.

"You like that, Sunshine?" his question came out muffled as he buried his mouth at her neck. His hand cupped her heat, and she needed the barrier of clothing gone.

Tori opened her eyes to demand he remove them and got a tongue to the face. Shrieking, she closed her eyes as Toby's wet slobber drenched her cheek.

Rafe lifted his head, shifting backward at the sound, but she missed his warmth. She opened her eyes and started laughing, which made the dog more excited. He jumped up, placing his front paws on her chest as he tried to lick her some more. "*Toby!* Off!"

With her lids shut in defense of dog kisses, she couldn't see Rafe, but she heard his chuckle before the weight of Toby's paws disappeared. She opened her eyes and smiled.

Rafe had the dog in a sit, a sheepish expression on his face. "I guess we have a chaperone."

She laughed as the lust left her brain. "He's letting me know it's dinner time."

Toby barked, understanding the word, which meant he'd be fed.

"I guess it is." Rafe scrubbed at his neck and avoided her eyes in a gesture that made it clear he was uncomfortable.

He better not be about to apologize.

After all, s*he'd* been the one who'd kissed *him.*

Feeling cold as the heat from their exchange fled, along with her confidence, Tori stood, wrapping her arms around her chest. "Maybe you should go."

His gaze whipped to hers, and for a second, she saw hurt before he nodded and rose. "Think about what I said?"

As her mood deflated, she acknowledged she didn't have the energy for another round of sparring with him. So, instead of starting another argument because she wasn't going anywhere, she agreed, "I will."

She walked Rafe to the door, regret churning in her gut, and couldn't help but think about what would have happened if Toby hadn't interrupted them.

CHAPTER 13

Tori

Tori's foot slid on a patch of wet leaves, nearly sending her sprawling down a hillside, so she slowed her pace. Her exhales came out in visible puffs that became increasingly harder to see. The sun set behind her, and she missed its warmth. When a shiver racked her, she glanced around as she continued to run.

She'd been here before, hadn't she? It started to feel like she was running in circles.

When more leaves shifted under her pounding feet, she stopped. The last thing she needed was to twist an ankle. Not when she was . . .

Where am *I?*

Eerie silence answered her.

Her chest heaved with something akin to panic as she realized she had no idea how she'd ended up in the middle of these woods. Desperation crawled in her belly, and she turned in a circle, searching for anything familiar.

But nothing was.

The chilly air made her wrap her arms around herself. As they encircled her, a thought struck.

My phone!

She patted herself down, searching for a pocket that would hold her salvation, but her running tights and T-shirt had neither. She had no wallet nor her bottle of mace. This felt wrong. She'd never go for a run without those items.

When she scanned the trees again, her heartbeat pounded in her ears, and it wasn't from the exercise. Fear, the oily, suffocating emotion, slithered over her, freezing her to the spot.

Her brain started shutting down when a glimpse of something broke through the icy haze.

What is that?

A flash of white, thirty feet ahead of her. She instinctively followed, a niggle at the back of her mind telling her she'd seen the flash before. Her feet moved faster, and the white became a coat.

Her mind registered it was attached to a person, and she opened her mouth to yell for help, to tell them she'd gotten lost, when the sound of a baby crying pulled her up short. Foreign and familiar all at once, it pierced her with the pain of a thousand pinpricks.

Where's it coming from?

After sobbing out a breath, she made another circuit of the trees with her eyes, but the night crept in, obscuring everything. Tori shook her head. Surely, it wasn't a baby. It was probably an animal, which sounded like—

A sudden noise from behind startled her, and she whirled around. Her heart lodged in her throat, her chest rapidly rising and falling with the effort of her breathing.

There was nothing there.

And to make it worse, she'd lost sight of the white coat. Tears blurred her vision as the last of the light dimmed. Fear crawled into her limbs, leaving her shaking in the spot she was glued to. Hopelessly, she wished for Rafe. For him to save her from the dark.

The echo of footsteps crunching on the leaves behind her sent her body into flight mode, and she took off in a sprint. Branches she couldn't see hit her in the face, arms, and legs, but she pushed past them, running and praying she'd find a way out. Her pulse drowned out any other sound, but she dared not stop to see who pursued her. Fear had driven out sense. The idea that whoever followed her could help her never entered her mind. She had but one thought.

Run!

Her legs pumped, and as her foot landed and lifted, she pushed herself harder with each spring.

Faster!

Her next step connected with air, and a scream ripped from her throat. Falling, Tori closed her eyes, waiting for the moment of impact.

When it happened, the sudden jolt made her open her eyes to see the ceiling of her living room. Startled, she jerked upright, her breaths still coming rapidly.

It was a dream.

She winced as her neck cramped. She'd fallen asleep

reading and had slumped over in an awkward position. Beside her on the couch, Toby whined and pawed at her leg.

As her mind settled, she reached for him, petting his head and letting the soft, shaggy feel of his fur soothe her. "It's okay, buddy. Just a bad dream."

A relieved chuckle tickled her lip despite a cold chill shivering over her sweat-dewed skin.

Not real.

No matter that it had *felt* real. She rarely remembered her dreams, but the scary ones always seemed to stay with her.

It wasn't surprising she'd dreamt of running. She did it often enough. She'd also recently gotten lost, though, then she'd been driving. Still, the parallels were there. Plus, she'd been reading a thriller novel as she'd drifted off.

Done convincing herself the dream showed her overactive imagination at work, Tori glanced down and noticed the book she'd been holding now lay in a heap on the floor. It had fallen open, and the pages were getting crinkled. Annoyed at herself for dropping it, she reached and picked it up, placing it on the glass-topped coffee table in front of her. The movement bumped the table and caused her phone to light up.

Curious about how long she'd been out, she picked it up and checked the time. It was nearly midnight. She'd slept for close to two hours already. Shaking her head, she stood, and Toby jumped off the couch, excited for his usual trip outside before bed. His tail wagged as he waited for her to follow him to the back door.

But after she took a step, she hesitated.

Would he still be there?

Surely, Rafe would have gone home by now. But the desire to know one way or the other pulled her to the window. She slid the white fabric to the side, then blinked as the image of the white coat flashed in her mind.

Not a dream but a memory.

She *had* seen a person when she'd pulled over that night after she'd gotten lost. Someone had been in the woods. But why? And who?

Excitement made her pulse jump as she realized she needed to tell Rafe. She could very well have seen whoever deposited the victim, or perhaps the person she'd seen had been the victim before they'd been murdered. She would have to ask what they'd been wearing. Focusing on the street, Tori relaxed, her tight muscles loosening.

He was still here.

Hours earlier, when she'd first noticed Rafe hadn't left, she'd wondered if he'd been staking her out—as a suspect or if he'd had another reason for staying. She sighed and rubbed at the ache piercing her chest.

The vines guarding her heart shifted when he was around, but more often than not, they pricked her as much as they protected her. In the face of his apparent interest, they constricted. But what exactly was he interested in?

Did Rafe truly want a second chance or only a roll in the sheets? How could she trust he wouldn't hurt her again?

Toby whined behind her, and she turned, stuffing those questions away as an idea formed. She'd put his leash on and take him out front with her. Then, he could have his before-bed bathroom break while she talked to Rafe. Provided the man hadn't fallen asleep.

She frowned, wondering if he intended to sleep in his car. It seemed like a horrible plan to her—stakeout or not. Although, if he was supposed to be watching her, he probably shouldn't be sleeping. She snorted, liking the idea of him watching her more than she should. Especially under the circumstances. She *should* be angry he felt the need to. Yet, she wasn't.

Toby barked and pulled her out of her needless thoughts. "Sorry, old man." She scratched behind his ears, and he smiled, forgiving her on the spot. "Let's get you hooked up. We're going out front tonight."

The labradoodle cocked his head to the side like he attempted to figure out why she wanted to deviate from their routine. She chuckled at the consternation on his face. But when she pulled his leash off the peg by the door, he understood, instantly jumping up to twirl excited circles in front of it.

Shaking her head at his antics, she let out an exasperated sigh. "You know I can't hook you up when you do that, silly. Settle down."

After a struggle, she finally got the leash attached. Grabbing her phone for a flashlight, she switched it on and headed out the door with Toby leading the way. He nearly pulled her down the stairs in his excitement as he raced straight to Rafe's car.

They were there in a matter of steps. His head lolled to the side, a ribbon of dark hair falling over his forehead.

So he is *sleeping.*

The smirk at finding him asleep disappeared when Toby jumped up, his heavy paws landing on the window with a thud, which woke Rafe.

He jolted up, his eyes going wide.

Oops.

* * * *

Rafe

Toby.

As Rafe recognized the shaggy snout pressed to his window, he relaxed the hand that had reached for his firearm.

Not a threat.

A quick glance at the clock in his dash told him he'd been out nearly an hour.

Shit. He hadn't meant to fall asleep. Scrubbing his hands down his face, he forced his brain into action and lowered the window.

Toby's head instantly poked through, trying to lick his face. In defense, he held up his arms. "A little help, please?"

He heard Tori snort before she pulled the dog off him and made Toby sit.

Finding it safe to remove his arms, Rafe sent her an appreciative grin. "Thanks."

In the dim glow from the streetlamps, he watched the half-smile she'd been wearing disappear before she glanced away.

Unsure what he'd done to upset her, he rubbed the back of his neck and broke the silence, "Seems a little late for a walk."

"Oh, no, we weren't . . ." Her eyes searched his face as she trailed off. "Why are you still here?"

When she finished her question, she chewed on her lip, and his gaze was drawn there like a magnet. A war raged within him. He wanted another taste of her, but at what cost?

Technically, she was a suspect, though he had no doubts about her innocence. But he'd already crossed the line with her once today. Doing it again would be harder to forgive. Particularly when he wanted to protect her.

Keeping her out of harm's way was more important than slaking his desire, and it came head and shoulders above any care he gave about being professional.

He pulled his gaze from her mouth. He owed Tori an answer, but should he tell her the truth?

Gazing into her emerald eyes, he admired how the green turned a deep hunter shade in the low light, pulling him under until he drowned within their dark pools. He wanted to watch them go blank as he made her—

"Because I'm a suspect?" She blinked, and Rafe was free.

He cleared his throat, swallowing to wet what had gone dry. "Yeah."

Wait, that's not what he'd meant to say!

She flinched, and he cursed under his breath. "No, I mean . . ." *Fuck!*

He couldn't have this conversation when she hovered over him. He needed to be able to touch her.

His hand flew to the door handle. "Hold on, I'm getting

out."

Tori backed up with Toby, putting him in another sit while Rafe climbed from the vehicle. As soon as he'd made it to the sidewalk, the dog sprang to his feet, but she held him firm.

Rafe was too frustrated to notice. The situation ate at him. His gut burned at seeing her wary gaze trained on him. He clenched his fists at his side, feeling useless and hating it. He wanted to catch this slasher, whoever the bastard was, and send his ass to prison where he couldn't hurt her or anyone else.

"I don't think you're a suspect. But you've gotten caught up in this. There's a serial killer out there"—his Italian side took over, and his voice rose as he threw an arm out to make his point—"looking for his next victim." His stomach knotted in fear at the possibility it could be her, and he grabbed hold of Tori. "I need you safe." He speared her with a look broadcasting just how badly he needed that.

Her eyes went wide, and Toby yipped, his head swiveling between them as he sensed the tension.

Gently, Rafe rubbed up and down her arms, soothing the spots he'd clutched. "If you won't leave town, you can get used to seeing me around because I'll be damned if I'm letting that *sick fuck* get anywhere near you."

He saw her swallow but didn't know if it was in fear of him or what he'd told her.

"I'm not letting you scare me away."

This time. He heard the words she implied but didn't voice, and they dragged hard on the weight around his chest.

He deserved it; he knew he did. But knowing she felt that way, that she still nursed the wound he'd inflicted, meant she wasn't likely to give them a clean slate. The slasher case notwithstanding, he wanted another chance with her.

Had wanted it. For a very long time. But he'd have to earn it.

Before he had a chance to respond, she shook her head. "This isn't why I came outside."

He frowned at her change in subject. "Why did you?"

She sighed and petted Toby's head, stroking his fur as if she needed comfort. "I remembered something."

Instantly, Rafe tensed. Sure, she meant something from their past, and he wouldn't like what she was about to say.

"After I left your place that night and got lost, I pulled over to look for directions with my phone. But while I was parked, I thought I saw someone in the woods. I brushed it off, thinking I imagined it, then Detective Gorsky showed up, and I forgot about it."

His muscles stayed constricted, but the cause became excitement now. "What did they look like? Where did you see them? What direction?"

She frowned at his rapid-fire questions. "I don't know, exactly. They were too far away, but they were wearing a white coat. It flashed like a light in the dark."

Okay, that was something. But he knew she had more if he could draw it out. "What kind of coat? Was it recognizable?"

She pursed her mouth in thought, and his eyes were drawn to her lips. They were paler than usual, and he wondered if she felt cold.

About to offer her his jacket, she spoke, "It was long, not a normal coat. Maybe like the kind a doctor would wear?" She shrugged, but the description started the wheels turning in his head.

The slasher he'd sent to prison had been a mortician who'd worn a white coat as part of his work uniform.

"Were they ahead of you or behind you?"

"Ahead of."

"Which side of the road?"

"The same side I'd parked on."

This meant they'd been west of her, heading toward Forest Grove.

"How far away were they? Approximately?"

Her nose scrunched up in the cute way she had as she tried to recall. "Maybe thirty or forty feet? It's hard to say in the dark."

"Okay. Good. That's good, Tori." He nodded as he pulled out his phone. He'd catch Gorsky up on this lead.

Slow down. It's midnight.

"Do you think it was the victim? Were they wearing a white coat?" Her hand reached tentatively for his arm to draw his attention.

He covered it with one of his own. "It could've been, but the body was bare when we found it."

She blanched, likely wondering if this victim had suffered the same treatment as the previous one.

He cupped her face. Wanting to pull her thoughts from the horrible possibility, he forced her eyes on his. "Hey, I think Toby's ready to do his business."

He relaxed when she sent a surprised glance at the dog. His tail wagged furiously, but he hadn't left her side.

"Oh. Sorry, bud. Let's go."

When she turned Toby, Rafe fell into step beside them. Another explanation for what she'd seen bounced around in his gut and made him nauseous. Tori peeked at him from the corner of her eye but didn't comment on his proximity.

After Toby relieved himself on a patch of grass near the park entrance, she headed for the home she rented. Rafe kept up with them. The possibility she could have spotted the killer—not the victim—and he could've seen her too churned Rafe's stomach. He swiped the back of his hand over his mouth before bringing it up. He hated that the idea would make her afraid, but if it meant she listened to him and left, it would be worth it.

He stopped her before she climbed the front steps. "Tori, there's another possibility."

She paused with him, turning to look at him with a confused frown. "For what?"

"The white coat. You could've spotted the killer, not the victim. And if he saw you . . ."

She nodded as if the thought had already occurred to her, which wasn't the reaction he'd expected.

"Don't you think that's another reason to leave? If he knows you saw him, it gives him more reason to come after you." He wanted to beg her to go, to plead until she gave in, but watching the anger she rarely showed come into her eyes, he doubted she'd listen.

"No! Wouldn't he find me in that case, no matter where

I went? I have a book to write, Rafe, and I'm not letting a 'what-if' keep me from finishing it."

Stubborn woman!

"Fine! If you won't leave, then you'll stay with me. You can write from anywhere, can't you?"

Her eyes had grown huge. "What?" Apparently, his offer had stunned her.

"Stay with me. Where I can protect you."

"But—"

He put a finger to her lips, cutting off any arguments. "Please, Tori. I need to know you're safe."

Her eyes were pulling him in again as she scanned his face. He didn't care what she saw there as long as she agreed. If he looked pathetic, if he practically begged her, it didn't matter. All that mattered was she wouldn't become one more woman he hadn't been able to save.

Her shoulders dropped with a sigh. "Why don't you stay with me tonight? You're not likely to get much rest sleeping in your car."

Now, he searched *her* face. Her eyes had lost the spark of anger; their expression held gentle understanding. But he didn't miss the fact she hadn't agreed to stay with him.

Still, her offer was a start. And he wasn't willing to pass it up. "Okay."

A slow smile curved her lips.

As Rafe followed Tori inside, he wondered exactly what her offer to stay entailed.

CHAPTER 14

Tori

Tori woke to the sound of Toby scratching at her door. Confused, she sat up and rubbed a hand over her eyes.

What time is it? Does he need to go out again?

After a glance at the clock, she groaned. She'd only been asleep for three hours.

"Come *on*, Toby. You went out a few hours ago. It's bedtime now."

As she spoke to him, the dog turned to look at her, whining in disagreement. By the light streaming in from the streetlamps, he managed to look pitiful with his big brown eyes. Toby was a creature of habit, so his waking her in the middle of the night was unusual.

She sighed, slinging her legs out of bed to take the dog outside. As soon as her feet hit the floor, she paused.

What was that?

It sounded like a shout. Toby whined; then she heard it again.

Could it be . . .?

Worried when the next one sounded louder, Tori moved quickly, opening her bedroom door and rushing to the living room where she'd left Rafe. He'd insisted on sleeping on the oversized couch instead of in one of the guest bedrooms. She wasn't sure why, but she'd been too tired to argue with him after he'd agreed to stay.

She was still a little surprised with herself for making him the offer, but she'd known he'd have slept in his car if she hadn't. The man was stubborn. His protective instincts had kicked in if he thought she might be in danger. They made him a good cop, but she felt they were exaggerated in this case. She didn't need to be on lockdown 24/7. She knew how to be careful and take care of herself, plus she had Toby.

At that, she inadvertently let out a snort. The dog was only good at protecting her from oversleeping. He woke her at the same time every morning, ready to go out and do his business.

But why *had* Rafe agreed to stay with her? To protect her, or was there something else? She wondered if he believed she wasn't a suspect, or perhaps he wanted to be close in case she remembered more of what she'd seen that night in the woods.

She wished she had a better read on his motive, but one minute, he blew hot, the next cold.

When she reached the living room, those thoughts fled as she found him struggling against the blanket covering him. Before she or Toby could act, Rafe shot up. His eyes were wide, his breathing labored. He scanned the room before visibly relaxing.

As if approaching a wounded animal, she held her hand out, saying soothingly, "It was just a dream, Rafe."

For some reason, his face twisted, his expression turning sour. "No. It's not."

Her steps faltered, and she dropped her hand. Softly, she asked, "It wasn't? Are you—"

"I'm fine," he bit the words at her.

She frowned at the harshness of his tone. Judging by how tightly he'd clenched his jaw, he was anything but fine. Gathering her courage, she closed the distance, sitting beside him. Because he appeared upset, the part of her that had never stopped caring for him wished she could comfort him.

"Want to tell me about it?"

The question earned her a quick and unequivocal no. Not that his response surprised her, but she'd had to make the offer. She could guess what his dream had been about, and her curious mind came up with its own answers, no matter how unlikely. But a feeling in her gut told her it had to do with the slasher.

He'd turned away from her, and though his breathing was less ragged, tension rode his shoulders.

Instinctively, Tori reached for him, rubbing her hand there. He didn't flinch or shrug her off, so she took it as a good sign. "I had a bad dream earlier, too. Actually, that's how I remembered seeing the person in the woods, so it wasn't *all* bad."

Rafe mumbled something she didn't catch before grabbing her hand, stopping its progress across his shoulders. Immediately, she stilled, waiting to see what he would do.

Slowly, he lowered her hand, turning to face her. When they met hers, his eyes were filled with grief, making her heart squeeze.

What made his eyes so sad?

He lifted her hand to his lips, kissing the top of it. Surprised, she stared until he lowered his forehead to hers. "*Sole mio.*"

His tender words caressed her lips, pebbling her skin as they traveled from her head to her toes. He'd called her his sun, which had never failed to set her heart—and ovaries—ablaze. She bit her lip to keep a moan from escaping, clenching her thighs against the fire kindling there.

Rafe played dirty; he couldn't have forgotten how his speaking in Italian affected her. Trying hard to ignore how close his mouth was, she breathed in his scent, taking the familiar note of smoky cedar with her as she forced herself to lean back.

A part of her heart crumbled in disappointment because she let fear keep her from what she wanted—to kiss him and watch it combust into so much more. But she wouldn't risk letting herself fall for him again without knowing where he stood. The last breakup had nearly destroyed her, and though she hoped she could survive another one, she saw no reason to put herself through such hell . . . at least not yet.

With the past and present weighing on her, Tori studied him. She *felt* tired, but he *looked* it. Whatever conversation they needed to have about this would be better after some rest. "We should get some sleep."

She thought she saw an echo of her disappointment flicker in his gaze before he nodded.

"Goodnight." Rising, she nudged Toby, who'd sprawled at their feet. The dog grunted at her before he stood to follow her to her bedroom.

"Goodnight, Sunshine."

Her steps wavered at Rafe's quiet reply, but she pushed the surge of longing down and kept walking.

Sun or not, she had to shine for herself first.

* * * *

Rafe

The shrill ringing of his cell phone pulled Rafe from a deeper sleep than he'd had in a long time. Groaning, he rolled to grab the offending device off his nightstand and face-planted onto the floor.

What the fuck?

Shaking off the vestiges of sleep, he pushed himself up and opened his eyes. This was not his apartment.

Yesterday's events replayed in his mind as he moved to sit back on the couch.

Tori's place.

His phone lay on the coffee table in front of him. It quieted, lighting up with a message notification. He scrubbed his hands over his face, wincing at the amount of stubble scraping his palms. He'd need to get his razor from the glove compartment of his car.

What the hell time is it?

Checking his phone, Rafe sighed. It was barely past six in the morning. He opened his messages to find a voicemail from Gorsky.

Before he could deal with the detective, he had to have coffee. Grumbling, he cracked his neck back and forth. The low gold couch had not made the most comfortable bed, but he'd wanted to be the first line of defense in case anyone had decided to come in uninvited. And he maybe—

Okay, definitely.

—didn't trust himself to give Tori the space she seemed to want with her sleeping in the next room. *He* should be the one keeping his distance. She was—technically—a suspect in his investigation, but all his thoughts involved kissing her again and finishing what they'd started the day before.

With the way she'd comforted him last night, he'd thought . . .

Rafe shook his head. At least he'd slept like the dead after.

Because of Tori?

Could simply being in the same house with her keep his demons at bay? In the past, her bright light had always washed away the stains of his job.

Perhaps it still could.

He smiled; her touch sparkled everywhere he looked. Despite this being a rental, she'd made it home. The fresh flowers on the mantle over the fireplace, the suncatcher hanging at the window waiting to catch the morning's rays and reflect them around the room. Even the books scattered on the coffee table launched a quiver of joy at his heart. He remembered how she'd lose herself in them for hours doing research for her next great story idea. He'd often found her that way when he came home from work.

Work.

Rafe massaged the back of his neck. It's what he had to deal with now. The same work that had caused his night to start fitful with the familiar nightmare plaguing him. The faces of the slasher's victims assaulted him again, and he shuddered before closing his eyes. At least once a week, he dreamt of them.

Shaking the images away, he stood. He needed coffee to clear his head, and he determined to raid her kitchen until he found the life-giving nectar.

As soon as his feet touched the kitchen tiles, he cursed. They were surprisingly cold. Maybe he'd gotten soft living in a brand-new apartment building, but he'd have thought there'd have been some insulation under the floor. He needed hot coffee and a hot shower. Pronto.

Grumbling, he was searching the countertops for a coffee machine when a voice made him spin around.

"I'd forgotten how much of a bear you are in the morning." Tori grinned at him as she removed Toby's leash. She'd clearly just been outside with the dog.

The realization he should have gone with her—should've protected her—seized his chest. Fear and anger toward himself threatened to choke him. Pushing it down, he focused on what she'd said.

Thinking about it, he raised an eyebrow, though secretly, her teasing pleased him or would have if he'd had caffeine in his system. "Coffee?" It wasn't so much a request as a desperate plea.

She chuckled and stepped to the side. Behind her, a full pot of coffee waited. Rafe nearly dove for the machine before he realized he didn't have a mug.

"Here." He turned to see her handing him a cup.

He almost kissed her out of gratitude before he stopped himself, merely taking what she'd offered. "Thanks."

As he poured himself a coffee, Toby sat at her feet and let out a pitiful whine. Her exasperated huff in response made his lips twitch before he took a sip of his drink and prepared to watch the show.

"This behavior is unbecoming, mister." Rafe had to hold back a laugh as she planted her hands on her hips to scold the dog. "You know very well I was getting your breakfast. There's no need to whine about it." Now, she tapped her foot. "Good boys wait patiently."

Toby managed to look contrite as he pawed at her leg for forgiveness. When her stance didn't falter, the dog resorted to nudging her with his head . . . almost as if it was his version of a hug. At that sweet gesture, she broke, bending to scratch the doodle's head. "Oh, all right, old man. You know I can't stay upset with you. Let's get your breakfast."

As she retrieved Toby's food, he commented, "He's got you wrapped around his finger. Not that I'm surprised. You always were a softie."

Tori snorted. "It's true, but Toby could charm anyone."

After another sip of coffee, he started feeling more human, and he had to admit he'd liked the dog immediately. "I think you're right."

She smiled before a line creased her brow. "You're up *early*. Did you have another, um . . ." She bit her lip. "Did you sleep well?"

His gaze fell to the spot where she assaulted her pink flesh. Watching Tori nibble her lip sent a shot of electricity straight to his groin. He didn't need coffee to wake up *that* part of his anatomy.

"Rafe?"

He blinked, then noticing she waited on his answer, pulled his eyes and thoughts away from her mouth. "Yeah. Like a log."

"That's good." She turned to retrieve the dog food from the pantry.

"Mmm," he hummed in agreement as she bent over, her perfect ass on full display through the leggings she wore. His fingers twitched around his mug as he fought the desire to grab her and pull her into him. He'd kiss the nape of her neck as his hands explored her sof—

Stop. Stop. Stop.

He had more control than this—usually. She innocently moved about the kitchen, and here he was, fantasizing about having his way with her. He wasn't sure how, but if they were going to make it with her staying at his place, he had to rein in his libido.

He cleared his throat and broached the subject, "I'm sorry I don't have a yard, but I figure you'll want to take Toby with you while you're staying at my place?"

Tori froze in the process of pouring out the dog's food. Only for a second, but he noticed. Her shoulders had tensed, too, and he took another sip of coffee, preparing himself for an argument. He wasn't taking no for an answer. If he had to carry her out of here in handcuffs, he'd do it.

Her voice came across calm and breezy, "I don't think that's necessary."

Testing her, he deliberately misinterpreted her words. "So, you'd rather leave him here? We can check on him twice a day, but it hardly seems—"

"No!" She spun around to face him. "I meant we don't need to stay at your place." Though she'd managed to sound more composed with the last statement, her eyes challenged him.

Maybe it was the coffee or the decent night's sleep he'd had, but he kept his cool. In fact, he felt exceptionally calm as he told her, "You *will* be staying with me, Tori. Whether of your own free will or"—he reached for his handcuffs, then cursed when he realized they were in the coat he'd discarded in her living room—"I take you into my custody."

Her eyes went wide, and she sputtered, "You, you can't do that!"

Secure in the knowledge he'd do whatever it took to keep her safe, Rafe set his empty mug on the counter and advanced on her. "Actually, I can."

CHAPTER 15

Tori

For the third time in the past thirty minutes, thoughts of Rafe intruded, interrupting her writing flow, which made her want to scream. Instead, she settled for a disgusted huff, pushing her chair back with more force than necessary as she gave up on the prospect of finishing the chapter she'd worked on.

She was angry.

That's not true, well, maybe a little—at myself.

But she *was* agitated. Nervous energy coursed through her veins, making her jittery as if she'd downed a whole pot of coffee. She'd tried to channel it into writing, but if the last hour proved any indication, she'd failed.

Damn him!

Tori popped up from her chair at Rafe's dining table, slamming the lid on her laptop in the process. Toby whined at her, but she sent him a withering look and started to pace. As far as she was concerned, the dog was as much to blame. He'd gone more willingly than she had—all prancing feet and excited tail wags.

"Traitor," the word left her lips without any real heat in her voice, but Toby knew he was in the doghouse. He lay down, staring at her with his big brown eyes in full-on pout mode.

The look twisted her heart, and she sighed. She was such a sucker for brown eyes. This morning, she'd known Rafe had been serious about taking her into custody from the dangerous gleam in his dark ones. Thinking about his threat to handcuff her, she absently rubbed her wrists. He hadn't because she'd given in.

The only way she wanted him handcuffing her was to the bed.

Seriously, Tor?

She shook her head and then stomped out a circle in his living room, angry at herself for going there when she should be mad at the man. The exercise—if you could call it that—didn't relieve any of the tension coiled within her.

She was a prisoner.

Sure, Rafe had been all *mi casa es su casa,* but apart from taking Toby out to relieve himself, she'd been given specific instructions not to leave. After he'd assured her there'd be a patrol outside for her protection, he'd left to go to the station.

Yeah, right. More like for her incarceration.

Beyond frustrated, she trudged to the window and pulled the curtain aside. She needed to run, but judging by the police car parked outside, it wasn't likely to happen. Dropping the fabric, Tori turned away from her dashed hopes, and her gaze fell on the bookshelf across the room. The last time she'd been here, it had been nearly empty. But it looked like Rafe had done some unpacking since then.

An idea sparked, and with it, a devious smile crossed her lips. She should at least investigate her surroundings if she had to be stuck here. She reasoned it wasn't snooping since he'd told her to "make herself at home."

What is he reading?

She moved to explore his bookcase. There were two flavors—crime and food. Rafe's penchant for police procedurals hadn't changed. The handful of cookbooks, one specifically for the Instant Pot, made her smile. He'd always enjoyed cooking, but it seemed his interest in it had expanded over the years they'd been apart. Hers had definitely not. Frozen dinners and takeout were her usual modes of sustenance these days. She'd learned long ago cooking for one person meant way more work than it was worth, at least in her opinion.

Another thought occurred to her, and a frown marred her lips. Did Rafe not mind making food for himself, or had he shared the activity with other women? The thought of Rafe in a relationship sent a sharp stab of pain to her chest. He may not be in one now, but they'd been apart for over a decade. Who had come after her?

Curiosity seized Tori, and she left the living room behind. If she wanted to know what he'd been up to since they'd parted, she wouldn't find it there. Feeling a little like a thief stealing into an unguarded home, she cracked the door to Rafe's bedroom.

When no alarm went off, and she didn't get struck down from the heavens, she smirked, pushing the door open wider. But she paused at the threshold.

The boxes stacked near the entrance told her he hadn't done much unpacking in here. His bed remained unmade, the dark covers tangled at the foot like he'd twisted them, tossing and turning in his sleep. A pang of sorrow reverberated through her as she recalled the nightmare he'd had at her house. Apparently, they were a fairly frequent occurrence.

Shaking off the melancholy brought on by that thought, she surveyed the rest of the room. The nightstand by his bed held a lamp and nothing more. Across from the bed, a low dresser spanned nearly the entire length of the wall. Curious about what sat upon it, she stepped further into the room. A scatter of loose change, paper, and foam earplugs decorated the top as though he frequently emptied his pockets there. Another glance around and what the room *didn't* have struck her.

No artwork, no photos, nothing personal—anywhere.

She twisted the necklace she wore around her neck. If she were going to do this, she'd have to look in drawers, potentially even the boxes he'd yet to unpack. It would be an invasion of his privacy.

Teetering on the edge of indecision, she drew in a deep breath, and Rafe's scent invaded her nostrils. Notes of cedar, wood smoke, and . . .

Is that Peroni? She closed her eyes as a memory assailed her.

Her stomach knotted as soon as she heard the door open.

Rafe was home, and while his arrival usually filled her with joy, today, she was full of trepidation. Biting back tears, Tori didn't turn from the counter where she chopped vegetables. It took her by surprise when she was suddenly spun in a circle. Her arm flew out, knocking over the bottle of Peroni she'd had open and waiting for him.

She screeched when she heard the crash, but it turned into laughter before Rafe set her on her feet. Then his lips met hers. His kiss soothed some of her nerves. She tried to hold onto that for as long as possible, but the pungent smell of malt flooded her nose, the thought of the mess they had to clean up intruding.

When he broke the kiss, his arms stayed around her waist as he smiled down at her. "Hello, Sunshine."

She smiled at the nickname and the warmth blooming in her chest whenever he used it. "Hi."

"How was your day?"

His eyes shone with concern when her face fell at the simple question. She turned away to mop up the spill, but he stopped her.

"Hey"—he brushed a thumb across the wrinkle in her brow—"what's wrong?"

She bit the inside of her cheek as her eyes flooded with traitorous tears. She tried really hard not to let them fall. Crying wouldn't help the situation. But inside, she raged.

This wasn't in the plan!

She hadn't finished school yet, and now . . .

She had to tell him. Her lip trembled, and she swallowed. All day, she'd worried over his reaction.

When the seconds stretched without a response, Rafe

cupped her face. "Tori, please. What is it?"

"I—" The words failed her.

What if this was the end of them?

She couldn't bear to think about it. Gripping her necklace like a lifeline, Tori pushed out, "I'm pregnant."

His hands fell from her face as he slowly blinked at her. "You're pregnant?"

Was he seriously going to make her repeat it? The knots in her stomach tightened as she nodded.

"How"—his Adam's apple bobbed—"how do you know?"

"You know I've been feeling off, and this morning I realized I was late so . . . I took a test."

His head moved up and down in response, but his face held a vacant expression. She could tell he was trying to process the news.

She nibbled on her lip while she waited. She'd had the better part of the day to come to terms with it, and though having a baby hadn't been in their immediate plans, there was no way she didn't want the child. She hoped Rafe would feel the same.

"Okay." His expression cleared as his dark eyes settled on hers.

"Okay?" She sniffled as the tears she'd been holding at bay threatened to break through. What kind of response was 'okay'?

He flashed a grin, and she blinked at the sudden change. "Okay!" He picked her up to spin her again but stopped almost immediately, setting her quickly on her feet. "Oh shit. I probably shouldn't spin you." His eyes shifted, and she saw the panic in them as he cupped her face. "Are you okay?

How do you feel? You should sit."

The rope that had been squeezing her insides loosened with his concern, and she chuckled, shaking her head. "I feel fine."

"Not nauseous or shaky or—"

"Hey." She took Rafe's face in her hands, then pulled his head down as she rose on her toes to meet his mouth. Relief, joy, and excitement poured out of her as the kiss heated. But fear still niggled, sliding in and out of her thoughts.

Tori lowered to her feet and took a deep breath, preparing to voice them. It didn't come out as strong as she would've liked when she gathered the courage, "Rafe, I'm scared."

The look in his eyes was so confident it seemed to promise her she had nothing to be afraid of. "We can do this, Sunshine."

A car backfired and broke Tori from her reverie. Something hit her hand, and she glanced at it.

A teardrop.

Numbness had settled over her. A natural defense against the pain of the past, and she struggled to shake it off as she reached for her cheeks to wipe away the droplets.

She hadn't yet turned twenty-two when she found out she was pregnant. She and Rafe had been together for almost two years, but there were things she'd wanted to do before ever thinking about having a child. Like finishing her degree.

They'd been careful but not careful enough. In the span of two minutes, one little test changed everything.

It was the beginning of the end.

An arrow pierced the wall around her emotions, and she

flinched. The numbness faded, and she didn't like the alternative. Her eyes scanned the room again while she forced the past back where it belonged, to the buried recesses of her heart.

This felt wrong.

No matter their history, she didn't have the right to invade Rafe's privacy. A loud bark sounded from the living room, and she jumped, knocking into the pile of boxes by the door.

They teetered, dangerously close to falling. Moving quickly, Tori struggled to right them, but she overcompensated and sent the top two crashing to the floor. She flinched instinctively, bracing for the sound of something breaking, but they barely made a thump. The carpet muffled the noise. Thankful the boxes had missed her feet, she rolled her eyes at her jumpiness, then bent to clean up the mess she'd made.

The small one on top had come open when it landed. An interesting array of objects littered the floor, but with her new determination, she squashed her curiosity, using her arm as a shovel to scoop the contents that had spilled out back inside. Once she'd secured it by tucking the flaps over and under themselves, she reached for the second box. It had fallen on its side. When she righted it, the sunlight coming in through the window across the room flashed over a familiar image. A bolt of surprise charged down her spine, and she opened the box all the way. It was full of books, but not just any books.

No way.

Inside, neatly stacked, lay every book she'd ever written.

Had he read them?

She lifted the top one out and opened the flap. It was a signed copy.

Interesting.

She checked all the others, and each one had been signed. People often bought signed copies from the publisher, but it surprised her he'd want them. Had he kept up with her career?

Or had he been keeping tabs on her?

Confusion rolled through her. She wasn't sure whether to be flattered . . . or concerned. She checked the titles and confirmed he had them all, from her first book to the latest release.

Not sure how to react to this information, she mulled it over when excited barking alerted her that someone was at the door.

Shit!

As fast as she could, she dropped the books into the box and rebuilt the tower she'd toppled. Toby quieted, then she heard the sound of a key in the lock. Panicking, Tori dashed down the hall to the bathroom. If Rafe was home, she didn't want to be caught snooping.

A few moments later, she heard a decidedly female shriek and rushed out of the bathroom. Toby had an elderly woman pinned to the counter about to drool all over her face.

Uh-oh.

"Toby, down!" The dog immediately dropped, and she rushed forward, praying he hadn't accidentally hurt the woman.

The poor thing's light blue eyes were huge, and her tiny chest heaved.

"I'm so sorry! I promise he's friendly. But he can be a little overly affectionate." She shot a glance at Toby, motioning for him to sit.

He obeyed, his mouth opening with a smile as his tail swished against the floor. Satisfied he wouldn't forget himself again, Tori focused on the woman.

She'd straightened, and her breathing had calmed—a little. One hand rested on her chest as if she had to hold in the heart Toby had nearly made jump out of it.

Guilt made Tori's shoulders droop. "I'm sorry he scared you. Is there something I can help you with?"

The older woman finally focused on her, but she didn't let Toby out of sight. "Rafe?" she squeaked out.

"I'm afraid he's not here."

She shook her head, her white bob bouncing with the movement. "Who are you?"

"Oh, I'm Tori, Rafe's . . ." *ex? hostage?* Neither was likely to go over well. She fought the blush rising to her cheeks. "I'm staying with him for a little while."

The woman's eyes narrowed as she looked her up and down.

It was disconcerting, like being sized up by his grandmother, and she fought the urge to fidget. "I'm sorry, he didn't tell me you'd be stopping by, Ms. . . . ?"

"Walsh. I'm his neighbor."

Tori forced a smile. "Nice to meet you, Ms. Walsh."

The woman harrumphed, shooting a glare at Toby, then dug into her bag. When she pulled out a small manila envelope, she waved it at Tori. "This is for Rafe. Please see that he gets it. And for goodness' sake, keep that animal under control." She sniffed at Toby.

Both chastised and affronted, Tori managed not to cry or laugh as she reached to take the envelope from the woman. "Yes, ma'am."

With a sharp nod for her and another glare at Toby, Ms. Walsh stalked out the door, closing it behind her.

Tori glanced at Toby. "Nice job, buddy. You made us persona non grata with the neighborhood watch." She got the feeling Ms. Walsh kept an eye on the comings and goings of this floor—a veritable nosy Nancy—and they'd just gotten on her bad side. She'd bet the elderly woman's head popped out whenever she heard the elevator ding.

The thought made her pause. She wondered if Rafe had asked Ms. Walsh about the day he'd gotten the slasher's envelope. Perhaps she'd seen something they hadn't.

Toby let out a playful bark, then went back to wagging his tail. Distracted, she shook her head at her silly dog and turned her attention to the envelope from Rafe's neighbor. She flipped it over, but nothing had been written on the outside. Not a piece of mail, then. It kind of reminded her of the one she—

Shit!

Tori dropped the envelope on the counter.

Shit! Shit! Shit!

It looked exactly like the one she had handed Rafe a few weeks ago—the one from the slasher.

Ugh! And now her prints were on this one, too. She started pacing as her adrenaline spiked. She had to tell him. She paused mid-stride and huffed out a breath.

Except, she was overreacting.

She hadn't even looked inside the envelope. Maybe this wasn't another playing card. Just because it looked the same as the previous one didn't mean it had to be from the slasher. Manila envelopes *were* common office supplies.

She picked it up gingerly, trying to touch it as little as possible. On a deep breath, she lifted the flap and peeked inside. The tension left her body when she did, and her pulse quieted.

Not a playing card.

CHAPTER 16

Rafe

"Hey, did you get the tickets?"

Rafe startled, sloshing the coffee in his mug over the rim and onto his hand. He was lucky it had gone cold, or he'd easily have gotten second-degree burns. Regardless, his mood strayed far from light.

He shook the liquid off and scowled at his lieutenant, whose booming voice had pulled him from his thoughts, causing him to spill the coffee in the first place. "Dammit, Jameson."

The big redhead shrugged, his lips tipping up in a sheepish smile as he moved into Rafe's office. "Sorry. But did you get 'em?" He sat in one of the chairs in front of his desk, folding one long leg across the other at the knee.

He blinked at his friend. *Get what?*

Jameson's smile fell away into confusion. "The tickets?"

"What tickets?"

"Daisy said she left them with your neighbor." Jameson

scratched at his chin. "What's her name, Ms. Walsh?"

Rafe wasn't in the mood for another mystery to solve, especially not one involving his lieutenant's wife and his neighbor. "I haven't seen Ms. Walsh in days."

"Oh, well fuck. I'm sure she has them." The lieutenant uncrossed his leg and leaned forward, excitement on his face. "It was supposed to be a surprise, but . . . we've got tickets to the home opener! Bulls vs. Cavaliers. How fucking great is *that*? It'll be like old times. Except for—"

When Jameson's words finally penetrated, Rafe slammed his coffee cup down. He didn't have time for basketball, not when a fucking murderer was going after women like Tori.

"Why do you look like you want to tear me a new one?" The lieutenant sat up straighter, though his tilted head merely hinted at curiosity.

Rafe's hands clenched into fists on his desk as he worked to keep his voice calm. "I've got shit leads on a serial killer case. Basketball is the furthest thing from my mind right now."

Jameson frowned, his eyebrows pinching. "I get it, and I'll help any way I can. With Tori in town, I just thought you'd want to go. Daisy wants to do a double date with you guys, so I figured—"

"Double date?" Surprise pushed him against his chair. Then his shoulders drooped at the reality of how far from dating he and Tori were.

"Yeah, I mean, it doesn't have to be the game, though. We could—"

He swallowed against the disappointment, burning his

throat like acid. "Tori and I aren't . . . she isn't, uh . . ."

Fuck! Why was this so hard to say?

Jameson's face fell. "Oh, shit. I'm sorry, I assumed . . ." He shook his head. "But, fuck, Alonso! Why the hell *aren't* you? This is *Tori*, and you've been hung up on—"

"I know! It's fucking complicated," he growled, and Jameson held his hands up in an apologetic gesture.

The big redhead cleared his throat. "Speaking from experience . . . it's probably less complicated than you think."

He raised an eyebrow at his ballsy friend. His patience for this conversation wore thin.

"Just tell her how you feel."

"Thanks for the dating advice, Dr. Phil. Would you mind leaving me the hell alone now? Unless you have actual *police work* that needs my attention?" Rafe figured the barb would deter Jameson, but the fucker only grinned at him.

"Think about what I said." The redhead stood, heading for the door, but before he left, he turned around. "*Captain.*"

"Fuck off, Lieutenant."

After a mocking salute, Jameson disappeared. It almost made him smile.

But his lack of progress in finding the killer and the stalemate he and Tori had come to was nothing to smile about.

Although, thinking about the heat in her eyes when he'd told her he'd handcuff her if need be stirred up more than regret. His pulse drummed in his veins, imagining using his handcuffs on her for another reason. He mentally kicked himself when his stomach tightened in anticipation at the image in his head.

Not fucking helpful!

What *would* be helpful is finding the damn killer. His expression changed, a deep scowl wrinkling his forehead as he dropped his head into his hands.

The call he'd missed from Detective Gorsky this morning had been another dead end. The medical examiner's office had identified the particulates found on both bodies. What should have been good news— something that could tie the two homicides together, turned out to be another fucking mistake.

Anger buzzed through Rafe, and he slammed his fists on his desk. The trace evidence they had was useless. The particulates were a combination of amylose, amylopectin, and magnesium oxide, which meant fucking nothing to him, but the tech had explained those were the common ingredients found in cornstarch used to powder latex gloves—the kind of gloves they all donned whenever investigating a crime scene.

Their evidence proved nothing more than contamination by someone at the scene. It could've been Dundy, Gorsky, or any other officers who'd responded. Hell, it could've been him.

Rafe scrubbed a hand down his face. It happened more often than it should, leaving behind residue, but the clencher, in this case, was it had been the only real lead they'd had to go on. Now, they were back at square fucking one.

At least he'd gotten a single piece of good news this

morning. Tori was no longer a suspect. The M.E. had provided the time of death on the second victim—a young male, as yet, unidentified—and she'd a damn good alibi.

His muscles twitched thinking about it. He'd been ready to bend her over his kitchen counter around the same time the poor kid had been getting murdered.

Fuck, what a thought.

With a groan, he closed his eyes, rubbing at the headache brewing in his left temple. He might have been interested in a basketball game if he hadn't kept running up against a brick wall. When he and Tori lived together in Chicago, Jameson would drive over to the home games with them. It had been fun—something he hadn't had in way too long.

Rafe sighed, opening his eyes to stare out the window. The overcast weather and its gloom suited his mood. The only bright spot in all of this was he got to go home to Tori.

Knowing she was safe was the one thing giving him a measure of calm. Which meant he had to make her stay at his place.

The weight hanging on him tugged at his chest. If she wanted to stay with him, they could pick up where they'd left off when she came to dinner.

With every splintered piece of his murky, damaged soul, he wished for a second chance. He needed her light in his life again to brighten the dark days and shine through the good ones.

Because he'd never stopped loving her.

His chest squeezed uncomfortably, sucking away his air supply at the thought she might not feel the same way.

Sure, people could change . . . but Tori was still his Sunshine. If only she'd give him a chance to show her. Focusing on that, he sucked in a deep breath.

He needed a plan because he knew she would argue about going back to the house she rented. His Sunshine had always possessed a strong mind and a stubborn streak. He couldn't keep leaving her to come into the station every day.

Maybe she could write here.

He glanced through his door, tuning into the noise of the bullpen.

Maybe not.

With the cacophony, it's a wonder anyone could work in this environment. He shook his head and supposed you got used to it after a while, learning how to drown it out. Most of the time, it didn't bother him. The ringing phones, the good-natured insults yelled across desks, and the slamming of file drawers all faded into the background for him. But he doubted it would for Tori. She was way too observant.

No, the only real solution meant finding the killer.

Which he couldn't do while moping at his desk. There were loose threads in Chicago he needed to pull on, and that meant it was time for some legwork.

* * * *

Tori

Toby's bark echoed in Tori's ears as she gasped awake. On instinct, she rolled away from the sudden noise and landed on the floor in front of Rafe's couch. "Ow!"

She'd managed to bang her elbow into the corner of his coffee table on her way down, and the stupid thing was sharp. A stinging burn spread up her arm, waking her up fully. She twisted her elbow to look at it, afraid of what she might find.

Not bleeding.

That was good, but it would no doubt leave quite a mark. Even if she hadn't been prone to bruising, a curse of having fair skin, no way would that kind of pain not have left her unscathed.

Groaning, she pushed herself up as Rafe walked in the door. She'd been too preoccupied to hear the key in the lock, but at least she knew why Toby had woken her.

"Tori?" He rushed to her side. "What are you doing on the floor? Are you okay?"

His concern had warmth simmering in her belly until she remembered she was mad at him for keeping her prisoner all day. "I'm fine," she snapped, pulling herself onto the leather sofa.

Rafe flinched at her tone, then turned away to give Toby his desperately desired attention. "There's a good boy." He alternated between scratching the dog's ears and rubbing his head.

She glared at Toby, muttering "traitor" under her breath, but watching them together softened her anger.

She sighed and offered an explanation by way of an apology, "I was asleep on the couch when Toby startled me awake. I rolled off and knocked my elbow on the coffee table."

"Let me see it." He reached for her with a gentle request.

She cradled her right arm. It had stopped hurting—mostly. "It's fine."

His fingers on her were not a good idea . . . trailing along her arm, caressing her skin. She blinked and pulled her gaze from his outstretched hand. Her cheeks heated.

Prisoner! You're his prisoner, Tori. Don't forget that!

"I'm really fine. Not bleeding or anything." She covered her embarrassment with surliness.

"Sunshine," he dragged the nickname out, the exasperation apparent in his tone.

Knowing he wasn't going to drop it unless she let him have a look, she offered her arm. "See? Told you it's fi— Ow!" She snatched her arm back.

Rafe had pressed on the spot and sent a throbbing ache pulsing through her.

"Why did you do that?" she scolded.

"I'm sorry." He held his hands up in an apology. "I was trying to make sure you hadn't broken anything."

She cupped her injured elbow and glared at him. "Oh, I'm happy to break something." She pointedly stared at his fingers. "Which hand do you shoot with again?"

"Very funny." He smiled and tweaked her nose.

The affectionate gesture made her see red. As the little embers she'd been stoking all day blazed to life, her anger spewed out at him, "I wasn't kidding."

Tori pushed to her feet, needing to put distance between them. "Rafe, you left me here all day. I was basically a prisoner!" Her chest heaved as she worked herself up. "I couldn't even go for a run!" Beyond frustrated, she paced in front of the coffee table. "I will not stay holed up here all day like some, some . . . ."

While she struggled to come up with an appropriate analogy, he stepped into her path. With him in the way, she stilled, propping her hands on her hips. When the word she wanted didn't come, she settled for a cry of frustration.

Apparently, that amused him because a small smile flitted across his lips. It momentarily distracted her, so she wasn't prepared when he lifted a hand to cup her cheek. "I know."

His quiet agreement dampened the flames of her temper, or maybe his touch did. A different kind of heat ignited within her, making her breath hitch. She was afraid to move and break the contact. When his thumb caressed her face, she fought the urge to close her eyes and lean into it. Instead, she stared into his dark orbs and really looked at him for the first time since he'd gotten home.

Poor Rafe. He looks like he could use a nap like I just had.

The shadows under his eyes had grown, and his shoulders drooped. What kind of day had it been for him? Compassion threatened to weaken her resolve, but she pushed it away. She *would not* be stuck here against her will.

It cost her, but she made herself lean back anyway. The sudden separation left her chilled, so she crossed her arms over her chest. "Then we agree I go home?"

He didn't answer her. He scrubbed his hands down his face, muttering something she didn't catch.

"What was that?"

He looked at her, and though he smiled, she could tell it was forced. "Are you hungry?"

As if on cue, her stomach growled loud enough to give her away. "Yes. You locked me up here and didn't feed me. At least real prisoners get meals." Her stance didn't change as she waited for his response.

She ignored the fatigue so clearly written on his face and the . . .

No, it couldn't have been longing she'd seen.

She swallowed against the uncomfortable thought.

"Let's fix that." He flashed a genuine smile this time. "Grab your coat."

Her stomach jumped at the prospect of being set free. "We're leaving?"

Her question made his expression turn hesitant. "Unless you wanted me to cook?"

"No! Please, I need fresh air." The only cure for her cabin fever meant getting out of this apartment. The fact that he offered the option made her want to weep with gratitude.

Except he's the reason you were locked in here all day, dummy.

Tori rolled her eyes at herself and went to collect her coat. No matter what she'd thought she'd glimpsed in his gaze, the facts were this: she would not be his prisoner, and she certainly wasn't going to kiss him—again—until she knew where they stood.

"Ready?"

She was shrugging into her jacket when his hands lifted her hair out. The simple gesture he'd performed many times for her in the past made her eyes fill.

Blinking the tears away, she cleared her throat. "Yes." She wanted to leave before he changed his mind.

She didn't turn around; she couldn't yet.

"Great"—his voice brushed across her cheek in a rasp—"I know just the place."

Tori nodded, and her eyes fell on his kitchen island. When the last time she'd been in his house for dinner flashed in her mind, she spun around and headed for the door.

Dinner in public with people and space—away from Rafe—was exactly what she needed.

CHAPTER 17

Rafe

Rafe was so tired. More mentally than physically. His hands were steady on the wheel, and his eyes didn't droop. But inside . . . his stomach burned, and his brain fried. His body operated on autopilot as he drove the familiar route to Daisy's Diner. The little man running the controls had given up hours ago.

He'd been glad Tori hadn't wanted him to cook. Right now, he wasn't sure he had the mental capacity to make anything edible, even if he tried. The heartburn he'd been dealing with for the past few hours meant food was the last thing he wanted.

But Tori was hungry.

And he didn't need to give her another reason to be upset with him. He was an ass for not realizing she'd feel like a prisoner, trapped in his apartment all day. They had to come up with another solution to protect her, but that would be a problem for tomorrow. He'd had enough issues he couldn't solve for one day. At least he could feed her.

She stayed unusually quiet in the seat next to him. He glanced over, and her heady floral scent teased his nose. He breathed in deeply, enjoying her smell. Sun-warmed daffodils filled the space around him. But the joy didn't last long. The tension was evident in her profile.

She's giving me the cold shoulder.

It's probably best he hadn't handcuffed her this morning, or she would've been more pissed at him. Although, if handcuffing her had led to a heated argument, Rafe imagined it could've quickly changed to a different kind of heat. Even the temptation in the thought and the memories it stirred weren't enough to stave off the defeat weighing him down. He felt its tug on his chest and rubbed the back of his neck.

After Jameson had left his office, he decided to make a quick trip to Chicago. He still had contacts in several of the districts, but after reaching out to each of them, he'd gotten no closer to solving his case than when he'd started. There hadn't been any similar deaths to the slasher victims reported in the city, which raised more questions than it answered.

Was the killer local to Rolling Brook? Or were they targeting people in the area for another reason?

He couldn't shake the feeling the murders were meant as a message for him. But who had sent it?

He gazed out the windshield and wondered if this was what a hamster on a wheel felt like, moving as fast as you could but getting nowhere.

Stuck–that's what he was.

He'd gotten stuck on the same damn wheel he'd deliberately stepped off of. His intention had been never to get back on. Yet, here he was, playing detective again, investigating another serial murder case. He'd thought he'd left all that behind, but it had followed him to this sleepy little town.

The acid in his stomach sizzled with his anger as his hands tightened around the steering wheel. Hadn't he seen enough senseless deaths? He wasn't sure what he'd done to piss off the powers that be, but apparently, they weren't done punishing him.

As if on cue with his thoughts, a sharp pain in his abdomen made Rafe suck in a noisy breath.

Fuck!

He rubbed at the spot, but the heartburn continued to spread until his chest felt like it was on fire.

"Rafe, what's wrong?" Tori had finally turned away from the window. She stared at him with worry in her eyes as he tried to breathe through the searing pain.

Damn, but it was intense. Pretty soon, he'd be spewing flames. He gritted his teeth against the scorching and managed to get out, "Tums," before another burning stab had sweat breaking out on his forehead.

Where the fuck had he put them?

Rafe patted his pockets, but he didn't feel the tiny roll. Had he gone through a whole one so fast?

He heard her rustling through her giant purse, but his focus stayed on the road as sweat beaded at his temples. They were almost to the diner. At least there, he could get a glass of milk to help tone down the reflux.

He swallowed against the acid, getting dangerously close to his throat. *If* he made it that long.

"Here. Take these."

At her soft demand, his gaze cut to Tori, who held up what looked like two antacids in the palm of her hand.

Holy mother, she'd saved him. He reached for the medicine, popping it into his mouth. After he'd swallowed, he smiled at her. "*Angelo mio,*" he whispered.

She *was* an angel. Her presence in his life proved truly divine as she settled the geyser, which had been about to erupt, coating it with calcium carbonate.

She didn't return his smile, but her eyes lost the tightness they'd held. "Better?"

He nodded, breathing became more manageable, and he added, "Thank you." If he hadn't been driving, he would've kissed her.

"How long have you been having heartburn?" Tori studied him closely, her forehead pinched in concentration.

He cleared his throat, embarrassed by his body's response to the stress he was under. "A few weeks."

Since the first homicide.

She frowned at him. "Since I came to town."

"No! It's not that." He couldn't have her thinking he didn't want her here because he did. So much. "Not because of you, Tori."

He wanted to reach for her, but the look in her eyes told him she'd likely bat his hand away if he tried.

On a sigh, he acknowledged, "But I guess it has been about the same amount of time—"

Holy fuck!

As what he'd said sunk into his exhausted brain, Rafe's body went rigid. Why had he not made the connection before? What if the murders weren't a message for *him* but for Tori? She *did* arrive in town at the same time the killer started leaving bodies for them to find.

When his blood pressure spiked, his stomach cramped, the acid fighting to resurface. This was bigger than him. If she was the target . . . he couldn't let her out of his sight.

"Is this where we're eating?"

He blinked and focused on the building in front of him. He'd been so lost in his thoughts he hadn't noticed they'd arrived. He didn't want to scare her unnecessarily. So, for now, he'd keep that frightening possibility to himself.

As he turned the car off, he forced a smile even though his pulse pounded in his head. "Yeah, Daisy's is the best food in town."

She stared at the restaurant and didn't respond. Neon lights made the red paint on the exterior glow, giving the classic-looking diner a nostalgic air. "I love it. It looks . . ."

"Like a blast from the past," as she finished her sentence, she met his gaze.

She'd been smiling, but the longer she stared at him, the more it fell. When she started to chew on her lip, his eyes were drawn to the spot. He wanted so badly to kiss her, to show her they could have a future no matter their past.

She drew him in like a moth to a flame, and he leaned toward her. He gently pulled her lip from her teeth with his thumb when they were inches apart. "Sunshine—" He wasn't sure what he wanted to say, but it didn't matter because Tori jerked away from him.

He got a glimpse of her big green eyes before she scrambled out of the car.

Did I scare her?

He scrubbed his hands down his face in frustration before following her out. "Tori, wait!"

She'd practically reached the door by the time he caught up. Maybe he needed to start running with her because the woman could move.

"Look, you don't have to run away."

Her eyes cut to him, and they were sharp as emeralds.

Okay, she didn't like that *comment.*

He quickly tried to backpedal. "Not that you were, or that you would, uh . . ."

She wasn't giving an inch. Her red hair crackled like flames from the buzzing neon, her eyes just as volatile.

He gulped. "I'm sorry." He wasn't sure what he apologized for, but he'd take the blame for anything to remove the daggers from her expression.

She scoffed and crossed her arms over her chest.

Somehow, he'd made things worse.

"Please, *sei la luce nella mia anima.*" Okay, maybe it was cheating, pulling out the Italian, but he needed his Sunshine again before the fireball she'd turned into blazed him to the ground.

Her gaze slowly softened, her stance losing some of its defensiveness. "What does it mean?"

* * * *

Tori

Ugh, this man.

Tori sat across from Rafe in the booth furthest from the door. The diner was busy enough, a low din of noise echoing off the tin ceiling from the many combined voices. She'd been momentarily distracted by it and the rest of the decor when they'd stepped inside. Shiny red booths played off the stained concrete floor while a long checkerboard counter stretched the length of the place. It was everything she'd expected in a diner that looked straight out of a movie set because it seemed too pretty to be real.

Despite being charmed by the retro atmosphere of the restaurant, she hadn't forgotten her beef with Rafe. As far as she was concerned, the man kept accruing strikes. Not only had he held her prisoner all day, but he'd made her feel sorry for him and then scared her by clearly having a severe reflux attack. But the kicker had been him not revealing what he'd said to her in Italian.

It's like he enjoyed infuriating her. She wanted to keep giving him the silent treatment, but he'd always been better at it.

She glared at him and drummed her fingers on the table. Already, she was bursting at the seams.

But she would not beg. She huffed out a breath in exasperation. If he didn't want to tell her what he'd said, fine. She could deny her curiosity in this case. Besides, it hardly mattered. If she wanted to know, she could look it up. She'd already committed it to memory with that intention, anyway.

Thinking about it, she replayed the phrase in her head. She knew a few words in Italian—the whispered endearments he'd used when they'd been together—but she had no idea what he'd said apart from "my," which didn't tell her much. Her fingers itched for her phone.

But she could wait.

With a derisive sniff for Rafe, she turned away from him—no need to waste a glare when it wasn't having the desired effect. And staying angry proved exhausting. No wonder why she rarely let herself get this worked up.

Where's the server?

She could use the distraction. As soon as the thought crossed her mind, Jameson walked through the swinging doors from the kitchen.

Relieved, Tori smiled, lifting her arm in a wave. "Jameson!"

At her shout, the lieutenant looked her way. A grin spread across his lips, and he headed for their booth.

Wait, why was he in the kitchen?

She intended to ask him, but as soon as he stopped at their table, he clapped Rafe on the shoulder and opened his mouth.

"Well, well, Alonso"—the tall redhead smirked—"glad you decided to take my advice."

Wondering what he was talking about, Tori stared at Rafe. He momentarily looked panicked before he covered it with a glare that seemed to say, 'Mention it again, and I'll kick your ass,' which only made her more curious. She glanced between the two men who were having a silent conversation.

Annoyed at being left in the dark, she spoke up, "What are you talking about?"

Jameson's grin didn't falter, but he changed the subject, "Hey, did Alonso tell you we got Bulls tickets?"

She blinked, momentarily thrown, but then remembered Ms. Walsh's envelope. "Oh! No, he didn't, but, Rafe"—as she addressed him, he raised an eyebrow—"I forgot to mention your neighbor dropped off an envelope for you today. The tickets were inside."

When he didn't respond other than to narrow his eyes at her, she looked back up at Jameson. "That'll be fun. Guys' night out." She smiled with genuine warmth, figuring Rafe could use a break from work, and the basketball game sounded perfect.

Jameson chuckled. "The tickets are for all of us. Alonso, you, me, and Daisy." He blushed at the woman's name, and she couldn't help but smile as he scrubbed at his neck. "She wants to meet you, go on a, uh, a double date."

Tori's smile fell. *A double date?*

With her and . . . Rafe?

"But we're not dating!" The words blurted out before she had a chance to think them through. Her cheeks turned crimson. Okay, she needed to remember she was supposed to be angry with him instead of thinking about them going out on a date.

"Kinda looks like—ow!"

Tori wasn't sure, but she thought Rafe might've stepped on Jameson's foot. "Where's Daisy? This place is pretty busy tonight."

"Shit! I was supposed to be bringing her the baby wipes.

I'll catch up with you guys later." The redhead turned on his heel without a backward glance.

She chuckled. "It's funny to think of him and baby wipes in the same sentence."

Rafe *actually* smiled, and her breath caught in her throat. If such a thing as good bone structure existed, he had it. The man was handsome from any angle but in an almost aloof sort of way. Except, when he smiled a real, genuine smile, *then* his beauty was devastating. It changed the light in his eyes, and the crease beside his mouth appeared. That little thing was dangerous. Something about it made her want to lick and suck until she knew what he tasted like there.

"They seem happy, and Daisy's great for him." His lips were moving, "You'd like her."

She reined in her salacious thoughts to focus on what he'd said. "Then, I hope I get to meet her before I leave."

His smile disappeared, the light in his eyes dimming. He opened his mouth to speak, but the server chose that moment to appear.

"Welcome to Daisy's. What can I get for you?" The young woman's sweet voice wasn't what Tori expected, with the short, spiky pink hair and the piercings in her eyebrow, nose, and lip.

She hadn't looked at the menu, so she picked it up now. The dishes blurred together as her thoughts strayed to what had made Rafe's smile disappear so fast.

"I'll have the fennel soup."

She frowned when he gave his order, wondering if his stomach still bothered him. She was no closer to figuring out what she wanted and hated to keep the poor girl waiting.

"You might like the special, Tor."

She popped her head up from the menu. He'd thrown her a lifeline when she'd been drowning in a sea of culinary confusion. "What's the special?" she asked the server.

"It's Cincinnati chili. If you've never had it, you should give it a whirl. You won't find better outside the city itself."

She didn't know if it was true, but she was intrigued nonetheless. "Sure, I'll try it. Thanks."

The young girl nodded. "I'll have your drinks in just a moment."

With the server gone, Tori stared at Rafe. The sadness had crept into his eyes again, and she didn't have the heart to refuel her ire with him. She wanted to ask him so many things—like how he felt about her—but she wasn't sure where to begin. "Do you come here a lot?"

Because that's what she really wanted to know, she internally rolled her eyes.

He shrugged. "I've met Jameson here a few times since I moved to town, but mostly, I cook at home."

A lightbulb went off in Tori's head. *Oh, Jameson's Daisy is* that *Daisy.*

The ensuing silence made nerves dance in her belly. She almost bit her lip before she stopped herself. It was too risky, and she'd already made the mistake once tonight. Not that she didn't want his mouth on hers. She did.

But she needed answers first *and* a guarantee he wouldn't lock her up again.

"Rafe?" She swallowed to wet her dry throat, then sat

on her twitching fingers. She felt like she vibrated from nervous energy, the electricity charging through her.

I need a shot of whiskey.

Not likely to get one, she took a calming breath. "Why did you want me to stay with you?"

He didn't hesitate. "To protect you."

But his answer didn't settle her stomach. "Is that the only reason?"

His dark eyes widened a little like he was surprised by her question. "No."

She sucked in a breath. "No?" She waited on pins and needles for the rest of his answer.

The server returned, placing their drinks on the table, but Tori couldn't tear her gaze away. So much indecision clouded his expression.

Please, please, just tell me!

"Sunshine"—Rafe laid his hand palm up on the table, and without a second thought, she placed hers in it—"I . . ."

"Here you go!" They both startled at the server's cheery voice, separating as she approached with their dishes. "Fennel soup and the special for you, ma'am." She set their food down and asked, "Can I get you anything else right now?"

Tori couldn't answer.

"We're good. Thanks." He glanced at the young server, and Tori's eyes fell to her plate.

"Oh, is this spaghetti? I thought I ordered the chili." Her nose scrunched in confusion as she stared at the meat sauce on top of the pasta.

Rafe chuckled, and her eyes flew to his. "What?"

"It's what you ordered. Cincinnati chili has noodles."

He grinned at her, and she was struck by the possibility he and Jameson could have played a joke on her. "Am I being punked?"

He laughed out loud. It was contagious, and she couldn't help but join in, enjoying seeing him without the weight of the world on his shoulders.

When they finally settled down, he told her, "No. It really comes that way. Try it."

She shrugged, willing to play along either way, when her stomach growled to remind her it'd been too many hours since she'd eaten. She took a bite, and her eyes widened in surprise at the flavors exploding on her tongue. It didn't taste like spaghetti, but it didn't taste like any chili she'd ever had. Was the meat sauce sweet?

She took another bite. No, not sweet, but the notes of cinnamon made her think of dessert, like pumpkin pie on cold fall days.

After she swallowed, she smiled at Rafe. "It's good. *Different* but good."

"That's what I thought the first time I had it." He took a tentative spoonful of his soup.

She worried his stomach still hurt but didn't want to bug him about it. "How's yours?"

He took another sip. "It's flavorful. I'm hoping it's mild enough not to attack me later."

She frowned, though she was happy he'd answered honestly. "Maybe you should see a doctor. I'm sure they have medicine that can help. Something better than

Tums," she muttered the last part under her breath. He'd probably been eating them like candy.

He sighed heavily, and she decided to drop it—for now.

When they'd finished their meal, his eyes caught on something behind her head. "What is it?"

She would've turned around to look, but he caught her hand. "Jameson's coming over with Daisy and the baby. Are you okay with that?" His rushed question and the concern in his eyes surprised her.

"I'll be fine, Rafe," she managed in a whisper before the couple appeared at her elbow.

Tori turned and found herself face to face with the most adorable chubby cheeks she'd ever seen. "Oh! Look at how cute you are." She grinned at the baby sitting on her mother's hip. When she raised her eyes to the woman, Tori blinked. Jameson's wife was stunning. She'd never seen someone with her copper skin tone, black-as-night hair, and sapphire blue eyes. "Wow, you must be Daisy."

Daisy smiled. "And you must be Tori. I love your hair."

She laughed. "I was thinking the same thing about yours."

"Hey, scooch over." Jameson made shooing motions at them.

"James!" Daisy scolded him, but he only shrugged as he folded himself into the booth next to Rafe. Tori moved over for Daisy and the baby to sit.

"What's this cutie's name?" She traced a finger down the baby's nose. Her bright blue eyes were taking everything in. They were lighter than her mother's, but she had the same coal-black hair.

Jameson answered, "Abby."

"Abigail," Daisy corrected him, and Tori couldn't help but grin. She knew what it felt like to have a name you wanted shortened.

"It's a beautiful name. How old is she, about six months?"

Daisy's eyes registered surprise before she answered, "Yes, good guess. Do you, um—"

"I have a niece and nephew." She saved her from framing the uncomfortable question people always asked. *Did she have kids of her own?*

A pang of sorrow sliced through Tori's defenses at the thought of having a child, but she pushed it away and pasted a smile on her face.

Daisy didn't seem to notice as she bounced the baby. "That's wonderful. I'm still waiting on my brothers to give me some of those."

"I know what you mean. I have two older brothers. No kids. But my sister has twins."

"Oh, that's great. I'm a twin." Daisy leaned in close and lowered her voice so the men didn't overhear, "I'm a little worried about trying again because I don't know if I could handle two at one time."

Another knife to her chest and Tori's ribs squeezed off her air supply. "I'm sure with Jameson, you'd manage just fine."

Daisy chuckled. "He's surprisingly good with her. Even changes diapers."

She coughed out a laugh, and it was mostly sincere. "It's funny to picture it."

Jameson's wife gave an impish grin. "It was funny to watch. But he got the hang of it before too long."

"What are you ladies saying about me?" The redhead's voice boomed at them, and Tori jumped.

Was it this hot in here before?

She felt sweaty all of a sudden, and her pulse sounded too loud in her ears.

Daisy spoke, but Tori had trouble focusing on the words. Did she have a fever? Because she was burning up.

The conversation continued around her, but she didn't catch any of it. Her dinner started to roil in her stomach, and she swallowed against a wave of nausea.

"Tori?" Rafe's hand felt cold on her cheek as he kneeled next to her.

When had he moved to her side?

"I'm sorry. I think I need to leave," her voice barely whispered, but it echoed in her head. She tried apologizing to Daisy and Jameson, but her vision blurred upon looking for them.

That fact freaked her out, and her heart skipped a beat.

Not only was it hot in here, but now she couldn't breathe. "Rafe?" she wheezed out his name, and his arm came around her.

"I've got you, Sunshine. Let's get some fresh air."

CHAPTER 18

Tori

Tori wanted to melt into the leather of Rafe's couch. She'd had a panic attack, which was embarrassing enough to admit, but having it in front of Daisy and Jameson was mortifying. She dropped her head back and closed her eyes, rubbing lazy trails along Toby's spine and tangling her fingers in his soft coat.

On the way to Rafe's, she'd calmed down, but something was soothing about the dog's shaggy hair gliding through her fingertips. If only her life could be as simple and carefree as her dog's.

She felt the cushions shift as Rafe sat next to her. He'd been wonderful on the drive home, giving her the space she'd needed to recover. But she'd known it would be short-lived.

He deserved an explanation.

Her stomach sank; she wasn't ready to open her eyes and face him yet. She stroked Toby's fur and thought that if reincarnation was a thing, she wanted to return as a well-loved dog. Then she'd have nothing but long walks, naps in the sunshine, and where the treats were hidden to worry about.

"I brought you some water," his voice stayed quiet, soothing.

Knowing she couldn't put it off any longer, she shifted, opening her eyes to face him. "Thank you." She didn't only mean for the drink, and Rafe nodded in understanding.

He ran a hand through his hair and blew out a breath. "Can you tell me about it? Was it . . . did the baby . . .?"

She gave a slight nod, resigned—but far from enthusiastic—about having this conversation.

When she didn't say anything more, he ventured, "Has it happened before?"

Drawing an unsteady breath, Tori felt tears welling and blinked them away. "Not in years." She hadn't had a panic attack like that since her niece and nephew had been babies.

Rafe reached for her hand. When his rough palm cradled hers, she sighed, grateful for his warmth. She forgot any lingering anger in his tenderness.

Lifting her eyes to his, she saw worry and wanted to banish it. "When Ron had the twins . . . it happened a few times. But I got over it." She shook her head, still confused as to why she'd had an attack tonight. "I've been around other babies since then and not experienced that. I don't know why this was different."

Unless it was because she'd already been rubbed raw from being near Rafe and having those memories stirred up.

"I'm sorry you had to go through that." He brushed a lock of hair off her face, pinning it behind her ear. The look in his eyes shifted, and pain pinched his face before he lowered his forehead to hers. "I'm sorry I wasn't there for you."

The anguish in his voice twisted the vines around her heart. She sucked in a breath, closing her eyes. She was so tired of fighting her feelings for him; it was painful either way. And right now, she wanted him to kiss her, to make her feel *anything* that wasn't loss or heartache. Their breaths mingled, and she licked her lips. When he tilted his head, her pulse sped in anticipation.

Kiss me!

As if he'd heard her silent demand, his mouth met hers in a gentle caress, his lips applying the softest of pressures. It was so incredibly sweet but the opposite of what she needed right now. She groaned, then attacked him. Gripping Rafe's head, she fused her mouth to his, licking the seam of his lips and plunging her tongue inside. He tasted sweet, like the sugary tablets he'd been popping, but she didn't care.

Yes, I need this. I want this.

Tori had control for maybe ten seconds before Rafe took over. His throat bobbed with a low, sexy growl as he gripped her backside and pulled her onto his lap. Their movement annoyed Toby, who let out a woof and then jumped from the couch. She would've chuckled, but she was too busy devouring Rafe.

Their kiss became all hunger and need from a decade of

longing. The years apart had created a ravenous beast, and it demanded to be fed. She surrendered to the primal part of herself and scratched her nails down his shoulders.

He roared and broke the kiss. When she would've gone back for more, he captured her hands, pulling them from behind his back. Then he raised them above her head, and she sucked in a deep breath as her shirt lifted enough to expose a sliver of skin. The chill in the room combined with the excitement over having her hands caught, pebbled her pale form.

He laid her on the couch, keeping her hands locked above her head. When he hovered over her, his eyes were as black as coal while they took her in. She thought she could feel their heat lapping at her, throwing fuel on a fire that had been burning for years.

Like a spark igniting, his lips crashed down on hers with a kiss that was anything but gentle. She moaned, bucking her hips as liquid heat pooled between her legs. When he freed her hands, she clawed at his shirt.

Why were they still dressed? She wanted his clothes off. *Now!*

Tori tugged the dress shirt from Rafe's pants, then snuck her fingers between them to work on the buttons. He was just as eager to take her top off, and their hands clashed, getting in each other's way. She stopped and helped him lift hers, then grabbed his and pulled. To her surprise, she'd ripped it open; a button flew past her head.

"Take it off!" she demanded, desperate to have the barrier gone.

Rafe didn't have to be told twice. He pulled off the ruined

shirt with the tee underneath it in one smooth move. And she got a good look at him. He was still in great shape. She'd always loved his broad shoulders and his arms, chest, and abs corded with muscle. Underneath a dark curling of hair, his olive skin glowed.

I love his chest hair.

She ran her hands through it, humming in pleasure when her fingers felt the ridges underneath. She wanted to explore those—later. She reached for his belt buckle, but he stopped her when her hands closed around it.

"Bedroom," he choked out.

She didn't need the bedroom. Slow was the opposite of what she wanted. She frowned and shook her head. "Here."

He groaned, "To-ri," dragging her name out, then clenching his jaw.

When she started to protest and reach for him again, he picked her up. She squeaked, but when he wrapped her legs around his waist and stood, her center hit the bulge in his pants. She moaned and clutched him tighter.

Rafe's breaths huffed out, tickling her ear as he carried her toward his bedroom. She licked his throat on the way to his earlobe, savoring his smoky scent and the spicy flavor on his skin. Wanting to taste him somewhere else, she ground into his hardness—repeatedly. Halfway down the hall, he stopped.

With a noise between a howl and a growl, he pushed her back against the wall and took her mouth again, licking and sucking until the pressure had built so much she would burst if she didn't get him inside her.

Desperate noises sounded from her throat. He

understood, or he'd become as crazed as she was because he lowered her feet to the floor while they both worked on removing their pants. At record-breaking speed, Tori undid her jeans and pulled her legs free. Then she helped him shove his trousers and boxers to his ankles.

Their eyes locked, animal answering animal. She jumped, and Rafe caught her. Their mouths crashed together again, and with her back pressed into the wall, her legs around his waist, he entered her.

It was like writing 'the end' of a story, which had dragged on much too long. Euphoria flooded her senses, bursting out of her in a glow brighter than the sun.

Joined with him, she felt free. The chains of the past fell off to be replaced with something better . . . *so* much better. Her eyes closed; her head fell back in ecstasy.

Until Rafe moved.

The second of stillness exploded into a frenzied race to completion. She made sounds she didn't know how to identify as her hips rocked, meeting each thrust of his.

Too long. It had been too long since she'd had this, had him. A volcano rumbled in her core, nearly ready to blow.

Her breaths were harsh rasps, her pulse drummed in her ears, and thoughts fled as feeling took over.

He had one hand braced against the wall, and he found the bundle of nerves between her legs with the other. It was all she needed to send her through the roof. Her back arched, and her toes curled.

"Rafe!" she gasped as the orgasm erupted.

His release came right behind hers. He grunted, and she fell apart with a cry, rushing down the mountain on a flow of lava as he emptied himself inside her. Her muscles turned to liquid magma, and she melted against him.

Rafe stumbled, but he didn't drop her. She squeezed him tighter, and he groaned into her neck, bracing his forearms on the wall to hold their weight.

They stayed like that for seconds or minutes. She wasn't sure how long it took for her brain cells to come back together.

"Holy fuck," he rasped out the expletive, and she giggled into his shoulder.

Holy fuck, indeed. That had been a long time coming. And, at the moment, she had no regrets.

He drew in a deeper breath. "I can't feel my legs."

His comment made Tori grin. "Me either."

She shifted, and he sucked in a sharp breath. "Sunshine," his voice was a warning, but it had the opposite effect on her.

They were still connected, so she wiggled and clamped him tighter, moaning as little aftershocks rumbled between her legs.

Rafe cursed, and she felt him quiver beneath her.

Teasing him, she straightened. "Want me to get down?"

His eyes were shut, his jaw clenched. She traced a finger along the tension there. "Should I get down?"

"No . . . yes," he bit out.

She laughed at his obvious struggle, making him wince with the movement. "Which is it?"

Apparently, he'd had enough of her teasing because before she knew what was happening, Rafe spun her around and pinned her against his hard body, facing the wall.

His breath tickled her ear before he told her, "You're not the only one who knows how to torment."

Her heart skipped a beat, but it wasn't in fear. No, what he'd said didn't scare her. It was excitement. The kind that had warmth pooling between her legs.

She bit her lip with a moan as his hand slid from her hip to cup her heat. When he traced a finger through her folds, the familiar throbbing spread from everywhere he touched.

His mouth landed on her shoulder, sucking and biting, then kissing up her neck. Tori leaned into him, losing herself in the wave of sensations. His other hand came up to cup her breast, and she whined in annoyance. They'd never taken off her bra.

He was already undoing the clasp before she could ask him to remove it. He slid it down her arms, trailing her skin with his fingers. She shivered from his light touch, her nipples hardening.

"So smooth, *così come crema*."

Her legs clenched. Rafe's deep voice speaking Italian was its own kind of aphrodisiac.

His mouth lowered to her neck again, and she tilted her head to the side to give him better access. As he nibbled on her, one hand massaged her breasts, the other deftly stroked her most sensitive spot.

She wanted to touch him, but the position didn't allow it. Reaching for anything she could find, she made a noise in complaint, but he grabbed her hands, splaying them against the wall.

"Spread 'em," he commanded in her ear, and a delicious shiver raced along her spine before she did as he asked.

"Good girl." His hands traveled up her hips to her waist and trailed across the sides of her breasts before moving back down. She'd never been frisked, but she didn't mind Rafe doing it, not one bit.

She had a flash of him handcuffing her and wondered what it might be like before the thought fled when he tugged her legs apart and kneeled underneath her. Starting at the inside of her knees, he placed open-mouthed kisses up her thighs.

Her legs started to shake. She vibrated with anticipation, but he didn't put his mouth where she wanted it.

"Ah, ah, ah, you're not ready for that yet." He nipped the sensitive skin of her bottom before laving it with his tongue.

She whined, knowing he teased her on purpose. But when he stood up and bent her against him, her protests evaporated over the fire he stoked within her.

Rafe's husky voice whispered in her ear, "No one touches you like this but me."

A shudder made her breath hitch. His possessive behavior wasn't a turn-off. No, it turned Tori on *more*. She didn't know if it was from his words or his hands, but she didn't want him to stop. He was the only one she wanted to touch her like this—only him.

He still knew how and where to touch her to drive her insane. The more he tormented her, the more she fought *not* to beg for release. Please teetered on the tip of her tongue. Before she surrendered, he pinched one nipple, tugging and twisting the way she liked as his other hand traveled to the apex of her thighs.

He entered her with his fingers, and she groaned in relief, "Yessss."

Finally!

His mouth found her neck again, his hands working her until the pressure she'd felt before climbed to that exquisite peak. Her breaths rushed out as her pulse picked up speed. She closed her eyes and leaned into him and the magic in his fingers. They played her like a finely tuned instrument until she was ready to sing.

As the song built, she moved her hips with the rhythm of his hand. "That's right, Sunshine. Come for me."

He hit the right note, and like a crescendo, Tori soared through the ceiling with a cry, collapsing against Rafe as the pleasure washed over her in a beautiful sonata of lights and sounds.

She heard him whispering to her in Italian when she came down from the clouds. It made her smile, and she hummed in satisfaction. Floating light as a feather, slowly drifting to the ground.

"Are you back with me, Sunshine?" He had a smile in his voice.

"Mm-hmm." At least, she thought she was—mostly.

Rafe shifted, and her eyes flew open when his hard length pressed against her hip.

Oh my.

She grinned and spun in his arms, hooking hers around his neck. "Maybe we should make it to the bedroom this time."

He smiled, and her breath caught. She wasn't sure she'd ever get used to seeing those again. "We're going to." He slung her into his arms and carried her bridal style the rest of the way down the hall.

Toby had been hiding in the living room, but he followed them now.

When they reached the bedroom, Rafe told the dog, "Sorry, buddy. Mom needs some privacy." Then he shut the door on him.

"Rafe!" Tori wasn't sure why she protested, but she felt bad for leaving Toby in the hall.

He chuckled. "Well, I didn't think you'd want him to watch."

"But—"

He dropped her on the bed, and she squealed. Then his mouth was on her thigh, and she closed her eyes. Toby would be fine by himself for a little while.

"Mmm, I guess not."

CHAPTER 19

Tori

Early morning sunlight warmed the back of her eyelids, but Tori refused to open them. She'd woken up a few minutes ago, and the reality of the night she and Rafe shared came crashing down on her. She wasn't ready to face it, face him. Not when she couldn't be sure of his answers to the questions plaguing her—like whether he wanted more. For her, he'd hacked a path through the vines around her heart, and she didn't want it to regrow.

His arm lay slung over her middle. The weight was both a comfort and a trap. She needed to get up and take Toby outside but didn't want to wake Rafe.

Part of her felt elated at what they'd done, but the other half stirred with a mixture of worry and anxiety. Her body reacted as confused as her brain. In sympathy with her thoughts, her stomach knotted. She wanted more than one night with him. Casual was not in the cards when it came to Rafe. At least it wasn't for her. But would he feel the same way?

She hoped she hadn't started something that would leave her bruised and broken again. A chill slithered along her spine, and she pushed the thought away.

Despite the uncertainty she battled, no way could she regret spending the night together, but she did wish they'd talked things out more before, well, before she'd jumped him.

Remembering how she'd practically attacked Rafe, her cheeks heated with a blush. Then a giggle tickled her throat, but she swallowed it down. He was sure to wake up if she started shaking with laughter.

But oh, my gawd.

She hadn't had that much sex in one night since . . . maybe ever. It's like they'd been trying to make up for lost time. They'd fallen asleep late; then he'd woken her up twice in the middle of the night. Her lips curved in a smile, her heart warming at how gentle the last time had been. They may have started at a race, but he'd slowed them down to a stroll.

Mmm, and what a stroll.

A soft sigh escaped her lips as she thought about how he'd made her feel—like a goddess. He'd worshiped every inch of her body with his mouth. In remembering, heat rushed to the juncture of her thighs. She clenched them and hummed low in her throat. He'd whispered to her in Italian, all those words she'd wanted to kno—

Tori's eyes flew open. The phrase he'd said to her at the diner the night before pounded in her head. Seized by a desperate need to find out what it meant, she searched the room for her phone. Where had she left it?

Ah! It lay on the nightstand next to his. She'd brought it in after they'd taken Toby out for the night. Could she manage to reach it without disturbing Rafe? She glanced over at him. His face smashed into the pillow, his mouth slightly open.

The man was out cold.

Her gaze softened the longer she watched him. She didn't want to wake him because the shadows were still there under his eyes, but her fingers itched to trace the stubble along his cheek.

Just a small touch.

When her palm met his skin, it instantly warmed. He had that ability. To make her heart glow and heat her from the inside out. His skin felt rough, but underneath . . . she remembered the soft spots. How gentle he could be. With a smile at the memories, old and new, her hand retreated. She was glad he slept so deeply; he needed it.

Very carefully, she inched her way out from under his arm. He grunted but stayed asleep when she laid it gently in the spot she'd vacated. She breathed a sigh of relief, then she picked up her phone and tiptoed out of the room, motioning at Toby for him to come with her.

He was such an intelligent dog, getting up from his bed on the floor without making a sound. When he entered the hall with her, Tori glanced at Rafe, taking in his muscled form outlined by the sheet lying low around his waist. She grinned, hoping she'd see more of it later, but then her stomach cramped with nerves over how things would go when he woke up.

She was a mess.

Quietly, she closed the door and searched for her clothes so she could take Toby outside to do his business.

After she'd gotten dressed, the doodle started to whine at her, his head turning to look longingly at the front door.

"Oh, all right. Let's go outside, buddy."

The dog perked up, racing toward the exit. She smiled and grabbed his leash from the spot on the floor where she'd left it in her haste to get back to bed last night. Once she had him hooked up, she slipped her phone into her pocket, deciding to wait until after taking care of Toby to find out what Rafe had said.

The labradoodle wasn't usually a puller, but he needed to go because she had to practically jog to keep up with him as he raced to the elevators. She shivered when they made it outside. It had gotten cold overnight. Now, she wished she'd grabbed something warmer than the blouse she'd worn to dinner.

"Let's make this quick, bud."

Rafe's apartment building had a grassy courtyard with a paved walking path around it. She'd used it yesterday as Toby's bathroom spot. Bracing herself against the chill, they headed there now.

When her teeth wanted to chatter, she clenched them and blew on her fingers. The temperature had dropped quite a few degrees. Toby made two circuits of the path before he decided to relieve himself. Her toes had gone numb by the time they headed for the building.

Halfway to the entrance, she froze, the hairs on the back of her neck standing up. Toby stopped with her, growling low in his throat. She spun around, positive someone would be there, but all she saw was a well-manicured lawn and young ash trees whose leaves were starting to change. Unease made her stomach quiver as her eyes continued to scan.

"What is it, Toby?" she whispered, wishing he could answer her. But the fact that the dog had sensed something freaked her out. Her hearing intensified while her heart pounded in her chest.

Nothing. There's nothing there, Tori.

Not at all convinced, she turned and ran for the building, Toby keeping pace. Before they'd made it, Rafe came outside. Her legs nearly buckled in relief as she launched herself into his arms.

"Tori! What the fuck? Why didn't you wake me?" He'd squeezed her tightly at first, but now he pushed her to arm's length, growling in her face, "Don't *ever* do that again!"

She blinked, taken aback by the anger in his voice. His jaw was set, his eyes hard. "What are you talking about?"

"Leave without—" His voice broke, and he closed his eyes. When he opened them, they were swimming. "I thought something happened to you."

Her heart squeezed, seeing the worry she'd caused. She cupped his face, pulling his forehead to hers. "I'm sorry. I didn't want to disturb you, but Toby needed to go out."

The dog yipped and wagged his tail at the sound of his name. Whatever threat he'd sensed was gone or forgotten.

Rafe leaned away, giving Toby a pat before focusing on her again. His forehead wrinkled. "Why were you running?"

The reason she'd been running eluded her. Her heart had stopped racing, but the exercise had warmed her up.

Yes, she was hot from the exertion. She nodded at herself. And *not* the fact Rafe stood in front of her in nothing but a pair of gray sweatpants.

They were slung low on his hips, leaving very little to the imagination, but then she already knew what he had under there. Her fingers itched to trace the indentation below his obliques.

"Aren't you cold?" She bit her lip as her cheeks turned red from more than the exercise.

He watched her closely, and she wondered if what she was thinking showed clearly on her face because she had an idea of how they could warm up. A hot shower sounded amazing right now with him lathering her—

He groaned; the same desire warming her blood simmered in his chocolate irises. "Sunshine, you're going to kill me."

She grinned, willing to give it her best shot, but he shook his head. Reaching for her hand, he dragged them into the building. They made it inside the elevator before he stopped, his mouth claiming hers.

The kiss was raw, hungry. She thought she could taste his fear over finding her gone as he unloaded it on her. While his mouth consumed her, his hands were everywhere, gripping, stroking. A moan sounded from her throat as she wrapped her leg around his, grinding against him where they both needed it.

Rafe clouded her senses, and she forgot they were in an elevator, forgot she'd sensed someone watching her, forgot what she'd been planning to look up. It all evaporated like steam in the heat of their passion.

The lift stopped; the doors dinged as they opened, but the outraged gasp caused her and Rafe to break apart.

"This is hardly the proper place for that!" Ms. Walsh's indignant declaration made Tori turn crimson. She had very little chance of getting back in the woman's good graces now.

Rafe wasn't so affected. He sounded as if he held in a laugh when he apologized to his neighbor.

Tori couldn't meet the woman's gaze. She tucked her head, pulling Toby behind her to Rafe's door. When she entered the apartment, she unhooked the dog and then collapsed on the couch, covering her eyes with her arm. If she and Rafe were going to talk, she couldn't look at him, at least not until he covered up all that deliciousness.

"What's wrong, Sunshine?" His voice was soft as he kneeled beside her.

She groaned. "Your neighbor hates me."

He laughed, but she didn't think it was funny.

Peeking at him, she couldn't help but smile at the joy on his face. He seemed less weighed down than he had been, his shoulders not so droopy, his eyes not so sad.

"She probably thinks I'm a tramp."

Rafe sobered, his gaze turning serious as he lifted her arm from her face. "Tori, I don't want—"

She cut him off, along with the conversation she wasn't quite ready for. "Can you get dressed? Then we can talk. I can't, um . . ." She squeezed her eyes closed. "I can't think when you're wearing those."

She felt him lean over her before his plush lips kissed her forehead. When she didn't open her eyes, he stood up, chuckling before his footsteps faded.

Sensing it was safe, she lifted her lids, then sat up and blew out a breath. Her thoughts were whirling in an endless circle of questions. What if they weren't on the same page? What if Rafe only wanted a casual thing? How could she stay here then? Would she?

With a frustrated sigh, she moved to stand up, needing to pace, but her phone fell out of her pocket as she did. When it hit the floor, she remembered she'd wanted to look up the Italian phrase he'd spoken to her. She grabbed it and quickly navigated to a translator to type the words in. A soft gasp escaped her lips, and her eyes filled.

You are the light in my soul.

It was beautiful. Hope ballooned in her chest. If he could say that to her, he must want more than . . . a *fling*?

He hadn't returned, but she needed to know—now. Tori jumped up and headed for his bedroom.

"Rafe!"

He wasn't there.

She moved to look through the door leading into the bathroom right as he stepped out of the shower.

Naked.

Wet.

Droplets flowing down his chest toward his perfect—

Stay with me, brain.

She shook her head and forced her eyes up, locking them with his.

He raised an eyebrow at her. "I thought you wanted me

to get dressed?"

She cleared her throat, then closed the distance between them, stopping two feet away. Safely—*hardly*—out of reach.

"You're the light in my soul?" She spoke the words softly, questioning him with her tone as she tried to see into *his* soul.

He stiffened, his eyes widening. "You looked it up."

She nodded, her stomach yo-yo-ing. "Did you mean it?"

Please say yes.

Rafe lifted a hand, stepping closer and lightly brushing his thumb across her cheek. His touch, for once, was hesitant, his voice hoarse when he told her, "Of course, I meant it."

Her knees wanted to give out.

He lifted a hand as though he would touch her, but he dropped it instead. "I love you, Sunshine."

He loves me?

The declaration careened into her, but Rafe wasn't done.

He drew in a deep breath, adding, "I never stopped."

He never stopped?

Her lips pursed as she struggled to take in all he'd said. A wave of dizziness washed over her, and her thoughts turned fuzzy from lack of oxygen.

Rafe clutched her shoulders. "Breathe."

She gasped in a lungful of air. "You love me?" Tori wasn't sure she was *actually* awake. She blinked rapidly up at him.

Had he really loved her all this time . . . like she'd loved him?

He smiled, but it quickly faded when she could only stare, dumbstruck. "You don't feel the same way." It wasn't a question as he backed away from her.

"No!"

Rafe flinched and tried to leave, but she grabbed hold of him. "I do! I love you, too. I never thought—"

His mouth cut off the rest of what she'd been about to say, but Tori didn't mind. As his hands cupped her face, she wrapped her arms around his neck and gripped his hair. Euphoria took over, and she surrendered to its sweet bliss. They still had hurdles to overcome, but they would jump them together. Because he loved her, and she loved him.

They'd never stopped.

CHAPTER 20

Rafe

Rafe's lips curled, but he had no will to erase the smile dancing across his face. He felt like a beam of Tori's light shone within his chest, warming his heart.

She loved him.

It was enough to make him grin for an eternity. All he had to do was think of her saying it, and the painful weight, which had been dragging on him for years, disappeared.

He reclined in his office chair and gazed out the window. The morning sun streamed in through the blinds. When it bounced off the bare tabletop below the opening, he made a decision. He would 'move in' and unpack the personal items he typically displayed on his desk.

His smile faltered as soon as he thought it, doubts intruding. Even if he wanted to stay in Rolling Brook, would Tori? Her life was in L.A.; if he hated anything more than criminals, it was California. The father, he couldn't remember, had left him and his mother for that home-wrecking state.

Rafe sighed and pinched the bridge of his nose. But if Tori wanted to stay in the City of Angels, he'd follow her. The most important thing to him was her being back in his life. If keeping her in it meant moving to L.A., well . . . fuck, he'd do it.

He'd do anything for her.

Because she was his home. A smile pulled his lips up again. A home he never wanted to let go of.

Last night with her had been *the* best night of his life. They'd burned up plenty of sheets in the past, but this . . . this had been different. Maybe the time apart had made it so much more intense. Whatever the reason, he couldn't wait to have her again. His muscles twitched thinking about it.

He'd fallen deep into a fantasy involving her, his handcuffs, and Amaretto chocolate syrup when Jameson knocked on his door frame.

"Hey, how's Tori?" The big redhead didn't wait for an invitation, entering and making himself comfortable in one of the chairs in front of Rafe's desk.

He tried to scowl at his lieutenant, but the images he'd conjured still teased him, making it impossible. He cleared his throat, but it didn't banish the tantalizing thoughts. "She's fine."

Jameson's eyes were tight, and he looked genuinely concerned. "What happened last night?"

As the multiple times he and Tori devoured each other replayed in his head, he fought the grin, making his lips tremble.

Before he could reply, Jameson's boisterous laugh cut him off. "You fucker." He shook his head, still chuckling, before his light blue eyes met Rafe's. "I meant at the diner, but I'm glad you two worked it out."

He scrubbed at his neck, sobering at the mention of the diner. As happy as he was to have her back in his bed, they still had the past to contend with. "She felt pretty embarrassed about that. I think it'd be better not to mention it in front of her."

Jameson's brow creased like he was trying to figure out a puzzle. "Was it a panic attack?"

He nodded, dreading what else the lieutenant would surmise. His friend knew about his and Tori's history and the trials marking it.

Sadness crept into Jameson's eyes. "Because of Abby? Can she . . ."

Rafe's muscles tensed. Jameson was his friend, the closest one he had, but talking about this with anyone other than Tori felt wrong. As if he somehow betrayed her.

"Can she not be around kids? Without . . .?"

He frowned and pushed past the knot that had lodged uncomfortably in his throat. "She says she can. The other night was the first time it had happened in a long time." Rafe flexed his hands on the arms of his chair, but it didn't relieve the tension winding him up. "Look, man, I'm sorry, but—"

"No." Jameson stood and clasped him on the shoulder. "*I'm* sorry." He stepped back with a wink. "Let her know Daisy and I would love to see you guys again."

He struggled to muster a smile when they had come so

easily a few minutes before. "Sure. I'll tell her."

After Jameson left, Rafe slumped over his desk, dropping his forehead into his hands. The loss he and Tori had sustained hung like an albatross around his neck, pulling his hopes into the void.

Life had thrown him a curveball all those years ago, but he'd fielded it. They'd gotten pregnant, and though he'd been scared shitless, never having had a father figure in his life, he'd been ready to face those fears with her at his side. She was a twinkling star; if anyone could shine a light on a child's life, it would be her.

But they'd never gotten the chance.

He closed his eyes on the lightning bolt of pain that struck him. It reverberated through his body, leaving a pulsing ache in its path. He'd lost not only the baby but Tori too.

The miscarriage had hit her hard, and no matter what he'd tried, he hadn't been able to return the light to her eyes.

But she'd found it again . . . *without* him. Maybe it was merely time that aided her healing. Yet he couldn't help but wonder if *he* had been the problem. Talking to the counselor had helped her where he couldn't. Bitterness twisted his lips as doubts plagued his mind, and the acid in his stomach flared up.

Could he and Tori have a future when the past still haunted them?

* * * *

Rafe

Rafe pulled up beside Gorsky, and as he put the SUV in park, he braced for the information the detective had insisted on telling him at this location—the parking lot of a veterinary office on the border between Rolling Brook and the neighboring town. He hoped the man had an actual lead this time, not another dead end.

At least Gorksy's call had pulled him from contemplating the whirlpool his day had become, giving him something else to focus on.

Staring through the windshield, he took in the two-story building. It looked relatively new, though its pale brick gave off a dated vibe, contrasting with the modern-style construction. Large, unadorned glass-front windows invited in the sun, while a rectangular pergola sat atop the flat roof. The overhang proved to be the only form of decoration on the building. It screamed 'hospital' to Rafe, and even though it was for pets, it made him uncomfortable. His fingers tapped out a restless rhythm on the steering wheel.

After what he and Tori had gone through, he had more than enough harrowing memories of places like this.

Pushing away the thoughts Jameson had stirred up, he noticed Gorsky waiting on him. Grumbling under his breath, he climbed out of his vehicle.

This better be good.

The detective leaned against the hood of his car, sipping a steaming to-go cup. "Been here before?"

Rafe raised an eyebrow. The asshole could've had a spare coffee since he'd dragged him all the way out here.

"No. Why am I here now?"

And where the fuck is my coffee?

The detective handed him a photograph. He took it with a scowl, then stared at the young man wearing dark scrubs, dusted with what looked like cat hair. The smile looked slightly off, though he couldn't pinpoint why. "Tell me who I'm looking at."

Gorsky grinned. "Peter Mosier. A-K-A, our latest homicide victim."

Rafe's gaze snapped to the detective's. The man was enjoying this. "So we've ID'd him. What else do we know?"

He studied the photo while Gorksy spoke, "The M.E. found pento in his system and confirmed the wound matches the one on Tegan Powell."

A line formed between Rafe's brows. Confirming the two murders were connected validated what he'd already known. They'd both been injected with the same sedative and died by the same method. But . . .

His head jerked up. "What about sexual assault on the male victim?"

Gorsky shrugged. "No evidence of it."

The line deepened on his forehead as he thought about this news. The murders were connected, but they didn't fit the same pattern: no sexual assault postmortem and no playing card for Mosier.

Rafe ran a restless hand through his hair. "What are we missing?"

The detective straightened and pointed toward the vet's office. "This is where Mosier worked. I'm thinking we start there."

A high-pitched whine met his ears when they entered the veterinary clinic. He winced in sympathy with whatever poor creature made the noise. Gorsky seemed unaffected, waltzing to the front desk as if he belonged there. While he chatted up the receptionist, Rafe glanced around the waiting room.

Apart from the wall art tending toward animal photos, it looked like any other doctor's office. Uncomfortable plastic chairs lined the walls, separated by tables littered with magazines.

Sterile.

If he had to come here as a pet, he'd probably cry too. It was the opposite of inviting. You'd think they'd dress up the lobby with a fake plant or . . . *something.*

"Captain?"

He spun toward Gorsky's voice. "Yeah."

The detective raised his eyebrow. "Pamela here—" He turned and winked at the woman staffing the desk, making Rafe want to punch him.

Is there a woman he won't *flirt with?*

"—is going to take us to the Doc. You ready?" Gorsky addressed him but smiled at the receptionist.

Rafe rolled his eyes at the man's back. "Lead the way." *Asshole.*

Pamela led them through a short hallway before veering down another one on the left. Two more turns and they stopped at a closed door with 'Susan Andrews, D.V.M.' engraved in a sign hanging on it. The place was a maze, and he'd already lost track of how to get out.

As Pamela knocked to announce them, he tugged on

Gorsky's arm. In a low voice, he told him, "I'll talk to the Doc. Why don't you see what you can glean from the receptionist."

The detective opened his mouth. Rafe expected him to argue, but instead, the man closed it with a smirk, giving a short nod in agreement.

Relieved to be rid of Gorsky, he stepped through the doctor's door, hoping the detective could charm something useful out of Pamela.

All the warmth missing in the reception area had been crammed into this small eight-by-eight room. Colorful art decorated the wall behind the veterinarian's desk, which was fronted by two bright green chairs with multicolored polka dots. Personal photos littered the bookcase to his left. Pictures of the doctor and what he assumed was her family, her pets, and . . .

One with people wearing scrubs made him pause. It looked like the vet and her staff, as he noticed Pamela and Mosier in the photograph.

His scan of the room had taken mere seconds before the vet's voice pulled his attention away. "Can I help you?"

He focused on the woman who stared him down as he hovered in front of her desk. Giving her a smile, he deliberately relaxed into one of the chairs. "I hope so, Doctor Andrews."

She didn't return his smile. Instead, her hazel eyes narrowed on him. "What's this about, Detective."

Rafe didn't bother to correct her. Since Gorsky had dragged him here, he was acting as a detective at the moment. "Peter Mosier."

That made her frown. She looked to be in her forties, but the expression accentuated the faint lines around her mouth. "What about him?"

He crossed his legs, his left ankle resting on his opposite knee. "He's your employee?"

Her eyes flashed in annoyance. "Not anymore."

Interesting.

Rafe decided to let this play out. "He quit?"

"Yes, I mean, I guess." She huffed out a breath. "He stopped showing up for work, but . . ." Her hands clenched together on top of her desk. "I was going to fire him."

Very *interesting.*

"How come?" The more ambiguous he made the question, the more telling the answer would be.

The doctor stared at him for a long moment before she unwound her fingers and leaned back in her chair. "I don't want this to count as a report because I'm not ready to file one. I don't have proof, just suspicions."

His body tensed, but he forced himself to stay reclined in the comfy chair. "Not a problem, Doc. Tell me what you think he did."

She ran a hand through her short blonde hair, and her eyes darted to the open door. He understood her hesitation. Rising, he shut out prying eyes and ears.

When he turned, the doctor visibly relaxed. She began as he sank into his chair, "A year ago, Pete changed. He started missing shifts, calling in sick often, and his attitude toward the female staff shifted."

When she paused, Rafe urged her to continue, "How so?"

The vet blew out a breath, tousling the bangs on her forehead. "He'd pick fights over petty things, like who had the biggest locker, and he'd complain whenever one of them forgot to do something." She shook her head. "Tensions were high, but I'd hoped whatever he was going through would pass."

"It didn't." Rafe's low reply wasn't a question but an encouragement for her to continue.

"No. But it wasn't why I planned to let him go." Her mouth thinned into a hard line, and she sat straighter in her chair. "About a month ago, he was responsible for checking in our pharmaceutical delivery when it arrived. He claimed they'd shorted us on Fatal Flush and told him they'd make it up in the next shipment." Her jaw tensed as she ground her teeth. "I've been using this company for years and never had an issue like this before. So I called them. They said there wasn't a shortage in the delivery. They'd had everything in stock when I'd ordered."

He steepled his fingers. "Which means Mosier was lying."

The doctor nodded. "Yes. I was going to confront him, but he disappeared." She shrugged. "I've been waiting for him to show back up. He never cleared out his locker, so I knew he'd come in eventually."

His pulse took off. He wanted to get a look at that locker. But first . . .

"What's it used for?" With a name like Fatal Flush, he had a pretty good idea, but he needed confirmation.

The doctor frowned at his question, so he changed tack.

"Does it have pentobarbital in it?"

Her eyebrows lifted in surprise. "Yes, it's the main ingredient."

Bingo.

Rafe smiled, ignoring the confusion marring the woman's face. "Doc, I'm going to need to see inside Pete's locker."

CHAPTER 21

Tori

Tori hummed along to the beat playing in her head as her fingers flew over the keyboard. She was at the library, her shadow—as she'd decided to refer to him—hovering at a table nearby. Rafe had loosened the reins on her captivity with the condition she didn't go *anywhere* without Officer Hale. Typically, she would've argued, but because she loved Rafe, she'd decided to humor him. Even if being under constant surveillance grated on her nerves.

She felt the tall young officer's gaze boring into her as if she might disappear in a puff of smoke. She rolled her eyes, and her fingers stilled. Thinking about this killed her groove, and she'd been in a really good one.

A smirk crossed her face. It's like sex with Rafe had blasted the lid off her creativity, and the story flowed faster than ever. Already, she'd made it halfway through her book, having gotten several chapters written over the last few days. She still needed to check with him on some procedural things, but she wasn't worried about it now. At least not until her agent wanted more of the manuscript.

A frown tugged at her lips. The woman would likely ask for pages within the next couple of weeks. But as she thought about it, Tori shrugged. At the rate she was going, she was confident she'd finish the book before the end of the year. The deadline she'd dreaded a month ago seemed far less scary now.

Deadline!

An idea sparked, and she rushed to type it up before it fled. She'd been chewing over how to get the two main characters of her novel together, and this could be it. The detective needed a deadline to push things into motion, something that would make her trust the man she was falling for because she needed his help to catch the real killer.

"Aha!"

At the shout, Tori jumped, nearly falling out of her chair, a noise—mortifyingly close to a shriek—leaving her lips.

Her reaction was met with an amused chuckle. "Meg said you were back here." Ben Gorsky perched on the edge of her desk and peered at her computer screen. His position caged her in, and she didn't like it. The man had no concept of personal space.

She scowled at him, debating whether she'd get in trouble for shoving a detective when her shadow intervened.

"Ma'am, are you all right?" The question was directed at her, but Officer Hale's eyes stayed trained on Ben, his hand creeping toward the firearm at his hip.

"Settle down, rook. The lady and I are friends." Ben's relaxed posture didn't change; his voice remained unperturbed.

She wasn't so sure about them being friends, but she wasn't worried Ben would harm her. Annoy her—yes. She fought the urge to clench her teeth and told her shadow, "It's fine. I know Detective Gorsky."

The officer relaxed at the title. With a nod for Ben, he headed for his table a few feet away.

"What's that about? Are you so famous you have to keep security with you?" Ben grinned at the thought, and she rolled her eyes.

"Hardly." But how did she explain?

My . . . lover is worried I'm in danger and won't let me go anywhere alone.

The word wasn't nearly strong enough, but she and Rafe hadn't exactly discussed what they were to each other.

Ben watched her closely, waiting for her to elaborate, so she shrugged. "It's just a temporary thing." Hoping he would drop it, she changed the subject, "What are you doing here?"

"As it happens, I was hoping to run into this pretty redhead I know." He smiled, his pale green eyes warming.

Oh no. Do not blush, Tori. He'll think it's from something other than how embarrassingly uncomfortable his comment made you.

Her body didn't cooperate with her brain. Her cheeks heated, and she prayed for a way to escape this conversation. But she had to say *something*! "Oh."

His eyes dimmed a little when she didn't return his smile. "I thought she'd want to sign this for me." He pulled her latest release from behind his back, and the tension gripping her dissipated.

She could've melted into a puddle of relief. *That* she could do. This time, she returned his smile as she reached for the book. "I'd be happy to."

As she finished her name with a flourish, Meg appeared. "Sorry, Tori. I told him not to bother you." She glared at her nephew from behind her cat-eye glasses, but he didn't bother to appear sheepish.

With a cheeky grin, he took the book from her.

"It's all right, Meg. I don't mind." She smiled at the librarian, trying to convey her gratitude because she'd cared enough to try.

Meg harrumphed and made shooing motions at Ben with her hands. But he wasn't ready to leave yet. "Really, Aunt Meg?" He clasped her hands and pulled her in for a side-armed hug.

Meg grumbled but softened when he kissed her on the cheek. "Oh, you stinker."

"Now, what kind of fans would we be if we didn't beg our resident author here to do a reading," Ben teased, grinning at her.

She groaned inwardly as Meg's eyes lit up. "What a wonderful idea. Tori, could you do it? We could hold it here in the library or . . . oh!" Her hands flew to her mouth; her face split with a grin when she removed them. "You could do it at the carnival next weekend. That would be perfect! It's Halloween themed, so you could rea—"

"Whoa! Let's slow down a minute." She forced a laugh through the alarm, constricting her throat. "As flattered as I am by your enthusiasm, I don't think that will work." She ran a shaky hand through her bright red hair. "My publicist handles that kind of thing, and right now, my main focus is finishing my current book. Maybe when it's done, we can talk about a signing or"—she gulped and forced the words out—"a reading."

Her hands had gone clammy, so she clenched them in her lap. The idea of reading her work in front of an audience incited her anxiety. The two times she'd been strongarmed into agreeing to do a reading, she'd nearly puked all over the pages. She had no issue signing her books for people. Still, something about speaking her words aloud to a large group of them made her stomach drop to her feet and sent her pulse racing as fast as a rabbit's.

Meg looked crestfallen at her response. She opened her mouth. "But . . ."

She needed to distract the woman and fast. Taking a deep breath, she hoped it would slow her racing heart. "Tell me about this carnival."

Ben chuckled as he stared Tori down, and she had a feeling he knew she was deflecting. "It's a pretty big one. They hold it in the fairgrounds outside of town. People from all over the county come. There'll be everything from a pie-eating contest to pumpkin carving."

"Oh, it sounds like fun." She forced a smile, scrubbing the sweat off her hands with the fabric of her dress. It *did* seem like a good time, and she wondered if Rafe would be willing to go with her.

"Mm-hmm, it is. My favorite part is the haunted hayride. Ever been on one of those?"

Before she could respond, an angry beeping sound met their ears. Meg groaned, then patted Tori's arm. "I've got to go deal with that." She gave her nephew a stern look. "Let the woman get back to work, Benjamin."

He chuckled at Meg's retreating form.

Tori wished he would, but her curiosity peaked since he made no move to leave. "What is it? An alarm?" The noise hadn't stopped. It wasn't so loud it hurt her ears, but it would be impossible to write with it going on in the background.

He shrugged. "My guess is the new self-service checkout they just installed."

Huh, she hadn't known that was a thing.

"Sounds like someone made it angry." She felt ridiculously glad it wasn't her. She had a love-hate relationship with technology, and self-service kiosks were the devil. The ones she'd dealt with had been possessed.

The detective didn't respond; instead, he leaned over to look at what she'd been writing. "What's this book about?" He was practically in her lap, and she moved to scoot her chair back when a gruff voice made her freeze.

"What's going on here?" Rafe appeared between the fiction stacks, and her heart swelled, a smile lighting her face.

Until she noticed the tension in his.

Though it wanted to falter, she kept her smile in place. "Hi, Rafe."

Ben straightened, all hints of teasing gone from his face and his voice. "Captain. What brings you here?"

He closed the distance between them, laying his hand on her shoulder. "I'm picking Tori up."

She glanced at the clock on her computer. It was five-thirty already; she'd lost track of time. He'd texted her hours ago to ask when she'd be finished.

Ignoring Ben, who hovered by her desk, Rafe leaned over and kissed her forehead. "Are you ready, Sunshine?"

When he straightened, she watched him and Ben stare each other down. She felt caught between their pissing match and wanted it to end as quickly as possible before Rafe blew up as he had in the past.

Closing her laptop with a decisive snap, she stood and gathered her bag. "Yes, let's go."

She attempted to pull him away when he took her hand, but he wasn't done with Ben. "Since I ran into you, any word on the warrant?"

The detective didn't answer right away, shifting into their path. She felt his eyes on her but refused to return his gaze. "We should have it in the morning."

She glanced up at Rafe. As curious as she was of the warrant they were talking about, she wouldn't ask now. His jaw clamped so tight his teeth had to be grinding together. "Let's go," she whispered.

He relaxed enough to tell the other man, "Great. Give me a call when you have it."

Ben nodded, then stepped out of their way. She breathed a sigh of relief as Rafe started to lead her out, but it was short-lived. The detective's voice pulled them up short, "Maybe I'll see you at the carnival, Tori."

Rafe tensed. She tried squeezing the hand he held in reassurance as she called over her shoulder, "Goodnight, Ben."

She didn't wait for the detective to respond. She tugged, and Rafe fell into step with her. On their way out the door, she waved to Meg.

The librarian turned and lifted her hand in response. When she noticed Rafe, she grinned and gave Tori a thumbs-up before turning her attention to the kiosk she'd been working on.

She delighted in Meg's approval of Rafe, but her stomach jumped with nerves. The silence added to her worry over his reaction to finding Ben hovering so near her. It had been completely innocent, but if the past was any indication, she wasn't sure he would see it that way. She'd just gotten him back and didn't want to lose him again, especially not over something like this.

* * * *

Rafe

Fucking Gorsky.

Rafe wanted to break every one of the detective's fingers for thinking he could touch Tori. A growl escaped his throat as he gripped the steering wheel tight enough to make his knuckles white.

She sat quietly beside him as he drove, but he felt her concerned stare trained in his direction. He relaxed his hands and tried to tone down his scowl.

He trusted her. He *did.* But it didn't make him any less jealous seeing her with Gorsky. It's like the detective wanted to piss him off.

Rafe grumbled a curse under his breath. Maybe he needed to have a chat with Gorsky so he understood Tori was taken. And if the man didn't like what he had to say, well . . . the use of force might be necessary to convince him.

He'd enjoy explaining things to Gorsky with his fists— maybe a little too much. But since he had to work with the man on this case, losing control and beating him into a bloody pulp wouldn't help his cause. He still waited on the warrant the fuck had filed so they could search Mosier's locker.

Dammit!

He hated this. He wanted it over—all of it. Then he and Tori could take a vacation and finally put the past behind them.

But until then, he had to tolerate Gorsky.

Rafe's hands clenched the wheel again as his teeth ground together. A punch to the detective's smug jaw would've been satisfying, but it would've made solving this case even more difficult. And he needed to see what was hidden in that locker. His gut told him it was important, and he'd learned to trust it with nearly twenty years on the force.

If Mosier had sold the sedative to the killer, there could be something in the kid's personal items that would give them a clue as to who that was. At the moment, it was the strongest lead they had.

Gorsky's conversation with Pamela had confirmed Mosier had burned all his bridges at the veterinary office. So Rafe had sent the detective to talk to Mosier's family and find out who his friends were, as it was apparent none of the people he'd worked with liked him enough to want to see him outside of the office.

But someone had known the kid had Fatal Flush; Rafe needed to find out who.

He pulled into a parking spot in the garage at his apartment building and let out a sigh. He still felt like a damn hamster on a wheel, but it turned too fast to risk jumping off.

"Are you . . . okay?" Tori's hesitant voice broke into his thoughts, and he noticed her worrying the bag strap in her lap.

Was he?

He stared into her eyes; their expression pinched. Reaching out, he stilled her restless fingers, sliding the bag from her grip and setting it in the seat behind them. "Can you come here?" the request croaked out of him in a somber plea.

He needed her.

She didn't hesitate, climbing over the center console as he slid his seat backward. He hugged her tightly when she was in his arms, closing his eyes as he breathed in her dusky floral scent. The sweetly dark smell soothed him with its sultry familiarity. Her face pressed into his neck, and her soft breaths tickled his throat, stirring his heart and his blood.

"I love you, Tori." All the warmth he felt spilled out of

his chest with those words.

"I love you, too." Her lips smiled against his skin.

"But seeing you with Gorsky . . . it makes me crazy." He'd tried not to growl with the statement, but it had come out rougher than he'd intended.

She tensed in his arms. "I know. I'm sorry. But I promise there's nothing there." Her voice hitched, so he squeezed her in reassurance while trying to get himself under control.

Just thinking of Gorsky again had the pulse in his head throbbing an angry beat.

"I can't—" A tear splashed on his shoulder.

"Hey, don't cry, Sunshine."

He lifted her head to look into her face, and she sniffled. "I'm not. It's just . . ." Her eyes filled, and he caught the next drop with his thumb when it spilled over. "I can't lose you."

"You won't." He took a deep breath and hoped to allay her fears. He'd made the mistake of not trusting her once and wouldn't do it again. "I trust you." He held her gaze, and when her eyes watered anew, he worried he'd said the wrong thing. His stomach tied itself in knots while he waited for her response. Brushing a strand of fire behind her ear, he begged her to say something, anything, "Sunshine?"

"Thank you," she warbled. Then she hiccupped, blinked back the tears, and swiped them from her face.

When she smiled at him, his heart stopped. Tori was radiant. And she was *his*.

He knew it not only in his heart but in his bones. The

past didn't define their future, and he'd be damned if he would let it tear them apart. With her in his life, he felt whole. Her flame burned the weight on him to ash, blowing it away like leaves in the wind.

Taking the hand she'd placed on his chest for balance, he gently kissed it. She sucked in a breath, then grinned at him, tracing a finger across the stubble on his jaw. His stomach tightened at her feathery touch, a line of fire igniting in its wake.

She rocked against him, and he gripped her hips. The end of her long shirtdress had ridden up, and the smooth flesh of her legs begged him to stroke it. "I know this wasn't really a fight"—she leaned forward and spoke directly in his ear—"but we should have makeup sex."

Rafe's pulse jumped at the suggestion. Her thin underwear would be too easy to remove, but they were in the parking garage. It was a dimly lit corner, but *still*. About to tell her they should head inside, the words fled as she nibbled his earlobe, her hand dipping inside his pants before undoing his belt.

"Here?" the question blurted unbidden from his lips. His hands found their way under her dress, gliding up all that soft alabaster skin.

"Yes," she murmured, then licked down the side of his neck. When her fingers closed around him, he swallowed a groan. "Commando?" She chuckled against his shoulder, and his body shook with the soft vibration. "It's a bold choice."

A haze of honey clouded his thoughts, but he tried his best to answer as he bucked under her hand. "Laundry," he managed to grunt.

"Mmm, I like it," she purred.

Rafe did, too. But she needed to lose the barrier between them. He grabbed the thin straps of her G-string and pulled.

The sound of ripping fabric filled the car, and she sat up with a pretty pout on her wide mouth. "You owe me a new pair of those. They were a favorite."

He smirked. "And you owe me a shirt." He quirked an eyebrow at her and loved it when a blush heated her cheeks.

"I suppose I do."

"Come here, and we'll call it even." He grabbed a handful of her long hair and tugged gently on the silken strands to bring her lips to his.

She stopped a breath away. Her green eyes danced, her teasing grin full of mischief. "We're breaking the law, Captain."

With a grin of his own, Rafe undid the handcuffs from the snap at his belt. Her eyes widened, then pulsed with heat hot enough to spark his already simmering blood. He dragged them across her wrists, and she hissed as the cool metal brushed her heated skin. He set them on the passenger seat with a look that promised trouble.

She was chuckling at his threat when his mouth captured hers. But when he slid his fingers along her slick folds, her laughter died on a moan.

Breaking the kiss, he whispered in her ear, "I'll arrest you for it—later."

CHAPTER 22

Tori

Tori shivered as a blast of cold wind caught under her open sweater. She pulled it tighter to her chest with her free hand. The other she'd wrapped in Rafe's arm, and she hugged closer to his side as they traversed the carnival grounds. The sun had set over an hour ago, and fall was in full swing. Leaves danced along the paths, ushered on by its incessant hand.

Though she wasn't used to the cooler weather, and her toes were slightly numb in her boots, she was enjoying herself. More so because Rafe was, too. Lately, he'd been brooding over his case, so this bit of merriment proved a perfect distraction.

"Ooh, candied popcorn! Can we get some?" She pulled him to a stop in front of a booth offering several varieties of popcorn, caramel apples, and other decadent goodies. When he didn't respond right away, she looked up at him, batting her lashes.

His warm chuckle rewarded her antics. "Anything for you, Sunshine."

He tapped the tip of her nose, and she grinned, giddy as a kid at Christmas. She couldn't remember the last time she'd had the sticky treat, but she'd always loved it as a child. It was messy and would likely cling to her teeth, but she didn't care. Tonight was about having fun and letting go of their worries, if only for a few hours.

She nudged him with her elbow. "You should get some, too."

"I'll pass, thanks." The look on his face was comical. With his lip curled in disgust, you'd have thought she'd asked him to eat live worms instead of a delicious snack.

She laughed and shook her head. "It's your loss then."

She took in all the costumes people wore as they waited in line. So far, they'd seen everything from scary to cute, but her favorite had been a dog and person combo. The man wore a poodle outfit, while his dog had been dressed as a man, complete with glasses and a bowtie. She'd pointed them out to Rafe, giggling, but he'd just smiled and shaken his head.

Someone in a rather convincing zombie costume shuffled their way, and she whispered to Rafe, "Okay, he's going to give me nightmares."

He caught the direction of her gaze and frowned. "It does seem a bit overboard considering how many kids are here."

She nodded, trying and failing not to look at the peeling flesh on the man's face. Fake blood oozed from a gash at his throat, trickling down to stain his white shirt. "There must be a pretty good prize for the costume contest because that guy's in it to win it with his getup."

"Next!" the loud bark startled her, and she jumped. It was their turn to order.

Rafe squeezed her arm and led them forward. "Can I get a butter and a candied popcorn?"

She raised her brow. At least he'd decided to get *something* for himself. As the vendor filled their order, he pulled out his wallet.

"That's ten dollars," the plump man's gruff voice boomed louder than it needed to. He clearly had one volume—high.

She rubbed her hands together as Rafe paid. She couldn't wait to taste the sweet and salty combo of the candied popcorn. When he placed it in her palms, she bounced on her toes, as much in anticipation as in an effort to warm them. "Thank you."

They moved out of line and continued to stroll through vendors' tents on either side of the dirt path. Rafe snacked on his popcorn as she unwrapped the plastic from around the sticky ball of goodness he'd gifted her with. She bit into it and moaned. It was better than she remembered.

He grinned at her. "I don't know how you eat that."

She scoffed. "And I don't know how you can't. It's delicious." She took another bite and savored the sweet flavor of the glaze, loving how it contrasted with the saltiness of the popcorn. "Orgasmic even," she added with a wink.

He smirked at her, but she hadn't finished teasing him. Her grin turned devilish. "Better than sex."

His eyes flared with her challenge before narrowing on

her. "You think so?"

"Mm-hmm, can't beat it." She took another bite to punctuate her point.

"We'll see about that." The promise in his voice sent a shot of heat straight to her core, and her appetite changed, suddenly hungry for something other than popcorn.

She swallowed, then licked the sweetness from her lips. His eyes tracked the movement of her tongue.

Mmm, maybe it is *overrated.*

Because right now, the only thing she wanted to taste was Rafe's mouth on hers.

"Tori!"

Groaning inwardly at the interruption, she glanced over her shoulder to see Meg waving at her from a stall away. Unease tightened her posture. She hoped Meg didn't bring up the idea of doing a reading again.

Forcing a smile, she lifted her arm to wave at the librarian. Then she tugged on Rafe's hand, pulling them further out of the flow of traffic as Meg made her way over to them.

When she approached, she slid a sly smile Tori's way before extending her hand to Rafe. "You must be Tori's beau. I'm Meg."

He clasped the older woman's hand with a smile. "Rafe."

"Nice to meet you, handsome." Meg very unsubtly wiggled her brow at Tori as if to say, "Wow."

She blushed and tried to cover it up by telling him, "Meg runs the town library."

"I do. But I'm also a big fan of T.E. Graham." She winked at him. "Though, I suppose you are, too."

Tori wasn't cold anymore. Her cheeks blazed hot enough to fry an egg.

He was enjoying her embarrassment because he grinned at her, then told the older woman, "I am."

"Well, thank you." She cleared her throat and forced herself not to fidget with the half-eaten snack she clutched in her left hand. "Um, so, how are you enjoying the carnival, Meg?"

Can we please talk about anything other than me?

"Oh!" The woman swatted her head with her hand. "I got sidetracked when I saw you. I'm supposed to be watching the pumpkin carving contest."

"It sounds like fun." Tori relaxed enough to smile. "Maybe we'll go check it out."

"Great! I've got to run, but I'll see you there." She spun on her heel and took two steps before she stopped. Grinning over her shoulder, she said, "It was nice to meet you, handsome."

"You too!" Rafe called after Meg before she hurried away. Then he smirked. "I'm your 'beau,' huh?"

She didn't know why, but that word made her blush like she was the heroine in a historical romance novel. "I suppose so."

He raised a dark eyebrow before stepping closer to her. "You *suppose* so?"

She rolled her eyes. "Yes, you're my 'beau'"—her cheeks flamed—"is that what you wanted me to say?"

His grin was wicked, so she swatted him. "You're incorrigible!"

When he laughed, her eyes narrowed, the emeralds

flashing. "You want to laugh, *handsome*?" With a smirk of her own, she announced, "Then we're watching the pumpkin carving."

Rafe stopped abruptly, his eyebrows kissing. "Pumpkin carving?"

This time, she had a mischievous grin. "Yep. Let's go."

He grumbled but let her lead him toward the contest. Posted signs told them where to go, the lights strung overhead buzzing brighter as they neared the large white tent where it was being held. It had started already; no one waited to get in.

As they reached the tent opening, she heard an announcer saying the contestants had half an hour left. Peeking in, a group of wooden folding chairs, half empty, invited them to sit. Tugging on Rafe's fingers, she pulled him inside, taking two chairs in the front row.

In front of them, five tables held pumpkins in various stages of carving. She was so focused on picking out what people created that she didn't notice Ben was a contestant until she heard Rafe growl "Gorsky" under his breath.

She tensed, her calve muscles cramping against the chair legs. Now, she realized why Meg was supposed to be watching. She nodded at her friend when the librarian glanced over.

Taking a deep breath, she flexed her feet to stretch her legs, then clasped Rafe's hand and whispered, "We can go if you want to."

He lifted their entwined hands and kissed the back of hers. "No, it's okay."

The sweet gesture warmed her heart and eased the

tension in her muscles. Squeezing his hand, she looked toward the tables again. Most of the designs faced away from the audience, making them difficult to see. Her curiosity built as she watched slivers of orange flesh fly off the pumpkins. The ground was littered with it, and she thought it would be a huge mess to clean up, even on the grass.

"The man to Gorsky's right?" She followed Rafe's direction to the balding, overweight gentleman, whose wire-framed glasses slid down his nose as he bent over the pumpkin he carved. Something about him struck her as familiar.

Have I seen him before?

"He's the county coroner." Her stomach fell, and she dreaded Rafe's next words. "I need to talk to him when they're done."

She sighed inwardly. They couldn't get through one night without him thinking about work. "Okay." She hated how much it weighed on him and hoped talking to the coroner wouldn't add to the burden. It worried her more than it should because he wouldn't tell her anything about the case. Not that he ever had in the past, but she thought things might've changed with her involvement in this one.

They hadn't. Rafe was keeping her out of it.

She frowned and fiddled with the ends of her sweater. She understood why, even if it irked her. Not so much because she was curious and wanted to know but because she felt she could ease some of his load simply by being his sounding board. But he wouldn't let her. As usual, he protected her, and to him, that meant not mentioning what he dealt with.

She could only imagine what it would be like if the roles were reversed, and she kept being confronted with dead men who looked like Rafe. Swallowing against the sudden surge of bile that came with the thought, she worried her lip, her hands continuing to fidget.

He reached over, stilling her fingers, then lifted her chin to meet his gaze, his dark chocolate irises wondering what bothered her. She shook off her thoughts, giving him a bright smile. Tonight was about helping him relax. She couldn't do that if she wound herself up over something she had no control over.

When his stare didn't change, she glanced at the contestants. "I can't wait to see what everyone's carving."

"Yeah, wonder what they'll be."

She breathed deep when he didn't press her and worked to infuse the enthusiasm back into her voice. "Not long now, and we'll find out!"

* * * *

Rafe

Rafe hated to admit it, but Gorsky's *calavera* was impressive. The detective had carved a sugar skull, which gleamed under the harsh floodlights illuminating the tent. But it paled compared to Dundy's wilting rose held aloft by skeleton fingers.

He wasn't surprised the coroner had won the contest with how intricate his design was. Each detail had been rendered visible, from the smallest thorn on the stem of the rose to the notches in each finger bone.

Impressive.

Next to him, Tori chatted with Meg about changes at the library, and his mind wandered. They stood behind the crowd, waiting to get a closer look at the carvings. He would have tugged Tori away, but he wanted to ask the coroner about the drugs Mosier had likely stolen.

Rafe was annoyed they hadn't been able to confirm the theft. A frown pulled on his lips. Last week, they'd finally gotten the warrant to search the kid's locker, only to find it empty . . . apart from one item.

The ten of hearts.

He felt like the killer was playing with him. He hadn't ruled out the possibility the slasher he'd apprehended last year was somehow orchestrating these new murders from prison. But with the pattern not being the same, he had his doubts. And no matter how hard he tried, he couldn't shake the feeling this slasher was here because of Tori. It woke him up in a sweat night after night.

"What do you think, Rafe?"

"Hmm?" He pushed the thought away and focused on her. She gazed at him with an expectant look.

What did she ask me?

Her smile slid, her eyes narrowing. "The haunted hayride? You want to do it next?"

He wanted to sit on scratchy hay and get bumped and jostled against other people about as much as he wanted a bullet to the chest, but he'd endure it—for her. For Tori, he'd do anything that would make her happy, so he forced a smile and shrugged. "Sure, Sunshine."

She clapped her hands and grinned. "Great!"

Meg chuckled as if she knew he felt less than enthusiastic about the prospect of a hayride. "You two have fun. My bones are too old to get tossed around in that thing."

Tori grinned at her. "You're not old, Meg. Not even a little."

She squeezed Tori's arm. "Thank you, but sometimes I *feel* it."

They'd finally reached the display table holding the finished pumpkins. Each carver stood behind their design. Gorsky and Dundy were at the opposite end, and Rafe was getting antsy. He ran a hand through his hair, wishing the line would move quicker.

Since they were both here, he figured he'd ask Gorsky if he'd had any luck tracking down Mosier's buyer. He had him talking to the kid's family and friends because it was their only lead. It had been a few days since he'd spoken to the detective, so he should have *some* new information.

Not surprisingly, people were enthralled by the coroner's pumpkin and kept asking him questions about the design. Impatient, Rafe drummed his fingers on the table, waiting for the crowd to shuffle out of the way. Like an itch he couldn't scratch, his irritation built the more he thought about the case. He knew he'd missed something, and the longer it took him to figure it out, the more likely another body would show up.

A loud shriek sounded outside the tent. Then a lanky teenager burst in, almost dragging a sobbing girl who clung to his arm. "Police! We need the police!" His eyes were wide, his chest heaving with each breath.

A collective gasp sounded at the outburst before he and Gorsky headed for the teenagers.

Rafe reached them first. "I'm a cop. What happened?"

The kid swallowed, then scrubbed a hand over his mouth. "There's a dead body in the woods."

CHAPTER 23

Rafe

Another redhead. As Rafe stared at the body under the high-powered beams from the mobile LED lamps, his gut turned hollow with the cold certainty of failure. She was one more woman he hadn't saved.

She'd been deposited in an area of tall grass not far beyond the path of the haunted hayride. Her eyes were closed, but the long gash across her neck made her look anything but peaceful. Like the others, her pale skin was exposed, her clothes gone, and he had little doubt the medical examiner would confirm she'd been treated the same.

Rafe's hands clenched into tight fists. Whoever this necrophile was, he needed to stop him before the bastard struck again.

Before *he* failed to save the next poor soul. And before he recognized the victim's face.

Rafe blanched at the possibility of finding Tori this way.

He'd sent her to his car with Meg and instructions to wait there until Officer Hale arrived to take her home. He didn't want her anywhere near the crime scene and the death permeating everything here.

Footsteps approached behind him. He glanced over his shoulder, expecting Gorksy. But it wasn't the detective. A line creased his forehead. Gorsky had been gone a long time taking the teenagers' statements.

Rafe figured the poor kids had snuck off for a makeout session but saw more than they'd bargained for.

Dundy approached after retrieving his gear. As he set down his medical bag, Rafe gave him a nod, then backed away from the body to allow him space to work.

When the coroner snapped on a pair of latex gloves, he frowned. "Are those powdered?"

Dundy looked confused for a moment before he understood what Rafe asked, then he nodded. "Yes, makes them easier to slide on."

"Just try not to get any residue on the victim. We don't need more false evidence," he grumbled, crossing his arms over his chest while he watched the man examine the body.

Gorsky appeared at his shoulder. "Word travels fast." He thumbed a hand behind him, and Rafe looked to see several curious onlookers being ushered away by the uniformed officers cordoning off the scene.

About time you showed up.

Despite his rancor, Rafe commented, "So it seems."

"She hasn't been here long," Dundy drew his attention away, and he focused on the coroner as the overweight man labored to his feet. "No debris on the body. Looks like she's been dead less than eight hours."

Before Rafe could ask, Gorsky piped up, "Does it look like the same wound? Think he used the same weapon?"

Dundy gave an unhelpful shrug. "It's possible."

Rafe had little patience for this. He ignored Dundy and growled at Gorsky, "You called the sheriff, right?"

The detective nodded. "They're on their way."

"See that we get her to the M.E.'s as soon as possible."

After giving the order, he walked away. He'd seen enough dead women for a lifetime, and whatever evidence they'd missed would be easier to see in the daylight anyway. He also had a feeling there was a piece only he would find, a piece that wasn't with the body.

Where would the card be this time?

Pondering the question, he strolled through the carnival. Excited shrieks met his ears, while in the distance, he could hear the low tones of a horror movie soundtrack, likely coming from the haunted house he'd passed on his way in.

People pushed past him, smiles on their faces. At least some carnival goers were blissfully unaware of the death at their feet. He'd forced the hayride route to shift, keeping people away from the scene. Though word had spread, Rafe hoped the happy families he saw wouldn't find out about the body until the news broke the next morning.

But he knew. And he had to live with it.

Trying not to flinch at the kids who bumped into him, screaming on their way to the next event, he stepped off the main path. He'd take the route through the tents where fewer people wandered.

"Dammit!" he cursed, grabbing a tent pole to keep himself upright as the problem with his plan immediately made itself known.

The lighting was sporadic off the path, and he'd tripped over an unseen power cord. When he untangled his foot, he realized he'd made it back to the carving tent. A peek inside showed the discarded art on the table where they'd left it. He walked inside to study Dundy's creation.

Rafe thought he should've followed an artistic career path because he wasn't a very competent coroner. At this, the man had talent.

Lifting the pumpkin, he heard something rattle. A tiny medical scalpel rolled along its uneven surface as he looked at the table.

That's an odd tool for pumpkin carving.

Curious if it belonged to Dundy or Gorsky, Rafe considered taking it to them, but as he continued to hold the pumpkin, the scalpel kept moving until it dropped off the table into the disgusting orange mush littering the ground. Grumbling under his breath, he set the artwork down and bent to look for the implement.

The damn thing had disappeared.

Cursing as he plunged his hand into the wet pile of pulp from the pumpkins, Rafe dragged his hand around, feeling for the tool. When the smell of overripe fruit got to him, he gave up. If it had been important, whoever had used it wouldn't have left it behind. He rubbed his hand in the clean grass, but the stringy innards refused to leave his skin. Scowling at the offending produce, he rose and headed for his car. The sooner he got home, the better.

As Rafe neared his SUV, his eye landed on something caught in the windshield. The closer he got, the hairs on his neck stood up, and his stomach tightened into equally tense knots.

Stopping a foot away, he took a deep breath and glanced around. No one was in the area. This part of the lot had filled up hours ago, and people had been forced to park elsewhere.

With no one to question about it, he steeled himself to reach for the manila envelope. His fingers grazed the stiff paper, and he paused. At least he had a time frame. Whoever put it on his car had done so after Tori had left and before he'd arrived back at the vehicle. It was maybe a two-hour window.

Anger surging over missing the bastard, he ripped the envelope from beneath his wiper. Grimacing at what he knew he'd find, he opened it. Carefully squeezing the sides to force the inside to gap, he stared at the card within, but from this angle, he couldn't tell what was on the face.

He unlocked his car, then opened the center console to grab a pair of gloves. With his fingerprints covered, he upended the envelope and slid the card into his waiting palm. When it lay there, damning him, Rafe swallowed and closed his eyes.

He'd located the jack of hearts.

* * * *

Tori

A loud gurgling noise made Tori jump, her stomach

dropping. She blinked to clear her vision; dots swam in her eyes after adjusting from the lighted screen of her laptop to the darkness blanketing the apartment.

Was that Rafe?

She'd left him in bed an hour ago when her characters had denied her request to sleep. That and her mind had refused to quiet, worrying about Rafe after the drastic turn in tonight's events. He hadn't spoken to her of the body, but from how troubled he'd looked, it had to have been another redheaded woman. Another version of her.

Straining her ears, she heard nothing. It had gone silent, but instead of returning to her story, she rose, sliding the dining room chair back as quietly as she could.

Toby had been snoozing at her feet, and she nudged him gently now. "Come on, buddy. Let's check on Rafe."

The dog stretched, then pushed himself to all fours, padding after her as she crept down the hall. Before she reached the bedroom, she heard Rafe shouting her name. Her heart jumped to her throat, and she flew the last few feet, bursting through the door.

"Rafe!" She flipped the switch, turning on the lamp by the bed. He was sitting up, his eyes wide, his breathing shallow. She rushed to his side. "What happened?"

He covered his face with his hands, his shoulders bowed. When she reached for him, he flinched. "Don't."

Surprised by the harshness of his tone, Tori dropped her hand. "What's wrong?" She knew he'd had a nightmare, but she didn't understand why he wouldn't want her to touch him.

More confused than hurt, she watched his eyes rake the

room, looking at anything but her. Toby paced in front of the bed, sensing Rafe's distress.

"What did you dream?" she asked softly, hoping he'd give her that much. To help her understand.

He finally met her gaze, and his eyes were haunted. Tori cringed, afraid of what he'd seen. He shook his head, his voice cracking as he told her, "I can't."

Turning away from her, he slung his legs over the side of the bed, leaving her to frown at his back. Whatever he'd dreamt had shaken him. She lifted to her knees and crawled over to him. Before he had a chance to tell her no, she wrapped her arms around his chest, squeezing tightly. He shuddered as her skin touched his, and she noticed sweat drenched him.

She kissed the top of his shoulder, the salt from his perspiration coating her lips. "I love you, Rafe."

His breath stuttered; then his hands covered hers. His response, when it came, bordered on desperation, "I can't lose you, Tori."

Her heart bled for him, and she wanted to soothe his fears. "I'm not going anywhere."

"No, I meant . . ." He scrubbed his hands down his face, and she understood.

"I'm safe." When he squeezed his eyes closed as if he could shut out the images disturbing him, she gripped his face and kissed his lids, whispering those two little words over and over until he relaxed.

With a slow, relieving breath, he opened his eyes. The fear had gone, replaced by a need so strong it stole the air from her lungs. An ache throbbed low in her belly—a hunger to match his. She'd take some of his burdens; however, he'd let her. If release were what he needed, she'd give it to him. And she'd fill herself as well.

Climbing onto his lap, Tori straddled Rafe and brushed the damp curls off his forehead. His hands gripped her hips, his fingers digging into her flesh as if to reassure himself she was real. Staring into his dark chocolate pools, she grabbed the bottom of the T-shirt she'd borrowed from him and lifted it off her body. Under his hungry gaze, her skin heated, her nipples tightening.

He trailed a finger between her breasts. "Not cold," he breathed the statement, and she recognized it as a comfort for himself.

Is that what he'd dreamt?

Reaching for his hand, she placed it over her heart, holding it in place with one of her own. Under their palms, the organ beat, thrumming with excitement from being near him. She hoped the steady drum of her pulse within her chest would assure him she was alive. She wasn't cold—not lifeless.

He stared at their hands, his breath shuddering out. She released his palm and cupped his face. Scratching her fingers through his stubble, she smiled. "Never cold with you around." Her words had more than one meaning.

As if he understood, Rafe traced the shape of her with his palms, dragging his hands up her sides, then cupping her face. He tilted her chin toward him, a hint of a smile turning his lips up before they met hers.

The kiss started soft, almost hesitant, like the feel of silk sliding over her skin. Craving more, Tori added pressure, wrapping her arms around his neck and plunging her fingers in his hair. He pulled her closer. A gasp escaped at the sensation of his chest hair tickling her sensitive peaks.

When his palms cupped her breasts, his thumbs teased, and she moaned into his mouth. The fire that had been smoldering blazed to life. It grew, consuming her from the inside out. She clung to him and knew he would burn with her.

His mouth released hers, his forehead meeting hers as their breaths mingled in harsh rasps. The sweet pause was but a moment of rest before he twisted with her in his arms. Her back hit the covers, and Rafe hovered over her.

A tempest brewed in his eyes, two warring systems vying for supremacy. She could tell he was frustrated, and she knew a part of him blamed himself for not finding the killer before he'd had the chance to take someone else's life. Because he felt that way, her heart ached for him. She watched, mesmerized, as lightning flashed in his eyes before he shielded them, and serenity seeped in. But even as their surface stilled, she wondered if this was merely the calm before the storm.

His mouth claimed hers again, and she tasted the salt that had transferred from his lips to hers. Breathing in, his smoky scent fed the flames racing along her skin. She wrapped her legs around his waist, and his erection swelled against her belly.

Take me!

He'd built the hunger within her, and using her body, she urged him to take what they both needed.

Words weren't necessary, not this time.

When Rafe slid into her, her spine arched in rapture, breaking their kiss. No one filled her so completely or fit her so perfectly. It was as if they were two parts of the same whole. Only joined did she feel unbroken.

He'd frozen, and she focused on his face. The war raged in his eyes again, and she waited to see who would be the conqueror. As she stared, a growl left his throat, the torrent spilling out from the depths of his irises. His hips pistoned into her, and she locked her legs around his waist, meeting the storm in his gaze with a squall of her own.

Their bodies met and clashed in a frantic rhythm like waves pounding against each other. With each impact, the pressure built until she would swear she heard the roll of thunder before its rumble shook her body. Her eyes closed, lightning flashing behind her lids. Unable to hold on any longer, a cry left her lips, and her limp legs slid from around Rafe's waist.

The dam had broken against the force of his storm, and she happily floated among the debris.

His quick breaths brushed her face; then she heard his low groan as his body clenched, emptying himself within her walls. He collapsed on top of her, and her breath swooshed out. Before she could pull in another, he grunted, rolling off her and pulling her against his chest.

His lips brushed the crown of her head as his arm tightened around her. "I love you, Sunshine."

Her mouth curved against the crook of his arm. Sated and exhausted, she hoped he would sleep peacefully the rest of the night.

CHAPTER 24

Rafe

The rubber band around Rafe's head kept getting tighter. He massaged his temples as he sat at his desk, but it did nothing to relieve the throbbing. As if it colluded with the headache, the acid in his stomach flared up, burning on the way to his throat.

Grumbling at the now familiar fire, he opened his desk drawer and rummaged for relief. He found a roll of antacids and popped two in his mouth before returning to the drawer for ibuprofen. When his hand closed around the pain reliever, he shook out three pills. Both medicines were becoming part of his regular diet.

Frowning over that fact, he swallowed the tablets, washing them down with a sip of coffee. It had been over three weeks since the latest murder, and he was no closer to finding the slasher. On top of his lack of progress, he was plagued almost daily by nightmares of Tori in the killer's grasp.

Sometimes, he found her mutilated body; others, he managed to save her before that horrific picture burned itself, once again, on his retinas.

Scrubbing a hand down his face, Rafe shoved those images from his mind. As police captain, he technically had to wait on Gorsky for the detective work, not that it had stopped him before. Still, he'd been letting his responsibilities at the station slip in favor of this case. The Chief had chewed his ass, so he'd spent the past few days making up for it, which had meant long hours and mound after mound of paperwork.

Gorsky was still tracking down the veterinary tech's friends, but so far, it seemed Mosier had primarily kept to himself. They'd identified the third victim and confirmed what Rafe had suspected. She'd had the same sedative in her system, and the same weapon had made the wound, though they still didn't know what it was.

Tracing a gun proved easy in comparison. Looking for a blade with no identifiable edge seemed near impossible. It could be a razor, a surgical implement, hell, anything thin and sharp. The possibility of a paring knife had even crossed his mind. But despite not knowing the murder weapon, there was no doubt this was another slasher victim because she'd been sexually assaulted after she'd been killed.

He sighed and leaned his head back, cracking his neck from side to side, but it did little to erase the lingering tension. He'd had Gorsky locate the woman's family. She'd been staying with a friend from college in the Northeast during fall break. When the young student hadn't come home, her friend had assumed she'd gotten lucky. But what the girl had scored was the opposite of luck.

Rafe ground his teeth as the truth of those words soured his already-roiling stomach. Shoving papers out of the way, he reached for the clear evidence envelopes he'd been pondering, hoping to find something he'd missed. So far, the three playing cards taunted him. They seemed ordinary enough, even upon further inspection. The backs of each had the same mass-produced pattern of cherubs riding bicycles in the center. The background was red, and intricate white swirls created a border, joining with a cherub at each corner.

Insignificant.

Not only were the cards themselves ordinary, but they'd all been free of fingerprints. They weren't evidence, but a jeer meant to piss him off, which sadly was working.

With a growl, he threw the jack he'd been holding into the air. He had no care where it went, only wanting to release some of his frustration with the toss. But as the back of the card found the sunlight streaming through the window, Rafe thought he saw a glimmer of something he hadn't noticed before. Rather unsatisfactorily, the card floated slowly to the ground, and he watched as the symbol he'd glimpsed appeared and disappeared with each ray it caught.

Pulse speeding with excitement now, he pushed to his feet. In two strides, he'd recaptured the jack of hearts. Adrenaline rushed through his veins, adding to the throbbing in his head, but he didn't care. Why he hadn't found this before burned in his gut, but he would sure as hell follow through on it now. As he held the paper to the light, what he'd been missing revealed itself.

Hidden within the swirls along the border, a wilted rose climbed, stretching over the cherub's flesh and pricking it with thorns.

He walked to his desk and picked up the other two cards. First, he held the ten of hearts to the light. When the same rose appeared, the weight on his chest became a fraction lighter. Reaching for the nine, he repeated the process, and the result was the same. Each card had the same hidden symbol.

But what did it mean?

Was this the real calling card of the slasher?

Rafe studied the design more closely. It seemed eerily familiar, but he couldn't quite place it. Setting them on his desk, he reached for his phone. Now that he had an actual lead, he needed a professional to examine this new evidence.

* * * *

Tori

Tori plopped down on Rafe's couch, the black leather molding around her in a comforting embrace. She stared at the phone in her hand and dreaded what she had to do. It was time to call Veronica. Having run out of days to stall, she had to tell her sister Rafe would be coming with her for Thanksgiving.

Toby whined at her feet, and she patted the spot beside her. "You can come up here, bud." His tail wagged, and he smiled at her. "Come on," she coaxed, "I could use the support."

Understanding, the dog jumped up next to her and licked her face before settling by her side. She laughed, wiping away his slobber. "Thanks for that." She rustled Toby's hair before her eyes strayed back to her phone.

Okay, you can do this.

Taking a deep breath, Tori hit the call button. Was it wrong to hope Veronica didn't answer so she could drop this bomb in a voicemail instead? Barely two rings and her hopes were dashed.

"Well, it's about time you called!" The chastisement in Veronica's voice carried clearly across the line, making Tori's shoulders tense. "Thanksgiving is barely two days away. Are you still coming tomorrow or what?"

"Hello to you too, Ron." She rolled her eyes, but it didn't help with the nerves tying knot after knot in her stomach.

Her sister scoffed, "You didn't answer my question." Tori could envision Veronica's glare even though she couldn't see it.

She glanced at Toby.

Brace for impact, buddy.

With another breath, which did nothing to ease her anxiety over her sister's response, she answered, "Yes, we're coming tomorrow."

Veronica had always been sharp; she picked up on Tori's use of 'we.' "*We're* coming? As in, you and Toby?"

She tried to laugh, but it came out sounding completely fake. "Yes, but, um, Rafe too."

She'd expected her sister to bluster over the news, but

her calm was deadlier. "Rafe is coming with you?" Veronica's voice sounded entirely too even.

Anticipating a blow, Tori closed her eyes and winced. "Yes."

"AND WHEN WERE YOU PLANNING TO TELL ME YOU TWO WERE BACK TOGETHER?" Veronica yelled, and Tori moved the phone away from her ear. She'd known it was coming, but it didn't make the outburst any easier to bear.

"I'm telling you now." She worked to stay composed in the face of her sister's anger.

"Mm-hmm. I hope you know what you're doing, Tor. I'd hate to see—"

She couldn't handle the nastiness that crept into her sister's tone, so she cut her off. "You know what, Ron? I *know.* And it's okay. We've talked about it."

Surprise colored her sister's voice. "You talked about the miscarriage?"

Tori dropped her head back, resting it on the cushions, and closed her eyes. "Yes. Gah, this is embarrassing even to tell you." She ran a hand down her face before blowing out a breath.

"You had a panic attack."

Of course, Ron would know.

"Yes." She sighed.

Concern replaced her sister's anger. "Are you doing okay?"

She relaxed enough to smile. "I haven't felt this good in years. I know it's hard to believe because of our past, but Rafe . . . he makes me happy."

She heard her sister's sigh through the phone. "I want

you to be happy, Tor. I just . . . I don't want you to get hurt like that again."

Her fears surfaced with her sister's words. Hadn't she stayed away from Rafe because of the same reason?

But we've grown, and he loves me.

Veronica's voice dropped in volume. "What if it doesn't work out again? Have you thought about that?"

She squeezed her eyes shut, wishing it was as easy to close out those thoughts as it was to drop her lids. "You're being very pessimistic."

"I'm not trying to be. But I want to know you're prepared for the possibility."

Was she? Tori frowned, and her anger stirred, building heat in her blood. Though she wasn't sure if it was at her sister or herself. "We love each other," she snapped.

Instead of getting angry again, Veronica sounded resigned. "Sometimes it's not enough."

Desperate to end this conversation, Tori forced cheer into her voice. "We'll see you tomorrow, Ron. Tell the twins I can't wait to squeeze them."

Her sister let it go, but that didn't cool the fire she'd started. "Can't wait. Love you, Tor."

Annoyed that Veronica had said those words as a half-apology, she didn't want to return them, but she wouldn't be so petty. "Love you, 'bye."

Disconnecting, Tori tossed her phone aside with a frustrated huff. Things with Rafe weren't perfect, especially with how stressed he stayed about this case, but she was happy. And not 'fake a smile until it feels real' happy. But filled with so much joy, she felt its beams could burst out of her at any moment. *That* was something she hadn't experienced since before the miscarriage.

She hugged her belly. Echoes of those long-ago cramps twisting her insides. She didn't like thinking about the child she and Rafe lost, and her anger renewed at Veronica for bringing it up. She pushed to her feet, disturbing Toby, who'd started to nap at her side. He grunted and rolled over.

Vibrating with a mix of hurt and worry, she paced across Rafe's living room. All those years ago, she'd blamed herself until the guilt and shame of it had nearly buried her. They'd been so young, and she hadn't felt sure she was ready for a child. Fate had answered her doubts by taking the choice out of their hands. It had still been the first trimester, but they'd already heard the heartbeat.

Silent tears made tracks on her face as the memories she so often repressed climbed to the summit of her mind. He'd been working when she'd called him on her way to the hospital. Dull cramps had concerned her, but the blood had sent her into a panic. Her hands had been shaking so badly it was a wonder she'd made it to the ER in one piece.

The day she'd spent there was a blur, punctuated by memories of endless tears, gripping pain, and a hollowness that had taken her a long time to fill back up. So quickly, the pregnancy had been over, and Rafe had expected everything to return to normal.

But *she* hadn't been able to.

She shook her head, wishing she could shake away those memories. Her stride ate up the floor, her feet turning to repeat the loop. But then he'd helped her find a counselor. Slowly, she'd learned to set the blame and guilt aside, to realize what had happened was nobody's fault.

Tingling started up her arms, and Tori shook out the hands she hadn't realized she'd clenched into tight fists. Her thoughts still swam through the past.

The moment she had started to feel better, she'd lost Rafe too, and all those dark feelings she'd thought she'd stemmed had resprouted. It had taken Veronica to pull her out of the sea of despair she'd been drowning in.

Remembering, a sharp pain stabbed her chest, and she stopped moving. When the ache spread, Tori sat back down. Rafe had always been jealous, but the way he'd acted the day he'd seen her with her counselor . . . it still scared her to know he could get so angry.

She worried her lip. What if he flipped out again? He'd said he trusted her. But would it be enough? She'd already seen him get wound up by Ben's attentions to her. Doubts crept in, and she hated that she'd let her sister put them there.

Wishing she could talk to him about it now, but knowing he wouldn't be home for hours, she popped up off the couch. She *had* to run. It was the only thing that would help her work through her worries. She hoped Officer Hale was up for a little exercise as she headed for the bedroom to change.

* * * *

Rafe

Rafe hung up the phone and reclined against his chair,

steepling his fingers. He'd just gotten off a call with an analyst at his former district in Chicago. The kid owed him a favor, and he'd had the perfect reason to cash in—the symbol on the cards.

As he replayed what Jett had found out, Rafe dropped his chin to his steepled hands, tapping them against his scruff, deep in thought. The wilted rose represented an association of necrophiliacs existing on the dark web—The Dead Hands.

Their website was a 'meetup' for necrophiliacs like the slasher, catering to everything from those fantasizing about it to those committing the act.

While learning there were enough people interested in sex with a corpse to need to create a space to share that with others creeped him out, Rafe tried not to pass judgment. But how exactly did you ask *a dead woman* for consent?

A shudder racked his spine, and he straightened in his chair, pinching the bridge of his nose. The psychology of necrophilia aside, when a necrophiliac committed homicide to procure the opportunity, they crossed a line. And he had a problem with that—a big one.

Which is why he wouldn't rest until he'd caught this fucker.

Jett would get him a list of all the people who used The Dead Hands' site. Despite the impending holiday, he'd pushed and hoped to have the names on his desk by tomorrow.

Because there was no doubt in his mind, one of them was the slasher.

CHAPTER 25

Tori

Tori wasn't the chef Rafe was, but she'd started dinner because she'd needed the distraction. The run hadn't helped except to exhaust her physically as well as mentally. Not even the soreness in her muscles could settle the nerves, making her skin itch. She felt raw, her emotions too close to the surface, and she worried one wrong move would bobble her boat, tossing her into churning water.

Staring at the pot she had simmering for pasta, she could commiserate. She felt just as tumultuous. Shaking it off, she rolled her shoulders and focused on the recipe. When she reread it, she realized she hadn't prepared everything for the Swedish meatballs like she'd thought.

She blew out a breath, tousling the fiery strands of hair, which had come loose from the quick braid she'd fashioned to keep it out of the way. Brushing them out of her face, she moved to the refrigerator, searching for the flat-leaf parsley she needed. Her head had strayed deep inside when Toby barked, startling her.

"Ow!" She'd knocked the top of her skull on the shelving. Giving up on the herb for the moment, she shut the refrigerator and scowled at her dog. Rubbing the sore spot, she asked, "Was that really necessary?"

She would swear Toby grinned at her before racing to the front door. Rafe walked in, and the dog immediately pounced.

He'd gotten used to Toby's hugs. Unfazed by the dog's feet planted on his chest, Rafe scratched behind his ears. "Hey, buddy."

As she watched them, her hands wanted to fidget, so she tucked them into her pockets. Smiling with half her usual brightness, she greeted him, "Hi. I started dinner."

His mood seemed buoyant, the grin he sent her way lighting his dark eyes and crinkling their corners. "Hi." He set Toby's feet on the floor and advanced on her.

When he reached her, Rafe pulled her up on her toes, planting his mouth on hers. The warmth was immediate; the excitement vibrating off him transferred to her lips while the pressure left her wanting more.

Then he released her, setting her on her feet. She stared up into his smiling face and wondered what had happened today. "You're in a good mood."

He tucked her flyaways behind her ear. "I got a break in the case."

She was glad, if only so it weighed a little less on him. But worry still overshadowed the relief his statement brought. Trying not to focus on her twitchy muscles, she returned his smile. "That's great!"

Glancing toward the counter where she had everything prepped, he sniffed the air. "What are you cooking?"

She hadn't actually started the cooking part and didn't think he'd be able to smell the dish. "Swedish meatballs."

Rafe surveyed her prep work out of curiosity—or fear—she wasn't sure. She may not be the best cook, but it's not like she would poison him. "That'll be good."

She nodded and chewed her lip. Should she try to talk to him before dinner? The way her stomach kept jumping, she didn't know if she could make it until after.

While she debated, his brow creased. "What's wrong, Sunshine?" His hands cupped her shoulders, his thumbs brushing the hair at her neck.

Tori took a deep breath and blew it out. "I told Ron about us. I figured she should know before we showed up at her door and—"

"Oh."

He'd stopped her mid-sentence to say *oh*?

"What is it?"

"About Thanksgiving . . ." When he trailed off, she wanted to scream.

Frustrated energy made her pulse throb, the beat a warning she didn't heed. "Yesss?"

Rafe dropped his hands from her shoulders and stepped back, putting space between them. She knew it wasn't a good sign, and her hands flew to her hips.

"We can't go, Tor. Not now. I have to follow up on this new lead."

Her stomach dropped.

Tell me this isn't happening.

"You can't be serious." Her whole uncomfortable conversation with Veronica could have been avoided.

Because He. Wasn't. Coming.

It was apparently the wrong thing to say as his jaw went tight. "I'm dead serious." He scrubbed a jerky hand through his hair. "I'm hunting a serial killer. Time's not on my side here."

Okay, she understood that, but could he not let it sit for a few days? "What are you going to be able to find out over the holiday weekend anyway? Everyone will be on break." Her anger started to stir in her belly. It bubbled like the water she'd forgotten about on the stove behind her. "Come on, Rafe. It's *Thanksgiving!*"

His eyes went hard as his nostrils flared. "Just because it's a holiday doesn't mean I can take a break! The killer fucking won't!"

Great, now they were practically yelling at each other. Her frustration, the worry she'd battled all day, fueled the flames of her anger. It started to spew out of her, and she couldn't stop it. "Is this what life with you is going to be like? An endless stream of cases that mean more to you than family?" Tears threatened, and she blinked them away.

Rafe flinched, and she instantly regretted her words. Before she could apologize, his whole body stiffened, and the vein at his temple twitched with the tightening of his jaw. Through clenched teeth, he told her, "I don't want to do this any more than you want me to. But I don't have a choice, Tori." His hands flexed at his sides, and she wondered if he wanted to reach for her or was imagining punching something. "I can't sit around and do nothing and let him kill another innocent woman or *worse*." His eyes held their haunted look again, making her wonder what he'd seen but wouldn't tell her.

Resigned, she shrugged as if her whole world wasn't close to crumbling. "Fine. I'll go without you."

"No!" When he reached for her, she glared, crossing her arms over her chest, and he dropped his hand. "You can't go alone. It's not safe."

She was so tired of this. Since the carnival, he'd become more paranoid. She knew he wanted to protect her, but his behavior bordered on obsessive. He wouldn't even let her walk Toby outside without an escort. She felt trapped, smothered almost, and the need for freedom was beginning to outweigh her willingness to humor his fears.

She opened her mouth to calmly tell him all this, but that's not what came out. The water on the stove boiled over, and as it started to steam and hiss, she did the same. "This is getting ridiculous, Rafe!" Her breath hitched, but she forced it out with her next words. "I can't take it anymore! There haven't been *any* threats against me." She threw her hands in the air. At her wit's end, she shook her head. "It's almost like you don't want me to do anything. Like you're afraid of me talking to anyone who isn't you."

The dark brown of his eyes went cold at her insinuation. His voice came out just as frosty when he said, "That's not true, and you know it."

"Do I?"

His shoulders fell at her response, but she wasn't sure

of anything right now except she needed some fresh air. She glanced at Toby, who pouted on the kitchen tiles, upset over their arguing. Sending him the hand signal to come, she walked to the front door, grabbing the dog's leash from the hook beside it. Without another word to Rafe, she leashed Toby and shrugged into her coat.

"Where are you going?"

With her hand already on the doorknob, she resisted turning around. "For a walk."

He didn't try to stop her. Maybe he knew she wouldn't let him. The best thing for both of them was a little space to think.

When she and Toby made it outside, Tori breathed easier. The cold air brought a rosy hue to her pale cheeks, and she welcomed it, hoping the chill would cool her anger as well as her blood. It was already dark out, but she barely noticed. She let Toby lead her along the walking path next to Rafe's apartment while her thoughts wandered.

Their talk had not gone at all as she'd pictured it.

Understatement of the year.

How had she gone from being blissfully happy to blindingly angry in the span of a few hours?

She couldn't blame Veronica. No, she'd done this to herself. The things she'd said . . .

Well, it was too late now to take them back. Maybe it was better she'd voiced her own fears. She'd been struggling against Rafe's for long enough. It seemed only fair.

But where do we go from here?

The thought of driving to her rental house crossed her

mind, but she didn't want to do that. Her heart already ached from the wounds she'd inflicted on both of them. Spending the night apart wouldn't ease it.

A gust of wind stole inside her coat, waking her from her musings. She grumbled at the cold air and paid attention to her surroundings. Every twenty feet or so, tall lampposts shone down on the leaves scattered over the circular path, but the shadows in between made her uneasy. A quiver in her gut had her straining her eyes, searching for anything that might be on the grounds with her. But as Toby tugged her along, she shook off the feeling. This was Rafe's doing. He'd made her paranoid, too.

Her anger revived with the acknowledgment. He'd made her afraid to do something as simple as taking her dog on a walk.

Annoyed with herself, she let Toby continue to explore. They'd not gone this far from the building before, and she glanced back, watching it shrink behind them. She was surprised he hadn't come after them yet. She'd thought for sure he wouldn't let her stay out here alone. He had to know Officer Hale was gone. Didn't he?

Still looking behind her, Tori tripped and tumbled to the ground. She lost hold of Toby's leash as she braced her arms to catch herself. A yelp tore out of her at the pain searing up her arms when she hit. The debris on the pavement cut into her palms, and her knees skinned against the roughness.

She'd managed to keep her face from connecting with the ground, but as she flexed her right arm, tears blurred her vision, a sharp pain warning her not to try that again.

She'd likely sprained it.

Just what I need.

Using her left hand, she gingerly pushed herself to her feet. She glanced around, grateful no one had seen her embarrassing fall.

Where did Toby go?

Tori's eyes searched the darkness. He wasn't one to wander off, but she didn't see him. Though, with his coloring, he could be blending in with the shadows.

"Toby," she called his name, but no shaggy face appeared. Worry clawed its way into her throat, turning her mouth dry as she tried calling his name again, louder this time.

"Toby, come!" she yelled into the night, her lungs threatening to constrict.

She heard a bark in the distance when she was about to dissolve into tears. Relief washed over her, and she ran toward the sound. Her stride was awkward, with her right arm hugged to her chest, but she pushed forward, still calling out the dog's name.

When she neared the next lamppost, she slowed to a stop. She could see someone there—a man. As he turned, she recognized him, and the tension, which had built in her muscles, flooded out. "Did you see a big shaggy dog run by here?" she panted.

The coroner was startled, and she apologized, thinking she'd snuck up on him. He pushed his glasses further up his nose. "I believe I did." He scratched at his balding head. "I passed a dead animal or something in that direction." He thumbed behind him. "Would the dog go after it? I can show you where it was."

Tori rolled her eyes. Toby was into anything smelly that could be food. She nodded at the coroner. "Please lead the way."

He smiled as she fell into step beside him. "I'm Ian, by the way."

"Tori. Thank you for this. Toby doesn't usually run off." They passed out of the beams from the lamp, and her eyes squinted, readjusting to the lack of light.

"Are you hurt? I noticed you were holding onto your arm."

She blushed in the darkness and was glad he couldn't see her embarrassment. "Oh, I tripped. It's probably just a sprain."

"That's too bad," he spoke so softly she wasn't sure she'd heard him.

"What?" When she glanced over, he wasn't there. Her scalp prickled right before something stung her neck. On instinct, her hand flew to the spot. "What did . . ." But she couldn't finish her question because her mouth stopped working, and her legs collapsed.

His hands caught her as she fell. "You're coming with me, my queen."

Queen?

Her eyes drooped, and then her thoughts slid away into the blackness, settling around her like a veil.

* * * *

Rafe

Well, his day had turned to shit. Rafe scrubbed his hands down his face and scowled at the door Tori had walked out of. He'd been on such a high, finally having made some progress on the case, only to have the one person who'd always offered support rip the rug out from under him instead.

The sizzling behind him penetrated his gloomy fog, and he stalked to the stove, turning off the burner under the boiling pot with more force than necessary.

Dammit!

He leaned against the counter, his fingers gripping it so hard his knuckles turned white. He didn't care about the mess in front of him. The one he *was* worried about wouldn't be as easy to clean up.

He'd fucked up.

Thanksgiving had never been a big deal for him. Growing up, it had always been just him and his mom. They'd make ziti and watch football, but it wasn't much different than what they did on any given Sunday. He'd known the holiday was important to Tori. For her to see her family, but he'd happily take a week or a month off and go with her. *After* he caught the slasher.

Rafe blew out a breath. He'd handled explaining it to her about as well as he snowboarded—poorly and clumsily. But the things she'd said . . .

He pushed off the counter and rubbed at his chest. They'd stung.

He'd been floating adrift, a boat rocked on a stormy sea, and each additional word she'd thrown at him had been a wave crashing over his hull with pounding force. He shook his head, wishing he could erase the past few minutes.

With a growl, he started to clean up the mess on the counter. If he kept replaying their conversation, it would drown him. But his mind wouldn't let it go. He'd tried to step away from cases like this. It's why he'd given up being a detective. He didn't want to have to be the one tracking down the killer. But he'd been pulled into the fucker's game. And he *wouldn't* forfeit. Not when lives were on the line and not when the threat came so close to the woman he loved.

The rag in his hands stilled as he stared into space. Did she really think he was that possessive? Not wanting her to talk to or hang out with anyone else.

He tossed the cloth away. He'd *never* treat her like that. It was as if she tried to push him away. But why? Did she want to leave again? Would he be strong enough to let her, if it's what she truly wished, to be out of his life for good?

A strangled noise escaped Rafe's throat as his heart cracked in two from the mere thought of letting her go. He had to fix this. If the last time he'd let her leave were any indication, it would be the wrong choice—for both of them.

The half-prepared dinner was forgotten as he rushed out of the apartment, expecting to see her with Officer Hale walking Toby in the courtyard. But as he pushed through the doors, the dark told him Hale had gone home.

It was his detail, and he'd let Tori out of his sight.

CHAPTER 26

Rafe

When Tori's bright red hair was nowhere to be seen, fear seized Rafe's limbs, making his muscles so tight they trembled. His eyes frantically searched the green space, straining to see through the shadows with no avail. He didn't see her or Toby in the courtyard by the apartments. The walking path around it proved empty. She'd either left or ventured into the wooded area beyond the apartment grounds. The latter seemed highly unlikely . . .

At least by choice.

His steps faltered. When the thought threatened to drench him in fear, he cut off the faucet, letting his training take over.

Using it now, he cautioned himself. It was dark; of course, he couldn't see her hair. It didn't mean she wasn't nearby.

Shoving down the panic, trying to incapacitate him, he started calling for her. His feet wanted to run, but he made himself walk the path. Otherwise, he could miss something or miss her.

"Tori!" Rafe cupped his hands around his mouth and called her name in every direction. When no reply came, the fear turned into a rock in his stomach. Ignoring it, he called for the dog instead.

A low bark met his ears, but Rafe was too tense to feel any relief. "Toby, come!"

Tori had trained the labradoodle well because he responded to the command. Like a bullet, he emerged from the tree line beyond the apartment grounds, running straight for Rafe.

When Toby reached him, he knelt to examine the dog. He still had his leash on, and as he touched Toby's face, he quickly pulled his hand back in surprise. Was that blood?

Grabbing the lead, he pulled the dog closer to a lamppost so he could get a better look.

As he neared the light, Rafe inspected his hand.

Shit, that's blood.

A cold wave doused him, and he shuddered. But as he knelt again to check Toby over, he found no wounds on the pup. His muzzle was a mess, but judging by the rancid smell of his breath, it had to be because he'd gotten into something he shouldn't have.

Rafe coughed at the cloying smell. "What did you eat, bud?"

Hoping it was an animal and not something . . . *worse,* he pushed to his feet, scanning for Tori. He called her name, and at the sound, Toby whined. Rafe studied the dog, wondering if he could lead him to her.

"Where is she, Toby? Where's mom?" The labradoodle wagged his tail, then nearly jerked Rafe's arm off as he lunged forward.

As he let Toby lead, he hoped the animal wasn't simply taking him to wherever he'd found his disgusting snack. When they'd gone so far past the path that the stars and a sliver of moon in the sky were the sole source of illumination, Rafe reached inside his jacket for his phone, turning the flashlight on as he let the dog continue to drag him forward. The further into the trees they went, the softer the ground became.

He shone his light on their route, noticing Toby's pawprints in the soft mud. If someone had walked this way, there'd be shoeprints. Looking for them, Rafe scanned to the right and left of the track Toby had made.

Finding no other footprints, he was about to give up searching for them when Toby abruptly stopped. The sudden change caused him to stumble, and then the dog sat and whined. Rafe frowned at him.

What's he trying to show me?

Moving his light from the ground to shine on the trees and branches close by, he noticed a spindly arm, almost even with his face, which he would have walked into. Intent on pushing it out of the way, he reached for it, but as he did, his eye caught on a few shiny strands of hair hanging from the bark. When he held the phone closer, they were red.

Rafe's heart ticked faster as a fresh surge of adrenaline flooded his veins. "Tori!" he called her name again and knew if she wasn't responding, she was either hurt or . . .

gone. Neither possibility settled his pulse. The rock in his stomach grew harder, and he swiped his hand over his mouth, swallowing against the panic. He *would* find her.

But if the slasher had her . . .

Terror like he'd never experienced caused his breaths to rasp out in cutting agony. Despite the cold temperature, he broke out in a sweat, which made his hands clammy.

My nightmare is coming true.

He squeezed his lids shut and gasped for air as his lungs constricted against the barrage of images assaulting his mind.

No! I won't let it.

Clenching his jaw, Rafe opened his eyes and pushed away the emotions keeping him from doing his job. Forcing several deep breaths in and out, he patted Toby on the head. "Okay. Show me where she is."

As if he understood, Toby again pulled forward through the copse of trees. They had to be nearing the other side because light from something started to filter in.

As his feet squished in the mud, he skimmed his flashlight back and forth. There had to be a sign that someone else had come this way. Tori had tiny feet, but he didn't see any evidence of her feminine bootprints. In that case, she'd likely been carried, so he kept looking for the marks from whoever had taken her.

Fear and panic continued to claw at him, but he shoved them away, knowing staying cool meant his only chance to find her before it was too late. He and Toby were nearly through the trees now. He could see a streetlamp and the road up ahead. Another twenty feet, and they would reach it.

Rafe pulled the dog to a stop, glancing again at the ground. His light had caught on a footprint. Something stirred in his memory as he bent over. He examined it closer, and recognition sent a shock through him, his stomach lurching.

He'd seen this shoeprint before. It looked exactly like the one Gorsky had collected from the crime scene of the first victim.

It's Dundy's.

With this knowledge, another realization slammed into Rafe. The carving of the wilting rose the coroner had made at the Halloween carnival flashed in his mind. It was the same flower from the playing cards. *That's* why it had seemed familiar.

He'd fucking seen it before.

His head snapped up, and he shoved to his feet. Beyond this footprint, a path of them marked the truth, damning him.

Dundy was the slasher.

He had Tori. He'd carried her through the woods.

Fuck, fuck, fuck!

How could he not have seen? It was in front of his face this whole time. Toby tugged him toward the street to an empty road as he berated himself. Still, he knew the fucker had lurked here, probably watching her, waiting for the perfect opportunity to grab her.

And he'd given it to him.

The weight on his shoulders nearly pulled him to the ground as he dialed the station on his phone, praying to any deity who would listen.

Let Tori get away.

Just let her survive.

Please, help me find her.

* * * *

Tori

The dark cocooning Tori slowly faded away, leaving her confused and uncomfortable. The first thing she noticed was the cold. She lay on something hard, its frigid temperature seeping into her bones through her exposed flesh.

Why am I naked?

Then, there was a light growing ever brighter behind her lids. Neither sensation felt pleasant, making her wish to return to the blackness. She thought she could glimpse its edges floating away, and if she could grab ahold of it, she'd be able to wrap herself up in it once more. But it eluded her reach.

And then there was no more tempting black veil. There was only pain.

The sharp slice of it at her neck forced her eyes open. As her arms lifted instinctively to defend, her pupils blinked furiously, assaulted by the bright overhead lamp. When they cleared, she saw the shocked visage of the coroner. Her motion had stopped the slice of his scalpel against her skin.

"How?" His light brown eyes were wide behind his glasses, his mouth opening and closing like a fish.

She didn't wait for him to recover. Mustering her strength, she rolled off the metal table. Using her arms to stop her fall proved a mistake as her right one buckled, another sharp stab of pain lighting her up and making her cry out before it dulled into a constant throb. A wave of dizziness followed, but she shook it off, forcing herself to her feet.

Where am I?

Her eyes quickly searched the room for a door, but the first thing they fell on was a wall of cabinets. It wouldn't have terrified her, except they were the kind used to store cadavers. She expected her fear to make her pulse pound, but it gave barely a sleepy thud in her chest despite the sight of the cold lockers.

How did I get here?

Her memories were jumbled, her head fuzzy. When she heard rustling behind her, she spun around and nearly toppled over. Catching herself on the table, she stared at the coroner. Despite her muddled state, she knew she needed to get away from him.

Ian had laid the scalpel on a tray and now held a syringe. His eyes squinted, studying her. "I suppose I need to up your dose."

The exit was behind him, and her eyes flitted to the door before landing on the needle. If she let him stick her with it, she wasn't making it out of there.

He took a step, and she went for the closest weapon. The embalming table she'd been on had a metal frame with four caster wheels. With a roar, she shoved it, hoping if she didn't tip it over on him, it would at least push him out of the way.

Ian yelped in surprise as it banged into his arm, making him drop the plunger. When he bent to retrieve it, Tori bolted for the door. But her coordination was off, and her legs weren't working as fast as they should. She stumbled into the tiled wall by the exit, close enough to grip the door frame for balance.

The coroner laughed at her. The sound made her shudder, and she chanced a glance over her shoulder. He was much too close. As she struggled with the knob, tears slid down her cheeks, salt mingling with the blood dripping from the wound at her neck.

Please, I have to get out of here.

She'd succeeded in making the handle turn right as she felt a prick in her arm. She pulled the door open, jerking her limb out of the coroner's grasp before he could finish sending whatever waited in the syringe into her bloodstream. Luck was with her because she managed to clock him in the face with it when he lunged after her.

A satisfying crack met her ears, followed by an angry howl as she emerged into a dimly lit hallway. The only illumination came from fluorescent sconces spaced high on the wall every ten feet. She yanked the hypodermic from her arm, tossing it away.

As she did, her eye caught on the rack of white coats outside the door, and she grabbed one, shrugging into it as she raced from the room. Ian would surely come after her; she *had* to find a way out.

Her bare feet flew over the pale linoleum, or she thought they did. But as she bounced from one wall to the other like a ping-pong ball, Tori realized she wasn't flying anywhere. The coroner would catch up to her at the rate she was going. Her only choice was to hide. Turning a corner, she found a shorter hallway and a dead-end.

Her knees tried to buckle, but she clung to the tiles on the wall with desperate fingers. Footsteps approached, and she knew he would find her if she didn't move. Fighting against the fog attempting to take her under, she pushed off the wall and shoved through a set of swinging doors. Her breathing and her heart rate were still too slow for the amount of fear coursing through her body.

The tears started again, and she blinked them away to clear her vision. Dark shrouded this room, hiding its contents from her. Wobbling forward on shaky legs, she fell. She couldn't stop herself, and her cheek crashed into the cold floor. The pain she expected never came. As she tried to push upright, a wave of hopelessness washed over her, and she collapsed.

She was going to die.

A loud bang sounded in the distance, startling her into a sitting position. Groaning quietly with the effort it took, she scooted to put her back against the wall by the swinging doors. They'd stilled from her entry, and she sighed with relief.

He hadn't found her yet.

She needed to let her eyes adjust to locate a better place to hide within the room. But as she sat there, the black veil returned, dancing at the limits of her vision. It crept closer and closer until she welcomed it with a plea.

Please, Rafe. Please find me.

CHAPTER 27

Rafe

Rafe pulled into a parking spot at the Dale County Morgue. The badge he wore on his hip became a shield he used to shutter his feelings and wall off his heart. If he was going to save Tori, he needed his head to be clear. After he checked his pistol, he climbed out of the SUV.

The primary part of the morgue was built in a square, with faded orange bricks decorating its tall facade. He'd been here before, and even though it wasn't visible in the dark, he knew the wide concrete steps had cracks in them. The white metal railing on either side had peeling paint in spots and rust stains in others. His stomach churned as a thought slipped past his defenses. He prayed he wouldn't be looking at another cold, lifeless body.

He needed Tori *warm* and *alive.*

The tall windows on either side of the building were dark, and no lights shone through the glass-fronted door in the center, which told him the coroner wasn't in his office. He had to be in the "L" of the structure, which branched off from the main square—the area where bodies were examined and stored.

He swallowed as bile rose in his throat. Instinct made him want to barge in, guns blazing, but that was the wrong approach and the approach most likely to get Tori killed . . . *if* she was still alive.

He ground his teeth against the pain, cutting at him with the possibility. Smothering his emotions for a case had never been an issue, but this . . . with the woman he loved on the line, he didn't know if he could manage it.

Inhaling deeply, he struggled to push all the fear, worry, and anger away with the exhale to concentrate on the task in front of him. It hadn't taken long for him to track the coroner here, but the minutes, which had passed, still felt like an eternity.

After calling the station for backup, Rafe dialed Chicago to speak to the analyst working the website angle for him. Jett had confirmed Dundy was on the list of users. Not only was *he* a member of The Dead Hands, but Mosier had been, too.

While Rafe was happy with the news because it helped build evidence against the coroner, his focus remained on Tori. She only had so much time until the fucker made her into the queen of hearts.

As Jameson and the cavalry pulled up, his stomach roiled, nausea threatening to escape, but he held his hand over his mouth and swallowed it back down. As the captain, he couldn't fall apart in front of his men, even if he walked a dangerously tight rope.

Jameson joined him at the base of the steps as a grumbling Gorsky and the other uniforms headed toward the remaining exits. The plan had already been put in place. He and the lieutenant would go in the front, make noise, and attempt to draw Dundy out while Gorsky ensured everyone else guarded any chance of escape. No one would go in until they were ordered to.

With a nod to Jameson, they climbed the steps together, firearms out, held low but at the ready.

The first thing Rafe did when he entered was flip the lights on. The fluorescent bulbs overhead illuminated the long hallway leading to the "L" of the structure.

"Hey, Dundy, you in here?" he called as he and Jameson swept the rooms they passed. "I need to talk to you about the latest victim." He made his voice as loud as he could without blowing his cover. He wanted the coroner to think he had no clue he was the slasher.

But he got no response. What if he was already too late?

His stomach dropped, but he pushed past the fear and the worries it brought with it. After they'd searched the main building, he and Jameson slammed through the double doors at the beginning of the "L," hoping the noise would bring Dundy into the open. The lights had been turned on there, the wall sconces flickering over pale green tiles leading to the dingy white floor.

"Dundy, are you here?" he kept shouting as they moved quickly toward the room where the coroner examined bodies.

They passed dark room after dark room until Jameson signaled at him. Rafe slowed and followed his lieutenant's finger, which pointed to several drops of blood splattered on the linoleum. Red colored his vision, and his hand tensed around his pistol. Rage proved stronger than fear, and he couldn't restrain both.

I'll kill Dundy for making Tori bleed.

Jameson gripped his shoulder, and he nearly elbowed him in the nose. "Stay cool, Alonso." His warning was quiet but stern.

His friend's voice pulled him out of the spiral he'd been about to go down like it had when they'd trained together at the academy. Bottling up the anger, he nodded at Jameson, who squeezed his shoulder before letting go, then Rafe knelt and swiped a finger through the blood. It felt warm, which meant if it *was* Tori's, she was likely still alive.

Standing up, he motioned for the lieutenant to flank him. They were right outside the room with the cold lockers. Taking a deep breath, he opened the door and stepped in with his weapon drawn. The lights were on, but no one was home. He quickly swept the room, then backed out of it.

"Where is this fucker?" he growled under his breath. He'd noticed the overturned table and hoped it meant Tori had fought and gotten away.

Jameson frowned and shook his head. Rafe knew he had the same thought. Dundy better not have already fled.

As the lieutenant radioed to the officers outside, he started following the blood trail. Behind him, he heard confirmation no one had left since they'd entered the building. He neared the end of the "L" and braced his back on the wall before checking around the corner. A quick look told him Dundy wasn't in the short hallway.

When he felt Jameson beside him, he passed the bend, tracking the splashes of blood to where they ended in front of a set of swinging double doors. He signaled to his lieutenant, and they prepared to enter the room. Either the coroner was in there, or Tori was.

Rafe's heart lodged in his throat as he pushed through the left side. He paused, unable to see a damn thing until Jameson slapped on the switch. A pale leg caught his attention when the room flooded with light, and he dropped to his knees. They'd found Tori.

His first reaction was horror as he took her in. The sterile room they were in, the potential danger at their backs, faded away as his world stopped. His emotions battered him like a ram as he stared at the top of her white coat. Her blood had stained it red, soaking it from the cut at her neck.

Am I too late?

His nightmares replaying in his head, Rafe's hand violently shook as he reached to check the pulse at her wrist. Her skin felt lukewarm, but where was her pulse? Impatient, he grabbed her in his arms, a dry sob tearing out of him as he laid his head on her chest, desperate to hear her heart beating.

There!

It was slow. The rhythm sounded faint and too far apart, but it *was* there.

"Is she . . .?" Jameson's quiet question trailed off, but he wouldn't have been able to say the words either.

Thankfully, he didn't have to. "She's alive."

His friend's hand gripped his shoulder. "Can you wake her?"

"Sunshine, can you hear me?" He tried gently shaking her but put his ear to her mouth when he got no response. Her breaths were as slow as her pulse. Panic crept up his spine, but he threw it off.

Tori was alive.

He reminded himself of that fact. Her heart might be slow, but it could result from the sedative the slasher had no doubt given her.

Despite trying to smother his worry in practicality, the boulder in his stomach grew heavier, and he worked to keep his voice from breaking as he asked, "Where are the paramedics?"

"They should be here any minute," Jameson answered. He'd called for them as soon as they'd found the blood.

"Can you find something to use as a dressing? We need to stop her bleeding." Rafe pressed his hand to the wound and applied pressure while he waited on Jameson. Tori didn't stir. Her lack of response made fear slither into his heart, boring holes in it like rotten fruit.

When his lieutenant returned, handing him a stack of gauze, they heard the creak of an old door being forced open. Rafe tensed; his whole body went on alert, knowing it was Dundy. The fucker came out of hiding.

Jameson pressed his hand over the cloth, nodding at Rafe's scowl. "I'll stay with her. Go get the coroner."

The need to make Dundy pay vibrated inside him, but the thought of leaving his Sunshine crushed him.

He brushed the back of his bloody palm over her face. With her eyes closed, she almost seemed peaceful, if not for the bruise forming on her left cheek and the blood at her throat. Her hair was its usual silky fire, and he lifted her up, breathing in its scent as he kissed her on the forehead. The smell of narcissus made him think of the flowers swaying in a gentle night breeze as if they danced under the moonlight.

Would they get to dance in the moonlight again?

As he stared at the battered body of his love, he felt the dam cracking. The one he'd forged to hold his emotions was going to burst. His eyes were burning from the effort of restraining them.

"Alonso, go. Arrest this sick bastard," at Jameson's low urging, his head snapped up.

Before he had a chance to respond, the sound of an ambulance siren forced him into motion. Tori would be saved, and he needed to finish this.

Nodding, he released her. Without another glance, for fear he wouldn't make it out of the room, he lifted his firearm and left, heading toward the noise they'd heard. Tuning out the whir of the sirens, he strained to hear any sounds of movement. Dundy had to know by now he was trapped. All Rafe had to do was find the mouse.

The fucker had turned out the lights, so he crept slowly toward the central part of the "L," his eyes tracking every shadow. When he reached the turn, he peeked around it, searching for his prey. Because that's what the coroner was.

Rafe was the hunter now and wasn't giving up until he'd

caught his quarry.

Something whizzed past his head, slicing his ear. He muttered a curse as the burn of the strike bit at him. Ducking around the corner, he felt for the wound and winced. Lifting his hand from his ear, it came away wet.

But he'd found the coroner.

"Throwing knives, Dundy? I didn't know you had it in you," he taunted.

"Not knives, Captain." The fucker chuckled, and Rafe tried to pinpoint how close he was. But the rage swimming in his blood made it difficult to focus. "A scalpel is much more effective at slicing."

"Is that so?" He attempted to keep the bastard talking so he could locate him. But the blood dripping in his right ear wasn't helping.

"Are you curious?" Dundy's footsteps receded, but his voice remained as strong as it had been before. "It's because they're so thin. The slightest pressure and the skin gives way."

Thinking about how the fucker had used one to cut into Tori's neck had him barely containing a roar. He wanted to end this. Now.

Reaching for his radio to unleash the officers outside, Rafe barked, "It's over, Dundy. Time to give yourself up." He made the call to his backup, then turned the corner, pistol at the ready.

The coroner waited in the hall in his white lab coat, backlit by moonlight streaming in from the window of the door to the room with the cold lockers. Something in his hand caught the light, and Rafe tensed. The coroner fondled a scalpel, running his finger along the blade's edge.

"Drop the weapon." He aimed his gun at the man's chest, but he didn't want to shoot. A quick death was more than this sick bastard deserved.

"Did you know the Suit of Hearts Slasher preferred a twenty-two?" Dundy held the scalpel up, showing it off to Rafe.

His whole body had gone rigid at the mention of the man he'd put in prison.

Dundy smiled, completely ignoring the gun trained on him. "This? It's a ten. Slightly smaller but just as effective."

Rafe slowly moved toward the coroner, ready to neutralize him. "Drop the weapon and keep your hands in the air."

Dundy ignored his command, pinning him with a confused stare. "What exactly is it you think I've done, Captain?"

He sneered, tired of playing this asshole's game. "You know what the charges will be. At least three counts of murder, among others."

At his jibe, the coroner grinned. To say it was demented would be an understatement. Maybe it was a trick of the moonlight, but he would swear he saw glee crinkling the bastard's eyes, making them shine with some unholy light. "And what evidence do you have that isn't circumstantial?"

Rafe growled, "The Dead Hands' symbol in the pumpkin. Your footprints where Tori was taken."

The bastard shrugged. "So I carved a rose and walked in the woods near your home. How does it prove I'm a murderer?"

His finger twitched on the trigger. Where the hell was his backup? Had the transmission not gone through? He was getting much too close to losing his cool on this fucker. "You didn't just carve a rose. You know the symbol was on the playing cards."

His laugh raised the hairs on Rafe's neck. "So you figured that out. I wondered if you'd be clever enough." Dundy pushed his glasses up his nose. "You certainly weren't clever enough to notice I'd taken an emetic to induce vomiting at Tegan's crime scene."

He kept his voice calm, though he was ready to shut this fucker up—permanently. "You were playing me."

The coroner lifted the scalpel again, his thumb caressing the blade. "I'll admit, watching the big city detective flounder was fun. Especially after I used Mosier to confuse things."

"I'm not floundering now." He took another step closer when he noticed Gorsky silently advancing behind the coroner.

"Aren't you?" Faster than Rafe could move, Dundy slashed across his own throat with the scalpel.

"No!" As he fell, the detective caught the coroner, and Rafe ripped one of the coats off the rack to press against the man's throat. "Get the paramedics!" he shouted to the uniforms behind Gorsky, then he roared down at Dundy, "You don't get to die. Not until you answer for your crimes."

"Motherfucker." Gorsky scowled, and Rafe wasn't sure if the comment had been aimed at him or Dundy.

When an EMT appeared at his elbow, he let the man take over the coroner's care. The paramedic worked with the other officers to triage his wound and load him on a gurney.

As he watched them wheel the man away, the rage he'd been holding at bay washed over him in a blinding haze. His jaw locked together as his chest heaved. He should've seen that coming. The fucker was obsessed with death; of course, he'd try and take the easy way out.

Slowing his breathing, Rafe reined himself in to finish what he'd started. He still had work to do if he wanted to make the slasher pay.

CHAPTER 28

Rafe

With a nod to a disgruntled Gorsky, Rafe left Dundy's hospital room, passing the officers stationed outside. The detective still stewed over Rafe not taking him inside the building, but he needed to get over it. Even though Gorsky had proven himself trustworthy, it didn't mean Rafe liked the man. Besides, he'd helped make the arrest; as far as Rafe was concerned, Gorksy could have all the glory. He didn't want it.

Shaking off the stare the detective had trained at his back, Rafe felt the edginess he'd been battling for the last hour recede. Dundy would live, but he wasn't exactly up to talking at the moment.

He blew out a breath and ran a hand through his hair. The coroner might not be ready to make a confession yet, but they'd found plenty to damn him.

After he'd checked on Tori and the paramedics had assured him she was stable, he'd reentered the morgue, searching for answers to the questions he still had about the case. When he'd opened a cold locker marked as 'Rose Mortemain,' he'd hit paydirt. No matter what the fucker tried to say, Dundy couldn't deny he had items in his possession that belonged to his murder victims.

The man had a thing for lanyards, which might've had something to do with the fact they were worn around the neck. The coroner seemed particularly fond of that body part and collected tokens from each. A Loyola lanyard from Tegan Powell, one with the name of the veterinary office Mosier had worked at, and a striped one from Brown, the university the latest victim had attended.

He'd discovered what was left of the Fatal Flush along with the mementos. Dundy had been siphoning it off, extracting the pentobarbital. His separation process hadn't been sound, though. Each victim had shown different levels of the chemical in their system. But Rafe was thankful for that, knowing it helped save Tori's life.

He strode on his way to see her now, though he'd been told it could be another hour or more before she woke up. Necessarily or not, he'd demanded her room be on a different floor from the coroner's.

Pushing the button for the elevator, he stared at the closed metal doors and wondered over the last item from the mortuary cabinet. He didn't know what to call it other than a manifesto.

Dundy had taken The Dead Hands' ideas to the extreme. To him, necrophilia was only pure if performed after a murder. He'd practically worshiped the Suit of Hearts Slasher, viewing himself as a disciple to that sick bastard's cause. And the coroner had wanted to finish what the fucker had started. To complete his suit.

A shiver raced down Rafe's spine, and he was happy he'd read only a portion of Dundy's document. Gorsky could have the privilege of delving into the mind of that psychopath.

He didn't want it.

The elevator dinged, and the doors slid open. What he wanted was to see Tori's bright green eyes smiling at him again. He stepped in, pushed the button for her floor, and leaned against the lift's metal railing. The last words he'd said to her had been in anger, and they were eating at his gut. As the elevator lurched into motion, pain sliced his chest.

I fucked up and nearly lost her for good.

Closing his eyes against that reality, his hand brushed across the box in his pocket, and he promised to spend the rest of his life making it up to her.

* * * *

Tori

"*Sole mio*, I need you. *Il mio cuore batte solo per ti.* Come back to me," Rafe's murmured words were a beam of light cutting through the dark waves Tori floated on.

She swam toward the sound like a beacon, pushing the murky water away with each stroke until she could make out his features in the distance.

"Her eyelids fluttered."

Whose eyelids?

She wondered who Rafe was talking to, but then she heard a second voice and felt pressure on her left wrist.

"Her vital signs are good." Material shifted before the hand on her arm disappeared. "Are you back with us, Miss Graham?"

Annoyed at being a bystander to the conversation, she pulled herself out of the depths and forced her eyes open.

"There she is," a nurse said, a smile in her voice.

At the same time, Rafe kissed the back of her hand. "Hello, Sunshine."

She gazed into his dark eyes, and her world shifted. With Rafe, she was home—safe and loved. She smiled, but something niggled at the back of her mind. A thought that she hadn't known if she'd see him again.

"Hi," her voice emerged as a croak, and she swallowed to wet her dry throat.

"Have some water, hun." The pretty, middle-aged nurse held a plastic cup to her lips.

Tori took a sip. Then two. When she'd had her fill, she leaned back in the bed. "Thank you."

The blonde woman nodded. "I'll leave you two alone for now. I'm sure you have a lot to discuss." She winked at Rafe, then pointed at the call switch on Tori's bed. "But you push that button if you need anything."

Without taking his eyes away from Tori's face, Rafe answered for her, "We will."

The nurse left, her feet squishing on the vinyl flooring, and she raised an eyebrow at Rafe. "What did I miss?"

His face fell, and he leaned closer, still gripping her hand. "What do you remember?"

Her nose scrunched as she surveyed her surroundings. "Why am I in the hospital?" With her question came her anxiety from being stuck in places like this.

As soon as her brain realized where she was, her body reacted. Her chest squeezed, and then her breathing became choppy. Ever since the miscarriage, hospitals and doctor's offices had made her uncomfortable. She bit down on her lip while tears stung her eyes. "Rafe, I can't stay here."

"Shh, *sole mio*, calm down." He squeezed her left hand, but her lungs refused to listen. "You're only here to rest for a little while."

She wanted out at the earliest opportunity. Her eyes darted around the room. A light blue curtain hanging from the middle had been cinched, so the rest of her sterile environment became visible. Next to the fabric stood an overbed table where the nurse had left her cup. Beyond it, a wide window showed her night still reigned, though she had no idea of the hour. Her eyes strayed to the mass of machines next to her bed, and she had to close them. It looked the same. All hospital rooms did.

Like pain and despair.

Her breaths were much too shallow. She tried to take a deep one, but she couldn't.

Rafe's hands clasped either side of her face. "Tori, look at me."

At his command, she obeyed, opening her lids. "What," she gasped.

"You're not alone. You hear me? I'm not leaving until you get to go with me."

She heard the reassurance in his voice, but the tears still spilled over. "I don't want to stay here."

"Please, don't cry," he crooned, kissing the drops from her cheeks. "It won't be long. I promise."

She sniffled, then looked at Rafe. She could get through this if she focused on him, not her surroundings. "Why am I here?"

His gaze fell to her neck, and she attempted to lift her dominant hand to the spot, only to find her right arm wrapped in an elastic bandage. She gasped, her eyes widening as the memories flooded in. Falling, hurting her arm, then . . .

"The coroner! He cut me." Her gaze flew to Rafe's. "He's the slasher!"

He squeezed her left hand. "Shh, I know. He can't hurt you anymore."

He knows?

That meant . . .

"You found me," she whispered the words in wonder. Rafe had saved her life. She said a silent thank you to the universe for answering her prayer.

But she had to know. "Where is he?" She hated when her voice trembled on the question.

"He's in the hospital too, recovering from a self-inflicted injury until he can be transferred." Rafe's face twisted with a sour expression, his tone growing harsh. "But he'll be charged. And put away. He's not hurting you or anyone ever again."

Despite knowing he'd apprehended the killer, she didn't feel relieved. Her shoulders slumped as guilt snuck in. Rafe had been right to worry for her—to be so overprotective—and she'd doubted him.

Swallowing the lump of tears in her throat, she tried to apologize, "I'm sorry. You were right, and I . . ." His eyes caught hers and held, the gleam in them hopeful. "I didn't mean it. Those things I said. I know you were just trying to protect me."

A slow smile spread across his face, and despite her bleary eyes, she could see it light up the hospital room, making it a little less gloomy. "I'm sorry, too. I know how important the holidays are for you, and . . ." He broke her stare and scrubbed at his neck. When he met her gaze again, he cleared his throat. "I, uh, I called Ron. So, your family knows what happened."

She groaned and shut her lids. "She's on her way here, isn't she?"

He chuckled softly. "She mentioned something about bringing Thanksgiving to you. It was the twins' idea."

Tori laughed. She loved her niece and nephew, but her sister used them as an excuse whenever it suited her. "Your apartment's going to feel *very* small *very* soon." She smirked at him, but he only shrugged.

She was thinking about it barely being big enough for the three of them, much less for her sister's family, when she realized she'd forgotten about Toby running off. She gripped Rafe's hand. "Where's Toby? Did you find him?"

He nodded. "I did. The pup helped me track you." Her eyes narrowed, unsure she believed him. She loved her silly dog, but he was not a tracker.

Rafe must have sensed her doubt because he added,

"I'm serious. Sherlock Holmes would've been proud. Although"—his expression turned sheepish—"he's going to need a serious bath. I don't know what he got into, but his face is a mess."

She looked pointedly at her injured arm. "I think you'll have to take care of it for me."

He gaped at her. "Shit, you're right. How do you wash him? He's a behemoth and refuses to sit still for me."

She had to laugh at the panic in Rafe's eyes. "Peanut butter is the secret. Lots and lots of peanut butter."

He shook his head like he didn't trust it would work. "I hope so."

A comfortable silence fell over them, and her breathing settled. Rafe holding her hand kept the anxiety at bay. The realization filled her with warmth.

Like a sunbeam, it radiated from her heart, traveling up and out through her smile. "I love you, Rafe."

He'd been gazing out the window, pensive, and as he looked at her now, his eyes widened.

A kernel of doubt sprouted in her stomach when he didn't respond immediately. "What is it?"

He blinked, his dark eyes dilating before drawing in a breath. "I wanted, uh . . . shit!" he muttered the expletive under his breath before clearing his throat and tugging at his hair with restless fingers.

He seemed nervous, and she wondered what made him stumble over his words. She was going to ask, but when he pulled a jeweler's box from his pocket, her throat closed up.

"Tori"—he squeezed her hand, then knelt by her bed—

"I'm butchering this, but I thought, what if we gave your family something else to celebrate?" He lifted the lid to the box, and her eyes filled. It was the most breathtaking ring she'd ever seen—an emerald cut diamond flanked by two emeralds set atop a thin gold band.

He blew out a breath, and she couldn't help the laugh bubbling out of her. He grinned as she clapped her hand over her mouth to keep the giggles in.

"Victoria Graham, my heart beats only for you. Be the light to my dark. The ray that chases away the shadows of the past. Marry me, Sunshine, and brighten all the rest of my days."

She was giddy with joy. It broke against her in an overwhelming wave, making her unsure if she wanted to laugh or cry. His proposal had been beautiful . . . apart from *one* thing.

"Oh, Raffaello," she couldn't resist snickering at him. He'd called her Victoria, so it seemed only fair. Then, she took a deep breath and told him her heart was his. It always had been. "*Il mio cuore è solo tuo,*" she struggled with the pronunciation, not having had enough time to practice it yet.

What felt like *ages* ago, she'd looked up a phrase she could say to him in Italian since he always used them on her. This one had struck a chord with her.

Rafe understood what she'd meant, though, because his eyes heated. His husky voice questioned, "That's a yes?"

Tori grinned and winked at him. "*Sì.*"

Faster than she could blink, he'd risen and captured her mouth with his. Frustrated that she couldn't wrap her arms around him, she leaned into his kiss, grabbing his dark curls with her good hand. The most delicious kind of heat licked at her, and she hummed low in her throat at the pleasure only his lips could give. She felt him smile before he pulled away, taking his dark and smoky scent with him.

Rafe plucked the ring from the box and lifted her left hand. His eyes were serious and a little sad when she met his gaze. "I'd planned to give this to you a very long time ago." Her heart squeezed in her chest as she understood the truth in his softly spoken words. "But it belongs on your hand and no one else's."

He slid it onto her finger, and the fit was perfect.

Just like we are together.

Tori smiled at the ring, turning it to admire the light as it bounced off the facets within the stones. After everything they'd been through, they'd gotten their second chance. Or maybe by now, they were on their third or fourth.

Lifting her hand to Rafe's stubble, his dark irises caught hers. The joy buzzing through her floated out with her soft response, "Some things are worth waiting for."

EPILOGUE

12 Months Later

Tori

Tori stirred, pulled from sleep by a deep voice softly crooning Frank Sinatra's "Fly Me to the Moon." Before she opened her eyes, her lips curved in a smile. Rafe was singing to the baby.

She stretched, lifted her lids, and then rolled over to turn the volume up on the monitor. Humming along with him, she climbed from the bed.

A glance at the clock showed her it was barely midnight. The little guy had to be hungry, but she appreciated Rafe trying to give her a chance to rest. Or maybe he'd never gone to bed. Looking at the mess she'd left on his side, she could see why. Her laptop, notebook, and books were scattered over the sheets. She'd been in the middle of outlining her next chapter when she'd drifted off.

Gathering it all up, Tori set her work on the dresser. She was writing a sequel to the book featuring her female detective. The added romance in the story had brought her a whole new group of readers who clamored for Moreno's next case. But it was slow going with a newborn. She chuckled, then winced. Her breasts were full, the milk aching to be released.

Gingerly, Tori slipped into a nightgown she could easily nurse from. Following the sound of Rafe's voice, she padded down the hall to the baby's room. Her heart filled when she paused in the doorway, then it spilled over as she stared at the three men she loved most in the world. The starry night carousel globe turned, causing the shadows to dance along with the notes of Rafe's singing as he rocked the baby. Toby dozed peacefully at his feet.

She watched them and thought what a whirlwind the past year had been. They'd gotten married, found out they were pregnant, and bought a house all within that timeframe. She'd been happy to leave L.A. behind for Rolling Brook. Her home existed wherever Rafe was, and this small town was exactly where she wanted to raise a child. Even if it had its own baggage.

A shiver racked her spine, but she shook it off, determined never to let his ilk dim her shine. The slasher had been sentenced to three terms of 25 years to life. One for each of the three victims. She'd testified and sat through his trial, a task which had proved harder than escaping him in the first place. But with Rafe holding her hand, she'd persevered.

He was her pillar, bearing the weight of whatever they

needed to weather until she became strong enough to hold it herself. The additional years the court had given Dundy for her attempted murder hardly mattered. He would rot in prison and be dead long before then. The important thing to her was he couldn't hurt anyone else—ever again.

She sighed. This past year hadn't been *all* rainbows and butterflies. But good had come out of it. She may have struggled through the first trimester, but they'd pulled through—all three of them. Despite the rocky start, at that milestone, her panic attacks subsided. With Rafe's calming presence, they'd made it to delivery day and beyond— *mostly* unscathed.

She chuckled under her breath. There *was* the chair incident, in which he ended up needing stitches, but she still contested it was an accident. Pregnancy hormones were no joke. Poor Rafe had learned that lesson the hard way.

As if he sensed her snickering, he stopped singing and glanced in her direction. He smiled at her, then brushed a kiss across the baby's head. "It's feeding time, *bambino*."

Rising with his son, he stepped over a still-dozing Toby, and she met them halfway. Holding her arms out, Rafe placed the tiny bundle of wonder into them.

Staring down at him, she asked, "How's our little moonbeam?"

He had his father's dark coloring but her bright green eyes. She'd wanted to name him something cool like Kade or Gage, but Rafe had wanted a more traditional name like Anthony or Matthew. In the end, they'd settled on Lucas. Because he was their little light. The star they'd created together, born into their hearts to shine on them through all the days to come.

Trailing a finger along the baby's cheek, Rafe chuckled. "Hungry. Like always."

She grinned and shook her head. They'd been home from the hospital a couple of weeks, and every few hours, Lucas let them know he was ready to eat again, no matter the time. She didn't mind; Tori was overjoyed at being gifted with him. The universe had a way of working things out, and even though the sorrow she felt over the loss of their first child would never go away, the happiness this new baby had brought kept it at bay.

"Let's fix that, huh, handsome?" She nuzzled her son, taking in his sweet scent—clean and warm like fresh bread. She'd never get tired of the smell.

With a glowing smile, she looked up at Rafe, who kissed her gently on the forehead. Then he nudged Toby to follow him to bed.

"Goodnight, Sunshine," he called from the door.

"Be in there soon." She made herself comfortable in the rocking chair, propping a pillow under her arm.

As Lucas's tiny fist kneaded her breast, Tori heard Rafe's voice through the baby monitor, "Goodnight, *Stellino.*"

Her heart soared like the star he'd called their son. Tori didn't know what tomorrow or the next week might bring, but she'd happily face it with her little family.

One baby step at a time.

A NOTE TO READERS

If you enjoyed this book, please consider leaving a review. They help spread the word about my books through the recommendation process and help new readers decide if they'll be a good fit for them. Reviews also contribute to my rankings on sites like Amazon, making my stories more visible to new readers. Even a one-line review makes a difference!

If you love second-chance romance and all the pent-up tension a shared history brings, you'll love *Wait for You*. This fast-paced cartel romance follows an undercover Texas Ranger whose past threatens to blow his cover. When the woman he walked away from five years ago shows up on the cartel's doorstep looking for her brother, it's up to him to keep both of them from ending up on the wrong end of a pistol.

If you haven't already, don't forget to take advantage of a free novella set in the Rolling Brook world. Subscribe to my newsletter, and by signing up, you receive an EXCLUSIVE book featuring a woman on the run and forced proximity with a troubled military hero.

Want more updates, teasers, and giveaways? Follow me on social media.

All my links can be found here: https://linktr.ee/blyedonovan.

Thank you for reading!

xoxo,

Blye Donovan

ACKNOWLEDGMENTS

This book has been such a long time coming that the list of people to thank is a long one. I will surely forget some, but I'll do my best to name those whose help made this book what it is.

For starters, I have to thank my husband, who still loves and supports me despite ignoring him for days on end to write.

My readers who fell in love with Tori and Rafe from the little snippets I shared. Your support helped push me to finish the book.

To the wonderful Shaders who recommended books when I was conducting research. Thank you! I took your advice and discovered that you *could* write a romance with a serial killer in it.

For help with technical questions, I'd be remiss if I didn't call out two amazing Facebook groups: Cops and Writers & Trauma Fiction. Your advice is always spot on, and any liberties taken for the sake of fiction are entirely my own!

My critique group. Dream Team stars, M.K. and Nina, I couldn't do this without you. Your suggestions are invaluable. You always know exactly what the scene or sentence needs. Plus, you help my readers understand my words when I have a tendency to write them backward. I can't say thank you enough to you ladies. I am so grateful to you! Thank you, thank you, thank you!

BOOKS BY
BLYE DONOVAN

Rolling Brook Protectors
Hunted at Whiteford Farm
Gifts from a Stalker
Small Town Frame-up
Condemned by Secrets
Marked as Queen of Hearts

Stand-alone Novels
Undercover Santa
Blaze of Glory

Texas Heat Shared Series
Wait for You

TOP Security Series
Going Rogue

ABOUT THE AUTHOR

Blye Donovan is a military brat and a veteran who resides in the Lowcountry of South Carolina with her husband and fur-child, Maximus. Besides books, she's addicted to coffee, peanut butter, and shoes. When she's not feeding these addictions, she writes books that are romantic suspense stories featuring strong heroines and alpha protector heroes overcoming dangerous villains. Her books are often set in small towns because she loves the atmosphere associated with them, especially when they  have historic architecture. She was supposed to become a historic preservationist, but . . . writing has always been her passion. You can check out her current series, follow her on social media, and more all at this link: https://linktr.ee/blyedonovan.